'I am Drew Exford, and I would know who you are.'

Bess looked down into his perfect face, and, giving him a smile so sweet that it wrenched his heart, she said softly, 'But I have little mind to tell you sir. You must discover it for yourself. Now, let me go, Master Drew Exford, for I have no desire to be behindhand with the day.' She rode off, leaving Drew to gaze after her.

'Was she real?' he demanded of Charles. 'Have you ever seen such a divine face and form? Dress her in fine clothing and she would have half London at her feet.'

'Now, Drew, you do surprise me,' drawled Charles as the pair of them remounted. 'I had thought that your wish would be for her to have no clothes on at all!'

Paula Marshall, married with three children, has had a varied life. She began her career in a large library and ended it as a senior academic in charge of history at a polytechnic. She has travelled widely, has been a swimming coach, and has appeared on *University Challenge* and *Mastermind*. She has always wanted to write, and likes her novels to be full of adventure and humour.

Recent titles by the same author:

THE BECKONING DREAM
THE YOUNGEST MISS ASHE
LADY CLAIRVAL'S MARRIAGE
AN AFFAIR OF HONOUR
EMMA AND THE EARL
A BIDDABLE GIRL?
THE LOST PRINCESS
NOT QUITE A GENTLEMAN
DEAR LADY DISDAIN

THE DESERTED BRIDE

Paula Marshall

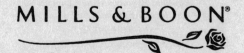

This novel is dedicated to my husband for his
constant support and encouragement in
more ways than I can list here.

*First published in Great Britain 1998
Harlequin Mills & Boon Limited,
Eton House, 18-24 Paradise Road, Richmond, Surrey TW9 1SR*

© Paula Marshall 1998

ISBN 0 263 80774 6

*Set in Times 10 on 11½ pt. by
Rowland Phototypesetting Limited
Bury St Edmunds, Suffolk*

04-9804-74572

*Printed and bound in Great Britain
by Caledonian International Book Manufacturing Ltd, Glasgow*

Chapter One

He was her husband. He had been her husband for ten years, and all she had ever had of him was the miniature which had arrived that morning.

And the letter with it, of course.

The letter which simply, and coldly, said, 'My Lady Exford, I am sending you this portrait of myself in small as a token of my respect for you. I am in hopes of paying you a visit before the summer is out. At the moment, alas, I am exceeding busy in the Queen's interest. Accept my felicitations for your twentieth birthday now, lest I am unable to make them in person. This from your husband, Drew Exford.'

Elizabeth, Lady Exford, known to all those around her as Lady Bess, crumpled the perfunctory letter in her hand. All that it was fit for was to be thrown into the fire which burned in the hearth of the Great Hall of Atherington House. At the very last moment, though, something stayed her hand. She smoothed the crumpled paper and read it again, the colour in her cheeks rising as her anger at the writer mounted in her.

About the Queen's business, forsooth! Had he been about the Queen's business for the last ten years? Was that why he had never visited her, never come to claim her as his wife, had left her here with her father, a wife and no wife? She very much doubted it. No, indeed. Andrew, Earl of Exford since his father's death, had stayed away from Leicestershire in order to enjoy his bachelor life in London, unhampered by the presence of a wife and the children she might give him.

The whole world knew that the Queen liked the handsome young men about her to be unmarried, or, if she grudgingly gave them permission to marry, preferred them not to bring their wives to court. And from what news of him came her way, the Queen had no more faithful subject than her absent husband.

How should she answer this? Should she write the truth, plain and simple, as, 'Sir, I care not if I never see you again?' Or should she, instead, simply reply as an obedient wife ought to, 'My lord, I have received your letter. I am yours to command whenever you should visit me.'

The latter, of course. The former would never do.

Bess walked to the table where ink, paper and the sand to dry the letter awaited her, and wrote as an obedient wife should, although she had never felt less obedient in her life.

And as she wrote she thought of the day ten years ago when she had first seen her husband. . .

'Come, my darling,' her nurse had said, on that long-gone morning, 'your father wishes you to be wearing your finest, your very finest, attire today. The damask robe in grey and pink and silver, your pearls, and the little heart which your sainted mother left you.'

'No.' Ten-year-old Bess struggled out of her nurse's embrace. 'No, Kirsty. Father promised that I should go riding with him on the first fine morning, and it is fine today. Besides, I look a fright in grey and pink, you know I do.'

Her nurse, whom Bess was normally able to wheedle into submission to her demands, shook her head. 'Not today, my love. I cannot allow you to have your way today. Your father has guests. Important guests. They arrived late last night after you had gone to bed, and he wishes you to look your very best when you meet them.'

Kirsty had an air of excitement about her. It was plain that she knew something which she was not telling Bess. Bess always knew when people were hiding things from her but, even though she might be only ten years old, she was wise enough to know when not to continue to ask questions.

So she allowed Kirsty to turn her about and about until Bess felt dismally sure that she looked more like a painted puppet dressed up to entertain the commonalty than the beautiful daughter of Robert Turville, Earl of Atherington, the most powerful magnate in this quarter of Leicestershire. She disregarded as best as she could Kirsty's oohings and aahings, her standing back and exclaiming, 'Oh, my dear little lady, how fine you look. The prettiest little lady outside London, no less.'

'My clothes are pretty,' said Bess crossly, 'but I am not. I am but a little brown-haired thing, and all the world believes that fair is beautiful, and I am not fair at all— as well you know. And my eyes are black, not blue, so no one will ever write sonnets to *them*.'

Useless, quite useless, for Kirsty continued to sing her praises of Bess's non-existent beauty until aunt Hamilton, her father's sister, came into the room.

'Let me look at you, child. Dear Lord, what a poor

little brown thing you are, the image of your sainted grandam no less.'

Far from depressing Bess, this sad truth had her casting triumphant smiles at the mortified Kirsty, who was cursing Lady Hamilton under her breath. Fancy telling the poor child the truth about herself so harshly. It couldn't have hurt to have praised the beautiful dress m'lord had brought from London for her, instead of reminding her of the grandam whom she so resembled.

For Bess's grandam had been the late Lady Atherington, who had always been known as the 'The Spanish Lady'. She had accompanied Catherine of Aragon when she had arrived in England to marry the brother of the late and blessed King Henry VIII, the present Queen's father. The then Lord Atherington had fallen in love with, and married her, despite her dark Spanish looks, and ever since all the Turville daughters had resembled her, including the brisk Lady Hamilton. Brown-haired herself, and black-eyed, she had still made a grand marriage, and the sonnets which Bess was sure would never come her way, had been showered upon her.

'Golds,' she was exclaiming, 'and vermilions, or rich green and bold siennas, are the colours which your father should have bought you. Trust a man to have no sense where women's tire is concerned! Never mind, child, later, later, when I have the dressing of you, we may see you in looks. This will have to do for now. Come!'

She held out a commanding hand, which Bess took, wondering what the fuss and commotion was all about. She had been living quietly at Atherington House as she had done for as long as she could remember—which admittedly at ten was not very long—until yesterday, when her father had arrived suddenly, with a trunkful of new clothes for her, and a train of visitors who had stared at her when she was brought into the Great Hall after they had dined.

Bess had never seen so many people all at once, but she had smiled at them bravely, relieved when, after being seated on her father's knee for a little space and been fed comfits by him, she had been allowed to retire to her room.

And now, if Kirsty was to be believed, another bevy of guests had arrived. Oh, she had heard the noise just as she was going to sleep, and could not help wondering what all the excitement was about. It seemed that she was soon to find out.

For, as she descended the staircase into the Great Hall, she saw that all the servants were assembled at one end of it, and a large body of finely dressed men and women were at the other. Her father was standing a little in front of them, her uncle, Sir Braithwaite Hamilton, by his side, with a pair of attendant pages hovering in their rear.

'Come, my lady,' her father said, smiling at her as her aunt Hamilton let go of her hand and pushed her towards him, 'we are to go to a wedding. In the chapel.'

At this, for some reason unknown to Bess, the company all laughed uproariously, led by uncle Hamilton. All, that was, except aunt Hamilton, who primmed her lips and shook her elegant head. Like all the guests she was richly dressed and Bess could only imagine that it was her father's wedding to which they were going with such ceremony.

Gilbert, the Steward, importantly carrying his white wand of office, marched solemnly before them. Tib, the smallest page, with whom Bess daily played at shuttle-cock, was his attendant, looking as solemn as Giles, not at all like the rowdy boy who was her shadow.

The processional walk to the chapel did not take long.

Not all the guests would enter it with them, for it was small. Above the altar was a painting brought from Italy, beneath a stained glass window showing Christ in his glory. Master Judson, the priest, stood before it.

But where was the bride?

Bess looked about her. Where the bride should stand were several richly dressed men—and a tall boy who appeared to be about sixteen years old.

The boy was as beautiful as Bess was plain, and he was as fair as the god Apollo on the tapestry in the Great Hall. His hair was silver gilt, and curled gently about his comely face. His eyes were as blue as the sky on a summer morning, and the pink and silver colours of his doublet, breeches and hose not only suited him better than they suited Bess, but also showed off a long and shapely body. He resembled nothing so much as one of St Michael's angels come down to earth to adorn it.

As she entered on her father's arm the boy was looking away from her. The man at his side, no taller than he was, whispered something in his ear, and he turned to look at her.

His eyes widened. The handsome face twisted a little. He swung round to the man who had whispered to him and muttered, 'Dear God, uncle Henry, you are marrying me to a monkey!'

No one else but Bess, and the man, heard what he said. Bess's father was a little hard of hearing and aunt Hamilton and the train behind her were too far away to catch his words.

But Bess heard. She heard every bitter syllable. And from them she learned two things. That it was not her father who was to be married, but herself. . .

And the beautiful boy to whom she was to be tied for

life thought that she was ugly and had not hesitated to
say so to his attendant.

No! She would not be married to him. She hated him.
She hated his beauty, and his unkindness. He had not
meant her to hear what he had said, and he was not to
know that her hearing was abnormally acute. Even so,
he should not have spoken so of her, and she would not
marry him, no, never! Never!

Bess wrenched her hand from her father's grasp,
swung round on him, and said, as loudly as she could,
her voice breaking between shame and despair, 'If you
have brought me here to be married, sir, then know this.
I have no mind to be married. Indeed, I will not be
married. Least of all to *him*!'

And she sat down on the stone floor of the chapel.

Such a hubbub followed, such an uproar as had never
before been heard in Atherington's chapel. Master Judson
looked down at her, astounded, nearly dropping his
prayerbook at the sight of such unmannerly behaviour.
The boy—and who could he be?—looked haughtily
down at her as she sat there, now weeping bitter tears.
He said, his voice like ice, 'And I have no mind to marry
you, either, but I obey my elders and betters at all times—
which plainly you have never been taught to do.'

Oh, the monster! She hated him. Yes, she did. A
monkey! He had called her a monkey. Well, she would
dub *him* monster.

'Handsome is as handsome does—and says,' she flung
at her as her father put his strong hands under her arms
and lifted her up.

'Shame on you, daughter, for behaving so intemper-
ately. You shall be beaten for this, I promise you. But
only after you have married Andrew, Lord Exford, whom
you have so vilely insulted. And since you are so free

with maxims, let me remind you of one which you have forgotten, "Little children should be seen and not heard." '

Sobbing now, and trying to hide her face, for she felt so humiliated that she could look no one in the eye, Bess found herself being gently lifted away from her father. It was her aunt Hamilton who set her upon her feet again, and bent down to speak softly to her so that none other should hear what she had to say.

'Come, niece. I told your father that he should have prepared you for this day, but he believed that it would be better for you not to be forewarned. See, it is a handsome boy you are marrying, and a great family. Your father has done well for you. Now do you do well for him. Dry your tears and behave as a great lady should.'

A great lady. She wasn't a great lady. She was simply poor Bess Turville who was to be married against her will to someone who despised her.

What of that? Could *she* not despise *him*? After all, it was likely that, after today, she would not see him again until she was old enough to be truly his wife and able to bear his children.

Slowly Bess nodded her head—to her aunt's great relief—to say nothing of her father's. The only person not relieved was Andrew Exford himself, who had been hoping that this unseemly child's equally unseemly behaviour might rescue him from this marriage which had been forced upon him by his uncle and guardian, the man who stood at his elbow.

It was all very well to talk of money and lands and the right to give the title of Earl of Atherington to his eldest son when the father of the heiress whom he was marrying died, but his uncle wasn't having to marry a midget who resembled a monkey. Useless for his uncle to murmur in his ear that the child would grow and might, when older, come to resemble her handsome aunt.

As Bess already knew, blonde was beautiful in Andrew Exford's world, and Bess was far from blonde.

But Andrew—as he had told Bess—knew his duty, and since his duty was to increase the lands and wealth of the Exfords, he would do it. But the good God knew that he would not enjoy the doing.

Her eyes dried, a cup of water brought to her to drink, her aunt's comforting hand in hers, and Bess was ready to be married. Her father snorted at Master Judson, 'Begin, man. Forget Lady Elizabeth's childish megrims—she will soon grow out of them—and do your duty.'

Thus was the Lady Elizabeth Turville married to the most noble the Earl of Exford. Later that day, after a banquet of which she tasted nothing, for all the beautiful food put before her might as well have been straw, she was ritually and publicly placed in her husband's bed, a bolster between them. For this short public occasion they had been granted the Great Bed of Honour in which Robert, Lord Atherington, usually slept.

Neither Drew Exford nor his bride had spoken a word to the other since the wedding ceremony. It was quite plain to Bess that he had tried to avoid looking at her at all. Bess, on the other hand, when she did allow her eyes to stray to his face, glared her hatred at him.

That he should be so beautiful—and she so plain! His beauty, which she should have joyed in, hurt her. She lay stiff in the bed, her back to him, and when, a little time later, the ritual having been performed, her aunt returned to take her away, she gave him no farewell.

Nor did he say farewell to her.

Two days later Bess had watched his train leave the

House, making for the distant south which she had never visited. Before he left he had taken her small hand and placed a kiss on it. His perfect mouth had felt as cold as ice, so cold that she wanted to snatch it away, but dare not.

'I shall see you again when you are grown, wife,' were his last words to her.

Bess had nodded at him, and curtsied her farewell. She could not speak, and sensed her father's exasperation at her silence, but for once she would not obey him. All that she could think of was that she would soon be rid of her unwanted husband, whom she would only see again when, as he had said, she would be grown, ready to be his true wife and bear his child.

Once he had disappeared down the drive, Bess knew that she must face her father's anger at her misbehaviour. Before Andrew Exford's arrival it would have saddened her to be at odds with him, but, all unknowingly, he had lost the power to distress her. It was, Bess thought, back in the present again, as though in one short moment in the chapel she had grown up, had learned the arbitrary nature of her life, and that her father's love for her had its limits.

What her aunt had said was true. He should have warned her, prepared her for such a major change in her life, but he had, as he told his sister when the Exfords had left, 'No time to trouble with a child's whimwhams. She should be grateful for the splendid match I have made for her—and for Atherington.'

'And so I told her,' Mary Hamilton said, her voice sad, 'but she is only a child after all, and for some reason which I cannot fathom, and which she will not confess to me, she has taken against him. Which surprises me not a little, for he is a beautiful youth, well-mannered and courteous. I would have thought she would have received him as happily as though he were a prince who had wandered out of a fairy tale, not met him with hate.'

'Hate!' exclaimed Robert Atherington. He was a choleric man, who loved his daughter but would never understand her. Since neither he nor his sister had heard Andrew Exford's harsh words about her, Bess's dislike of him seemed wilful and beggared belief. They were both united in that.

'Hate,' he repeated. 'Well, Lady Elizabeth must learn to tolerate her groom. It will not be many years before he returns for her, and she must be ready for him.'

But Andrew Exford did not return. The years went by. Bess's father died of an ague, leaving Bess mistress of the House and all the Atherington lands, with her uncle Hamilton as her guardian. Soon afterwards he had a fall in the hunting field, and became a cripple, helpless and confined to his room. Aunt Hamilton became her niece's constant companion, and if Bess was a queen in Leicestershire, much as her namesake, Queen Elizabeth, was Queen of England, aunt Hamilton was in some sort her Queen Mother.

With the help of the vast staff, numbering over three hundred souls, which Robert Atherington had trained, Bess reigned over her small kingdom. Accounts and details of the estate which he owned, but never saw, were sent to her husband, and occasional monies which he needed to keep up his position at court. They were all acknowledged by his secretary, never by him. So far as Bess was concerned, he did not exist, and she had no wish to see him.

Looking back over the years to her wedding day, Bess stifled a sigh. How different her life would have been if she had not overheard Drew Exford's sneering comment.

Not that she had any quarrel with her life. There was always so much to do, so little time to do it. She had become expert in the running of her estate, and enjoyed herself mightily in performing all those duties which her husband would normally have carried out. Never having known him, she did not miss him, and hoped that he would stay away forever, as her distant cousin Lucy Sheldon's absent husband had done.

One thing which she never did was look in a mirror. And if, occasionally, aunt Hamilton said, 'Bess, my dear, you grow more handsome every day,' Bess put such an unlikely statement down to her aunt's kindness. Her aunt had mellowed with age, and she and Kirsty were a good pair of flatterers, as Bess frequently told them.

And now Drew Exford was proposing to visit her—if she could believe him. Useless to worry about how she was to greet him. 'Sufficient unto the day is the evil thereof,' she said aloud. 'I'll think about that when he arrives.'

'Damn it, Philip. Why can't I be like you, unencumbered?'

Drew Exford was towelling himself off after a hard game of tennis against Philip Sidney, who had been his friend since they had spent part of the Grand Tour of Europe together shortly after Drew had been married.

Philip smiled wryly. 'Unencumbered is it, dear friend? I think not. I am most encumbered since the Queen took Oxford's part against me after our recent fracas on the tennis court. I am encumbered by her disfavour and her dislike, particularly since she knows that I am much against her flirtation with the notion of a marriage to the French Duc d'Alençon. I am thinking of retiring to Wilton. Why not come with me? The air is sweet there, and most poetical. But what is it that troubles you? After all, you retain the Queen's favour, you are your own master and may do as you please.'

Drew buried his face in his towel. Philip was a good fellow, and although his pride was that of the devil he had a sweet nature, and a kind heart.

'If you must know, I am envying you your single state.'

'Eh, what's that?' Drew's voice had been muffled by the towel and Philip was not sure that he had heard aright. 'I thought that you were single, too. And I am beginning to lament my single state.'

Drew emerged from the towel. 'Oh, I was married in a hugger-mugger fashion ten years agone, before we posted to Europe together and spent our wild oats in Paris.' He paused, and made his confession. 'I have not seen the lady since.'

His friend stared at him. 'Ten years—and not seen her since? That beggars belief. Why so?'

He might have known that Philip's reaction would be a critical one. Philip Sidney liked—and respected— women. If he had affairs, he was so discreet that no one knew of them. His kindness and gentleness in his relations with the fair sex were a byword.

'She was but ten,' Drew said, almost as though confessing something, he was not sure what. He could not tell Philip that for some little time his adventurous life had begun to pall on him, and the game of illicit love, too. He had begun to dream of the child he had married. Strange dreams, for she was still a child in them, who must now be a woman. A woman who could be the mother of his children. His uncle had railed at him recently for not providing the line with an heir.

'She didn't like me,' he said, somewhat defiant in the face of Philip's raised brows, 'and she. . .' He stopped.

He could not be ungallant and repeat exactly what he had said ten years ago to his uncle—'You are marrying me to a monkey'—but he thought it.

'And all these years, whilst you jaunted round Europe and sailed the Atlantic, and ran dangerous diplomatic errands in France for that old fox Walsingham, I thought you single! Was she dark or fair, your child bride who didn't like you? I thought all the world, and the Queen, liked Drew Exford!'

'Well, *she* did not. And she was dark. I remember at the banquet after the wedding ceremony, she ate little—and rewarded me with the most basilisk stare. I thought that the Gorgon herself had brought forth a child, and that child was trying to stare me stone dead!'

'And did you bed the Gorgon?'

'After the usual fashion. They put a bolster between us for some little time. She turned her back on me, and never looked at me again. For which I was thankful. She was not pretty.'

'Poor child!' Philip's sympathy for Drew's neglected child bride was sincere. 'And where is she now? I suppose you know.' This last came out in Philip Sidney's most arrogant manner, revealing that he thought his friend's role in this sad story was not a kind one.

'At Atherington House, in Leicestershire. Her father died; her uncle acts as a kind of guardian to her in my absence.'

He strolled restlessly away from Philip to stare across the tennis court and towards the lawns and flowerbeds beyond. He remembered his anger at the whole wretched business. His uncle had sprung the marriage upon him without warning, and had expected him to be overjoyed. He had not felt really angry until that fatal morning in

Atherington House's chapel when he had first seen his bride.

An anger which had finally found its full vent when he had been left in the Great Bed with his wife. I have been given a child, he had thought savagely, not yet to be touched, and what's more, a child who will never attract me. I do not like her and I fear that she does not like me because, somehow, she overheard what I said of her.

Lying there, he had made a vow. In two days' time he would journey to London to take up his life again, leaving his monkey wife in the care of her father until she was of an age to be truly bedded. Once he had reached London and the court he would make sure that he never visited the Midland Shires again, except on the one occasion in the distant future when he needed to make himself an heir.

Now, in his middle twenties, that time had come, compelling him to remember what he had for so long preferred to forget. For to recall that unhappy day always filled him with a mixture of regret, anger, and self-dislike. His friendship with Philip Sidney had made the boy he had once been seem a selfish barbarian, not only in the manner that he had treated his neglected wife, but in other ways as well.

'*Preux chevalier*', or, the stainless knight, he had once mockingly dubbed Philip—who was not yet a knight— but at the same time he had been envious of him and his courtly manners.

Drew flung the towel down, aware that Philip had been silently gazing at him as he mused.

'What to do?' he asked, his voice mournful. 'The past is gone. I cannot alter it.'

'No,' returned Philip, smiling at last. 'But there is

always the future—which may change things again. A thought with which I try to reassure myself these days. We grow old, Drew. We are no longer careless boys. I must marry, and I must advise you to seek out your wife and come to terms with her—and with yourself. The man who writes sonnets to imaginary beauties, must at the last write one to his wife.'

'Come,' riposted Drew, laughing. 'Sonnets are written to mistresses, never to wives, you know that, *chevalier* Philip. But I take your point.'

'Well said, friend.' Philip flung an arm around Drew's shoulders as they walked from the tennis court together. 'Remember what I said about visiting me at Wilton some time. It is on the way to your place in Somerset. Tarry awhile there, I pray you.'

'Perhaps,' Drew answered him with a frown. For here came a page with a letter in his hand which, by his mien, was either for himself or for Philip. He stopped before them to hand the missive to Drew.

'From my master, Sir Francis Walsingham,' he piped, being yet a child. 'You are to read it and give me an answer straightway.'

Drew opened the sealed paper and read the few lines on it.

'Simple enough to answer at once,' he said cheerfully. 'You will tell Sir Francis that Andrew Exford thanks him for his invitation and will sup with him this evening.'

Philip Sidney watched the boy trot off in order to deliver his message. 'Well,' he said, smiling, 'at least, if Walsingham knows that you are already married, he will not be inviting you to supper in order to offer you his daughter, who is still only a child!'

Drew made his friend no answer, for he suspected that Sir Francis Walsingham was about to offer him something quite different. Something which might require him to journey to the Midland Shires which he had foresworn, and to the wife whom he had deserted ten years ago.

Chapter Two

'I cannot abide another moment indoors, Aunt. I have ordered Tib to saddle Titus for me. I intend to ride to the hunting lodge and break my fast in the open. The day is too fair for me to waste it indoors.'

Aunt Hamilton raised her brows. Bess's teeming energy always made her feel faint. That her niece was wearing a roughspun brown riding habit which barely reached mid-calf, showing below it a heavy pair of boots more suited to a twenty-year-old groom than a young woman of gentle birth, only served to increase her faintness.

'Must you sally out garbed more like a yeoman's daughter than the Lady of Atherington, dear child? It is not seemly. If you should chance to meet. . .'

She got no further. Bess, who was tapping her whip against the offending boots, retorted briskly, 'Who in the world do you imagine I shall meet on a ride on my own land who will care whether I am accoutred like the Queen, or one of her servants? I am comfortable in this, and have no intention of pretending that I am one of the Queen's ladies. Everyone for miles around Atherington knows who I am—and will treat me accordingly.'

Useless to say anything. Bess would always go her own way—as she had done since the day she was married. Mary Hamilton sighed and walked to the tall window which looked out on to the drive and beyond that towards Charnwood Forest. She watched Bess ride out; Tib and Roger Jacks, her chief groom in attendance.

If only her errant husband would come for her! He would soon put a stop to Bess's wilfulness, see that she dressed properly and conducted herself as a young noblewoman ought. Her niece behaved in all ways like the son her late brother had never managed to father, and the dear God alone knew where *that* would all end.

Bess, riding at a steady trot towards the distant hill on which the lodge stood, was also thinking about her absent husband. It was now a month since his letter had arrived and there was still no sign of him. She had hung his miniature on a black ribbon and wore it around her neck when she changed into a more ladylike dress on the Sabbath in order to please her aunt.

Occasionally she looked at the miniature in order to inspect him 'in small' as he had called it in his letter. She saw a slim, shapely man with a stronger face than the one which she remembered. If the painter had been accurate, his hair had darkened from silver gilt into a deep gold, and his mouth was no longer a Cupid's bow but a stern-seeming, straight line. It would be as well to remember that he was twenty-six years old, was very much a man, no longer a child. Bess felt a sudden keen curiosity to know what that man was like: whether the spoiled boy—she was sure now that he had been spoiled—had turned into a spoiled man.

They were almost at the small tower, which was all that the lodge consisted of. It stood high on its hill above the scrub and the stands of trees, for Charnwood Forest was thin on Atherington land, merging into pasture where cattle grazed. The open fields of nearby villages had been enclosed these fifty years and charcoal burning had stripped the forest of many of its trees. Over the centuries, successive Atherington lords had run deer for the chase, and the deer had attacked and stripped most of the trees which the charcoal burners had left.

'Shall you eat inside the tower—or out, mistress?' Tib asked her.

He had called her 'mistress' since they had been children together, and Bess had indulged him by allowing him to continue the custom when the rest of her servants had learned to call her Lady Bess. Another of her many offences, according to her aunt.

'After all,' Bess had said sensibly and practically, 'my true title is m'lady Exford, but since I do not care to use it, then any name will do, for all but *his* are equally incorrect.'

Aunt Hamilton knew who *his* referred to and was silenced. A common occurrence when she argued with her niece.

'Outside,' Bess told Tib, 'at the bottom of the hill. My uncle Hamilton once told me that the Queen picnicked in the open, and I am content to follow her example. All that will be missing will be her courtiers.'

Tib grinned at her. 'Roger and I will be your courtiers, mistress.'

Roger grunted at that. 'You grow pert, lad, and forget yourself.'

Really, to bring Roger along was like bringing her aunt with her! He was nearly as insistent on reminding her of her great station as she was. Nevertheless, Bess smiled at him as she shared her meal with them. Inside a wicker basket lined with a white cloth were a large meat pasty, several cold chicken legs, bread and cheese and the sweet biscuits always known as Bosworth Jumbles, and wine in a leather bottle. A feast, indeed, all provided by the kitchen for her and her two grooms. All her staff were agreed that the Lady Bess was a kind and generous mistress.

'Food in the open always tastes much better than food in the house,' she declared, her mouth full of bread and cheese, 'and wine, too.' She threw the bread crusts and the remains of the pasty to the two hounds which had followed in their rear, before lying back and sighing, 'Oh, the blessed peace.'

She could not have said anything more inapposite! The words were scarce out of her mouth when the noise of an approaching horse and rider broke the silence Bess had been praising. They were approaching at speed through the trees, and as they drew near it was apparent that the horse, a noble black, which was tossing its head and snorting, was almost out of his rider's control.

Foam dripped from its mouth: something—or someone—had frightened it, that much was plain. But its rider, a tall young man, was gradually mastering it, until, just as he reached Bess's small party, his steed suddenly caught its forefoot in a rabbit hole, causing it to stumble forward. His master, taken by surprise, was thrown over his horse's head—to land semi-conscious at Bess's feet.

She and her two grooms had sprung to their feet to try to avoid a collision. Their horses, tethered to nearby trees, neighed and pranced, whilst Bess's two hounds added to the confusion caused by this unexpected turn by running around, barking madly.

One of them, Pompey, bent over the stunned young man to lick his face. The other, Crassus, ran after the black horse which, hurt less than his rider, had recovered itself, and was galloping madly away. Roger untethered his mount and chased after it. Bess and Tib joined Pompey in inspecting the young man, who was starting to sit up.

Bess fell to her knees beside him, so that when, still a trifle dazed, he turned his head in her direction, she looked him full in the face.

Could it be? Oh, yes! Indeed, it could! There was no doubt at all that sitting beside her was the husband whom she had not seen for ten long years. He had stepped out of the miniature, to be present in large, not in small. If he had been beautiful as a boy, as a man he was stunningly handsome, with a body to match. So handsome, indeed, that Bess's heart skipped a beat at the mere sight of him, just as it had done on the long-ago day when she had first seen him.

What would he say this time to disillusion her? To hurt her so much that the memory of his unkind words was still strong enough to distress her?

He gave a pained half-smile, and muttered hoarsely, 'Fair nymph, from what grove have you strayed to rescue me?' before dropping his head into his hands for a moment, and thus missing Bess's stunned reaction to the fulsome compliment which he had just paid her.

It was quite plain that though she had known at once who he was, he had not the slightest notion that she was his deserted monkey bride!

Drew Exford had left London for Atherington a few days earlier. His supper with Sir Francis Walsingham had, as he had suspected, brought him a new task.

After they had eaten, and the women had left them alone with their wine, Sir Francis had said in his usual bland and fatherly fashion, 'You can doubtless guess why

I have summoned you hither this night, friend Drew.'

Drew had laughed. 'I believe that you wish to ask me to do you yet another favour. Even though I told you two years ago that I had done my duty by my Queen, and would not again become involved in the devious doings of the State's underworld, as I did when I was with the Embassy in France.'

Sir Francis nodded. 'Aye, I well remember you telling me that. Nor would I call on you for assistance again were it not that you are singularly well placed to assist me to preserve our lady the Queen and her blessed peace against those who would destroy it—and her.'

Drew raised his finely arched brows. 'How so?'

Sir Francis did not speak for a moment; instead, he drank down the remains of his wine. 'Your wife, I believe, lives at Atherington on the edge of Charnwood Forest. There are many Papists in the Midland counties who are sympathetic towards the cause of Mary, Queen of Scots, and would wish to kill her cousin, the Queen, and place Mary on the throne instead. Each summer the Queen of Scots is allowed by her gaoler, the Earl of Shrewsbury, to visit Buxton, to take the waters there. Her sympathisers from the surrounding counties visit the spa, and plot together on her behalf.

'I have reason to believe that this plotting has become more than talk. It is not so long since another party of silly Catholic squires from roundabout were caught trying to rebel against the Crown—and were duly punished for their treason. Alas, this has not, we now know, deterred others from trying to do the same.'

Drew leaned forward. 'A moment, sir. Are you telling me that my wife is one of these plotters?'

Sir Francis shook his head vigorously. 'No, no. The Crown has no more loyal servant than the Turvilles of

Atherington. Your wife's father was a friend of the Queen and helped to seat her on the throne. What I wish you to do is to go first to Atherington and thence to Buxton to find out what you can of this latest piece of treason—and then inform me through one of my men who will arrive some time after you do. You will know that he is my man and that you may trust him because he will show you a button identical with those I am wearing on my doublet tonight.

'You may give it about that your real objective in the Midland counties is to take up your true position as the lady's husband. Consequently, no one will suspect that you have an ulterior motive for journeying there. Thus you will kill two birds with one stone. You will do the state some service—and get yourself an heir at the same time.'

'Most kind of you,' riposted Drew somewhat sardonically, 'to consider my welfare as well as that of the Crown.'

'Exactly so,' returned Sir Francis, taking Drew's comment at face value. 'It is always my aim to assist my friends, and despite the difference in our ages, you are my friend, are you not?'

Drew thought it politic to signify his agreement.

His host showed his pleasure by pouring his guest another drink, and saying, 'You are a promising fellow, Drew. You have outgrown your youthful vanity—if you will allow me to say so—and you have a commendable shrewdness which has been honed by your journeyings to both the New and the Old World. I would wish to think of you as one of my inheritors. England needs such as yourself when Burghley and I are gone to our last rest.'

Drew laughed, his charm never more evident. 'There is little need to flatter me, sir. I will do your errand without it. But this will be the last. I would prefer to perform upon a larger stage—and not be suspected of being a common spy!'

'And so you shall. I repeat, I would not ask you were it not that your presence near to the Queen of Scots will be thought to be the result of your family circumstances—and for no other reason. Drink your wine, man, and pledge with me confusion to that Queen. I fear that, as long as she lives, our own Queen's life is not safe.'

That was Walsingham's coda. Afterwards they joined Lady Walsingham and her daughter and talked of idle and pleasant things.

And so Drew had no other choice than to see again the wife whom he had avoided for ten long years. He was not sure whether he was glad or sorry that meeting her was part of the duty which Walsingham had laid upon him. Each mile that he covered once London was left behind found him still reluctant to commit himself to Atherington House and its lady.

So much so that, when he had come almost to its gates, he and his magnificent train had stopped at an inn instead of journeying on, and he had taken Cicero out into the forest to try to catch a glimpse of the House, as though by doing so he could gauge the nature of either his welcome, or that of the greeting he would give her.

Except that Cicero, usually the most well-behaved of horses, saw fit to take against the whole notion of riding through the forest, and whilst trying to control him, he had lost control himself. As a result he was now sitting, shaken, not far from the House, and looking into the great dark eyes of a beautiful nymph who seemed to have strayed from the Tuscan countryside which he had visited with Philip Sidney and whose glories he had never forgotten.

By her clothing she was the daughter of one of the yeoman farmers who frequented these parts, and he wondered if they knew what a treasure they had in their midst. Well, if boredom overtook him at the House, he would know where to look for entertainment!

Something of this showed on his face. Bess, agitated, turned away from him in order to rise to her feet, so that she might not be too near him. He was altogether so overwhelming that she was fearful that she might lose the perfect control which had characterised her life since the day she had married him. He was not so shaken that he was incapable of putting forward his perfect hand and attempting to stay her.

'Nay, do not leave me, fair nymph, your presence acts as a restorative. You live in these parts?'

Bess, allowing herself to be detained, said, 'Indeed. All my life.' She had suddenly determined that she would not tell him her name, and prayed that neither Tib nor Roger, when he returned, would betray her.

'Send your brother away, my fair one, and I will give you a reward which will be sure to please you.' The smile Drew offered her was a dazzling one, full of promise, and he raised his hand to cup her sweet small breast, so delicately rounded.

Tib! He thought Tib her brother, not her servant! Aunt Hamilton had been right for once about the effect her clothing would have on a stranger. For was he not promising to seduce her? He was busy stroking her breast, and had blessed the hollow in her neck with a kiss which was causing her whole body to tremble in response. Oh, shameful! What would he do next? And would she like that, too?

She was about to be seduced by the husband who had once rejected her! Was not this strange encounter as good as a play? Or one of Messer Boccaccio's naughty stories?

She must end it at once. Now, before she forgot herself. Bess escaped his impudent hands and rose to her feet, putting her finger on her lips to silence Tib who, full of indignation at this slur upon his mistress, was about to tell their unexpected guest exactly who she was.

'Not now,' she murmured, smiling coyly at Drew, her expression full of promise. 'Another time—when we are alone.'

'Ah, I see you are a practised nymph, but then all nymphs are practised in Arcadia, are they not?' smiled Drew, enjoying the sight of her now that his senses had cleared. For not only was she a dark beauty of a kind which he had learned to appreciate in Italy, but she had a body to match, of which her rough riding habit hid little, since she was wearing no petticoats under it, nor any form of stiffening designed to conceal the body's contours. He had not thought Leicestershire harboured such treasures as this.

Bess's reply to him was a simper, and a toss of the head. She was astonished at herself: she had not believed that she could be capable of such deceptive frivolity.

But I am, after all, a daughter of Eve, she thought with no little amusement, and, faced with a flattering man, Eve's descendants always know how to behave. Perhaps it might be the thing to flounce her skirt a little as she had seen her cousin Helen do when she visited her and wished to attract one of the gallants whose attentions Bess always avoided, she being a married woman.

Also present was the gleeful thought, How shocked he will be when he learns who I really am, and that he was offering to seduce his own wife!

She watched him stand up with Tib's help, which he did not really need, although he courteously accepted the proffered arm. By his manner and expression he was about to continue to continue his Arcadian wooing, but, alas for him, even as did so he heard in the distance a troop of horse arriving.

Drew stifled a sigh. It was almost certainly part of his household who had followed him at a discreet distance to ensure his safety, even though he had repeatedly told them not to.

'Yes, it must be another time, I fear, that we dally among the spring flowers,' he said regretfully.

His cousin Charles Breton, his mother's sister's son, arrived in the small clearing, at the head of his followers, exclaiming as he did so, 'So, there you are, Drew. But where is your horse?'

'He unshipped me most scurvily,' Drew told him, no whit ashamed, Bess noted, at having to confess his failure to control his errant steed. 'But I have been rescued by the shepherdess you see before you—and her brother,' and he waved a negligent hand at Tib. 'They have not yet had time to offer me a share of their picnic, else my pastoral adventure would be complete. Ah, I see that they have even rescued Cicero for me.'

So they had, for Roger rode up, his face one scowl, with Cicero trotting meekly along beside him, apparently unharmed.

'Here is your horse, young sir,' he growled, 'and another time show the forest a little more respect. It is not like the green lanes of the south where a man may gallop at his will!'

'How now, sirrah?' exclaimed Charles. 'Do you know to whom you speak? Show a proper humility towards your betters!'

Roger opened his mouth, ready to inform him that he knew who his betters were, and furthermore, that they included Lady Exford who stood before them, and around whom Drew had now placed a familiar arm. In vain, before he could speak, his lady forestalled him.

'Oh, my groom has a free spirit, sir, as all we dwellers in these parts have. And now I must bid you adieu, for my duties await me. The cows must be fed, and the day wears on.'

Adroitly, she wriggled out of Drew's half-embrace and, without either Tib or Roger's assistance, swung athletically on to her horse. Seeing Roger about to speak again, she said smartly, 'Silence, man. You must not offend these great ones. And you, too, brother.'

Tib's answer to that was a grin. He possessed to the full the countryman's desire to make fools of townies and, by God, these were townies indeed, with their fine clothing and their drawling speech. Particularly the one whose horse had thrown him, who had been so busy making sly suggestions to his mistress.

He and Roger mounted their horses, whilst Drew, seeing his nymph ready to abandon him—rather than simply turn herself into a tree, as Daphne had done when pursued by Apollo—seized the bridle of Bess's horse, and exclaimed, 'Not so fast. I am Drew Exford, and I would know who you are.'

Bess looked down into his perfect face, and, giving him a smile so sweet that it wrenched his heart, she said softly, 'But I have little mind to tell you, sir. You must discover it for yourself. Now, let me go, Master Drew Exford, for I have no desire to be behindhand with the day.'

He could not be so ungallant as to insist, especially with Charles's amused eyes on him, and the snickers of her two companions, who were enjoying his discomfiture plainly audible. There was nothing for it but to stand back and watch her tap her whip smartly on her horse's flank and ride off, the two men behind her, leaving Drew to gaze after her.

'Was she real, or are we dreaming?' he said, turning to Charles, who had dismounted and was staring at him as he added energetically, 'Come, let us follow them.'

Only for Charles to place an urgent hand on his sleeve. 'Nay, Drew. You have had a fall, the day grows old and we must ready ourselves to be at Atherington on the morrow. You do intend to visit your wife, do you not? Hardly the perfect start to your visit, to seduce one of her tenant's daughters before you even bid her good day.'

Drew nodded his head reluctantly. 'I suppose that you have the right of it. But have you ever seen such a divine face and form? Dress her in fine clothing and she would have half London at her feet.'

'Now, Drew, you do surprise me,' drawled Charles as the pair of them remounted. 'I had thought that your wish would be for her to have no clothes on at all!'

Chapter Three

'So, he is here, at last,' twittered aunt Hamilton, shaken out of her usual calm when a courier arrived with m'lord Exford's letter for her husband, Sir Braithwaite Hamilton, informing him that he was lying at an inn nearby and proposed to arrive at Atherington House shortly after noon. He would be grateful if Sir Braithwaite would apprise his niece, Lady Exford, of the news, and also make Atherington House ready to entertain his train.

She continued excitedly, half-expecting her niece to refuse to do any such thing, 'And when you meet him you must be dressed in something more appropriate to your station than that old grey kirtle you have seen fit to wear today.'

'Indeed, indeed,' agreed Bess equably and surprisingly. She had every intention of being as splendidly dressed as possible to receive her husband, if only to disconcert him the more when he realised who the nymph of Charnwood Forest really was.

'Does he not know that my poor husband has been unfit to arrange anything these past five years?' aunt Hamilton continued, still agitated, and quite unaware that Bess had kept this interesting fact from her husband lest he send a steward—or, worse still, arrive himself—to manage Atherington's affairs. He was quite unaware that Bess had been in charge since Sir Braithwaite had lost his wits after his accident—another surprise for him, and perhaps not a welcome one, was Bess's rueful thought.

He was sure to demand that some man should replace her, even though Bess had managed Atherington lands more efficiently than her uncle. In that she was similar to another Bess, she of Hardwick, who was also Countess of Shrewsbury, and who ruled her husband as well as their joint estates.

'He has probably forgotten,' prevaricated Bess, who had long developed a neat line in such half-truths. 'He has such a busy life about the court—and elsewhere,' she ended firmly, although she had not the smallest notion what her husband had been doing during the long years of his absence.

'Nevertheless. . .' Her aunt frowned, prepared to say more had not a well-known glint in Bess's eye silenced her. She decided to concentrate instead on arranging for her usually wild niece to look, for once, like the great lady which she was by birth and marriage.

'And you will receive him in the Great Hall as soon as he arrives, I suppose?'

'Nay.' Bess shook her head. 'I am sure that he and his train will wish to change their clothing and order themselves properly after their long journey. Only after that shall I welcome him—and then in the Great Parlour. I have given Gilbert orders to lay out a meal in the Hall for a score of us. Lord Exford—' she would not say 'my husband' '—writes that he is bringing six gentlemen of his household with him, as well as his Steward, and Treasurer, and Clerk Comptroller—to inspect our finances, no doubt. His servants, of whom there are a dozen, may eat in the kitchens. It is fortunate that since he wrote that he might visit us I have arranged for a greater supply of provisions than we usually carry. I suspected that he might arrive without warning.'

Aunt Hamilton said, almost as though regretting it, 'You are always beforehand with your arrangements, my dear.'

'Oh, I have a good staff who only cross me when they are sure I am wrong,' returned Bess, who had spent the morning with her Council discussing how to ensure that m'lord Exford's visit was a success. They were all men, so Bess's lady-in-waiting, Kate Stowe, always sat just behind her to maintain the proprieties.

At first, when Sir Braithwaite had become incompetent, they had been wary of Bess taking his place, but she had soon shown how eager she was to learn and, despite her lack of years, had shown more commonsense than Sir Braithwaite had ever displayed—even before he had lost his wits. Three years ago she had insisted on reducing her household from nearly three hundred people to little more than a hundred and fifty, arguing correctly that Atherington was beginning to run into needless debt by providing for so many unnecessary mouths.

'But you have a station to keep up, my child,' aunt Hamilton had wailed. 'We great ones are judged by the number of those we gather around us.'

'Nothing to that,' Bess had replied firmly, 'if by doing so we run headlong into ruin. If we continue as we are, we shall eventually arrive at a day when we shall lose our lands, and scarcely be able to employ anyone. How should that profit Atherington?'

Nor did her household know that she had failed to inform her husband of Sir Braithwaite's misfortune, for she had quietly destroyed the letters of her Clerk comptroller telling of it, and substituted others with the documents and accounts which were sent south.

And now, at last, the day of reckoning was here, and to the half-fearful excitement of meeting her husband in her proper person was added that of facing both him and her staff when they discovered her deceptions. Unless, of course, she managed to conceal them. How, she could not imagine.

No one could have guessed at the contrary emotions which were tearing Bess apart. She seemed, indeed, to be even more in command than usual when she spent her early morning with her Council. And this unnatural calm stayed with her during a late-morning session with aunt Hamilton and Kate Stowe—as well as sundry tiring maids—being dressed to receive the Exford retinue in proper style.

Usually Bess greeted being turned out 'like a maypole in spring', as she always put it, with great impatience. Today, however, aunt Hamilton was both surprised and gratified by her willingness to please, and her readiness to wear the magnificent Atherington necklace which her niece had always dismissed as too barbaric and heavy, even for formal use. Perhaps it was the prospect of meeting her husband which was causing her to behave with such uncharacteristic meekness.

If so, aunt Hamilton could only be pleased that Bess was at last going to behave like the kind of conventional young woman whom she had always wished her to be.

She was not to know that her niece was gleefully preparing, not to be counselled and corrected by her husband, but rather to wrongfoot him with the knowledge of exactly who it was that he had been so eager to seduce on the previous day!

*　　*　　*

Contrary emotions were also tearing at Drew Exford. The flippancy of his cousin Charles—which he usually encouraged to lighten the burden of his great station— grated badly on him the nearer he approached the time to meet his long-deserted wife.

Of what like was she now, m'lady Exford? Was she still as plain as the child he had abandoned? He prayed not, but he feared so. But this time he would be kind, however ugly she might prove to be.

He remembered Philip Sidney saying of a plain woman, 'She does not deserve our mockery, but our pity. For we see her but occasionally, whilst she has to live with her looks forever. Always remember, Drew, that she has a heart and mind as tender as that of the most beautous she. Nay, more so, for she lives not to torment our sex by using her looks as a weapon, but practises instead those other female virtues which we prize not in youth, but value in age. Loving kindness, charity and mercy—and the ability to order a good household!'

Easy enough to say, perhaps, but hard to remember when a young man's blood is young and hot. Perhaps here, Drew hoped, in leafy Leicestershire, away from the temptations of London and the court, he might find in his wife those virtues of which Philip had spoken.

'You're quiet today, Drew,' Charles observed as he drew level with his cousin who had ridden ahead of his small procession. 'Thinking of your bride, no doubt, who probably does not resemble the Arcadian shepherdess of yestermorn very much.'

This was too near to the bone for Drew to stomach. He put spurs to his horse and left Charles and the rest behind, and stayed ahead of them until Atherington House was reached.

And a noble pile it was. Square and built of red brick,

a small tower had been added on each corner to remind the commonalty that although a castle no longer stood on high to menace them, power and might in this part of Leicestershire still belonged to the Turvilles.

There was a formal garden on one side of the house, and stables at the back. It had been built around a central quadrangle filled with a lawn which was bordered by beds of herbs and simples. An arcaded walk had been added to one wall. A small chapel stood at a little distance from the main building.

But all this was yet to be discovered by the visitors. Drew waited for his people to catch him up, whereupon he sent the most senior of his pages before him as a herald to inform Atherington that its master had arrived. But even before the page reached the main entrance with its double doors of the stoutest oak, they were flung open and a crowd of servants appeared, opening up an avenue for Drew and his gentlemen to walk through when they had dismounted. A burly Steward, carrying a white staff of office, came forward to meet them.

He bowed low to Drew and his company. 'My mistress, your good lady, bids me greet you, my noble lord. Knowing that your journey from London has been both long and hard, she has arranged to meet you, m'lord, and your gentlemen, in the Great Parlour, after you have had the ordering of yourselves. I most humbly beg you to follow me to your quarters.' He bowed again.

Drew heard Charles give a stifled laugh. Himself, he wanted to fling the man on one side and demand to be taken immediately to his wife. His self-control and temper hung in the balance—and, what was more, Charles and the others knew it. Self-control won. After all, what matter it that he met his wife early or late, when as soon as they did meet he would make it his purpose to show her that he was the master at Atherington.

'I thought,' murmured Charles in his ear, 'that you told me that your wife's uncle was Regent here for you. But yon popinjay made no mention of him. Would you wish me to remind him of who rules at Atherington?'

Charles was merely saying aloud what Drew was thinking. Nevertheless he shook his head. 'No, I do not wish my own rule to begin in dissension and unpleasantness. Later we will arrange things to my liking. For the present we go with the tide.'

Again, easy to say, but hard to do.

It was, therefore, some little time before Drew and his gentlemen were escorted by the same Steward from their quarters in one of the towers down the winding staircase towards the entrance hall and the double doors which led first to the Great Hall. From thence they processed to the Great Parlour—the room where the owners of Atherington took their private leisure. These days the Great Hall was reserved for more formal functions.

Drew had dressed himself magnificently in cloth of the deepest silver with a hint of cerulean blue in it. The colours emphasised—as they were intended to do—his blonde beauty. His doublet had the new peasecod belly. His breeches were padded with horsehair, and his long stockings of the palest cream were visible until just above his knee where they were supported by garters made of fine blue and silver brocade.

His ruff was also of the newest fashion, being oval in shape, rather than round, and was narrow, not deep. It was held up behind his head by an invisible fine wire frame. His leather shoes had long tongues and small cork heels. A sapphire ring decorated one shapely hand; a small gold locket hung around his neck, its case adorned by a large diamond.

Charles and his other gentlemen were similarly dressed, but not so richly. They formed the most exquisitely presented bevy of young male beauty such as Atherington had not seen for many a long year.

They marched in solemn procession through the Great Hall, already laid out for a formal banquet, and then through an oak door richly carved with the Tree of Life, and into the Great Parlour, a large splendidly furnished room, whose leaded windows looked out on to the central quadrangle.

Facing them was a group of people as richly dressed as themselves, although not quite in the latest fashion. All but two of them were men. In front of them, with another, and older woman, standing a little behind her, stood a young woman of middle height as richly and fashionably dressed as he was, in a gown whose deep colours of burnt sienna, rich gold and emerald green were in marked contrast to the pastel hues of Drew and his train.

As though she were the Queen she made no effort to walk towards him, but stood there, waiting for him to approach her, her head held high, her face concealed by a large fan, so that all that Drew could see of her was her rich dark hair, dressed high on her head, and a single pearl resting on her forehead above the fan's fluted edge.

At last, reluctantly, he moved forward, bowing, as did his followers. Straightening up, he found that he had no wish to see the face which was hidden behind the fan. He had a form of words ready for her, which would contain no reference to what had passed between them ten years ago, or to her looks—for that might be tactless.

'Madam,' he began—and then paused for a brief moment before he spoke the words which flowed from him almost against his will. 'We meet at last, m'lady Exford.'

On hearing this, his wife slowly lowered the fan to show him her face for the first time.

Drew stood there paralysed. For the face before him was that of the beautiful nymph whom he had lusted after—and had offered to seduce—in Charnwood Forest on the previous day.

But the nymph had worn rough clothing and had moved and spoken with the wild freedom of a creature of the woods. This woman was a lovely icon, standing stiff and proud in her formal clothing. But, oh, her face was the perfect oval he remembered, the lips as crimson, shapely and tender, the eyes as dark, and her complexion, yes, her complexion, was of the purest and smoothest ivory, with the faintest rose blush to enhance its loveliness. And beneath her stiff clothing her body was surely as luscious and inviting.

Drew, standing there, dumbstruck, all his usual rather cold command quite gone, heard his cousin Charles give a stifled groan—turning it into something between a cough and a laugh as he, too, recognised the woodland nymph. The sound brought him back to life again, even as he wondered what in the world had happened to the dark monkey-like child of ten years ago.

Had his wits been wandering then? Or were they wandering now?

Had it been a changeling he had seen? Or was this woman the changeling? Without conscious thought, courtier-like, as though greeting his Queen, Elizabeth herself, he went down on one knee before her and took into his own hand that of his wife's which was not holding the fan.

Turning it over, he kissed, not the back but the palm

of the hand—a long and lingering kiss—and thought that he detected a faint quiver in it. But as he looked up there was no sign of emotion in the cold, aloof face of the woman before him.

Why did she not speak? As though she had picked his thought out of the air, she said at last in the wood nymph's honeyed tones, 'As the old adage has it, better late than never, m'lord. Permit me to introduce you to my good counsellors—and yours—who have served you well these many years.'

She had looked him in the eye for one fleeting moment before she began to name the men around her. Her manner reminded him again of that of his Queen. But that Elizabeth was a ruler, and this woman ruled nothing. He waited, as she introduced them one by one, for her to name the Master of her Household, Sir Braithwaite Hamilton, but although she introduced his wife to him, his name did not pass her lips, and he was not one of the men around her, either.

He murmured his acknowledgments, as did those gentlemen of his train whose duties matched those of the men around his wife, before he questioned her.

'And Sir Braithwaite Hamilton who rules here, where is he?'

Drew was not prepared for the manner in which his question was received. The heads of Atherington's male Council turned towards him in some surprise. His wife gave him a cool and non-committal smile.

She raised her fan and said to him over it, 'You forget, m'lord. As I informed you at the time, Sir Braithwaite has been an invalid bereft of his wits these five long years, and my Council and I rule in his place.'

Bess had expected his question, and was prepared to offer him a brazen lie in answer to it. Oh, this pinked and perfumed gallant who plainly thought that every pretty woman he met was his rightful prey, who had recognised her immediately, and on whose face she had read the shock he had received on learning what his ugly child bride had turned into during his absence, did not deserve that she should be truthful with him.

Drew's face changed again, as he received this second shock—the first having been the changed face of his wife. It was as though he were standing on one of the Atlantic beaches which he had visited during his merchant adventurer years, watching the surf come rolling in, each wave bigger than the last.

How he kept his composure he never knew. The hot temper which he had so carefully controlled these many years threatened to overwhelm him. He mastered himself with difficulty as he bade it depart, so that, like a dog retiring to its kennel, it slunk into a corner of his mind where it might rest until he was ready to indulge it.

He said, or rather muttered to her, 'I see that we have a deal of matters to discuss in private, madam.'

If he had thought that visiting—and disposing of— his wife was going to be a simple matter beside the duty which Walsingham had laid on him, he was rapidly being disabused of any such notion.

The smile his wife gave him in reply was, he noted, as false as Hell, as false as the letters he had received from her over the years. 'Indeed, and indeed,' she murmured sweetly, lowering her fan, and showing him the glory of her face, 'there is much of which we have to speak.'

'Beginning with honesty.' He made his voice as grim as he dare without causing an open affront. He had no mind for a public altercation with the double-dealing bitch before him. But, oh, how he longed for them to be private together!

'Oh, honesty!' Bess carolled, displaying animation for the first time. 'It is a virtue which I prize highly. Like chastity. Another virtue which I am sure, knowing you, that you prize also, my dear husband.'

He heard Charles's stifled laughter behind him again.

Drew thought of yesterday's unconfined behaviour of the demure woman before him. 'You would give me lessons in it, wife?' he riposted, his voice now dangerous as well as grim.

'Aye, sir. If you think that you need them. My acquaintance with you is not sufficiently lengthy for me to be able to make a judgement on the matter.' She paused, leaned forward and tapped his chest provocatively with her fan. 'They say that first impressions are frequently faulty, m'lord! What do you say?'

Drew wanted to say nothing. What he wanted to do was to place the impudent baggage across his knee and give her such a paddling as she would never forget.

But he was hamstrung by the formality of the occasion, and by the fact that so far she was wrongfooting him at every turn, so that he was finding it difficult to gain any verbal advantage over her. Much more of this and Charles would be openly laughing at him—and he could well imagine the smirks of his gentlemen.

Oh, what a fine play this whole wretched business would make with a title along the lines of, *The Nymph and the Satyr, or, the Man Who Tried to Seduce His Own Wife*. How much he would enjoy this situation if only some other poor fool was in the middle of it, and not himself.

He spoke at last, conscious that he had been silent for some time. He was surprised at how bored and indifferent he sounded. 'Why, madam, that is one matter which I would prefer to discuss in private with you. I cannot say how much I look forward to doing so.'

He let his gaze rove around the room, taking in the men standing watching them, more than a little bemused by this byplay, and said, in a low voice which none other but she could hear, 'And your youthful escort, madam, who follows you to play with you in the woods, where is he? I see him not here.'

What, was he jealous? This was delightful, was it not? Bess could see that every word she uttered was a dart striking home. He had come to lord it over her, to stress his superiority and by his own wilful and lustful behaviour, and her wicked conduct in not enlightening him as to who she was, she had him at a disadvantage— who should have been at a disadvantage herself.

'Oh, you shall see him soon—when you are introduced to the rest of my servants. In the meantime I have instructed my Council to have ready for you and your Comptrollers all the books and accounts relating to Atherington's affairs. First, perhaps, we should eat. A feast has been prepared in your honour.'

'So I see, madam.' He was glacial now. 'But permit me to correct you. First I should like to be taken to see Sir Braithwaite—to reassure myself as to his condition.'

Aunt Hamilton, who had been listening with increasing agitation to the hostilities being conducted in her presence, took it upon herself to say, 'Oh, m'lord, I can assure you that his condition is as was described to you when he first fell ill after his accident. He has not improved.'

Drew's blue gaze was stern. 'I thank you for that reassurance, Lady Hamilton, but I would prefer to see him for myself. My cousin Charles, who is my Chief

Comptroller, will accompany me. There is no need for either of you two ladies to do so. Only after I have paid him my respects shall I break bread. Pray order the Steward, Lady Exford, to conduct me to him.'

'Willingly, husband,' Bess said, dipping him a deep curtsey. 'I am always yours to command.'

'See that you are, madam, see that you are. I do not care for wilful, forward women who think they know better than their husbands.'

Oh, yes, she had stung him, and seeing his grim face Bess knew that she was going to pay for it. But for the present she had enjoyed herself mightily—and in the end everything had to be paid for. Which was a maxim her father had taught her. What he had been unable to teach her was what form payment might take!

Charles began to speak to his cousin the moment that they were safely out of the Great Parlour and walking towards the main staircase. Drew stopped, took him by the arm and said roughly, 'Not now, later. When we are alone. For the present we are to see Sir Braithwaite Hamilton, who, until a few minutes ago, I thought was in charge of my lands here. After that we may talk.'

Sir Braithwaite was, as his wife and niece had said, a helpless invalid. He was incapable of coherent speech, and physically little more active than a baby. He stared affably at Drew and Charles from a great chair placed before a window overlooking the kitchen gardens after his attendant had nudged him and pointed to his visitors. He spoke, but his speech was a babble. Drew thought that by his appearance he was not long for this world, but later the doctor attending him said that he had been of this countenance since his accident.

So, his lady wife had been deceiving him—and by the looks of it—her own Council, ever since Sir Braithwaite had become witless, by not informing him of her uncle's condition! He was certain that she had never sent him any letter reporting the true facts of it, however much she said to the contrary.

He dismissed the Steward when he reached the bottom of the stairway which led into the entrance hall, and pushed Charles into a room which opened off it.

'Now, Charles, what the devil has been going on here? The man I thought was my Comptroller is a blinking idiot, and my lady wife is not only running the household and the estates, but is riding around the countryside dressed like a milkmaid inviting seduction.'

Charles said, choking with laughter, 'Your face, Drew, your face when you saw that the nymph you tried to seduce was your own wife! A beauty, though, a very Helen of Troy. Whyever did you tell me that she was plain?' and he began to laugh helplessly.

Drew grasped his cousin by the shoulders and turned him so that they were face to face, eye to eye. Charles was still trying to control his amusement, whilst Drew was as grim as Hercules about to embark on another of his labours—as Charles told him later.

He hissed at his cousin, 'If you laugh, Charles, I shall kill you! That is a promise, not a threat!'

Charles rearranged his face, and said, as solemnly as he could, 'What, laugh? I laugh? No, no, I merely choked a little—from surprise, you understand. This is a grave matter, a very grave matter, m'lord.'

'And do not m'lord me, either. Damnation and Hell surround me and every devil with a pitchfork is sticking me with it. How in God's name was I to know that that wanton nymph in the woods yesterday was my wife? And he I thought her brother—in Hell's name, who was he? Was she wantoning with him in the greenwood? I can believe anything of her after the way in which she taunted me just now.'

'Most strange,' agreed Charles, his face solemn, but his eyes had an evil glint in them as he savoured Drew's discomfiture. 'As I said earlier, repute had it that she was plain, and you did not deny it, on the contrary.'

'Hell's teeth,' roared Drew who had lost all his usual calm control and the measured speech which went with it. 'She resembled naught so much as a monkey ten years agone. What alchemist has she visited to turn herself into such a...such...?' He ran out of words.

'A pearl?' Charles finished for him, still as grave as a parson.

Drew raved on. 'I was prepared to be patient with her, and kind, because she was so plain, you understand. But what shall I do with her now that she has caught me trying to seduce a woodland maiden who turned out to be my own wife? She never said a word to enlighten me, into the bargain, but inwardly enjoyed the jest at my expense. And after *that*, she had the impudence to twit me with her chastity—and my lack of it.'

Charles could not help himself. He began to laugh until the tears ran down his face. 'Confess, Drew, what a fine jest *you* would think this if it were happening to someone else!'

Drew stared at him, and then, as his cousin's words struck home, he began to laugh himself at the sheer absurdity of it all. Laughter dissipated his rage—it slunk back again into its kennel. When he spoke, his voice showed that he had regained his usual cold command.

'Merriment purges all, Philip Sidney once said. You were right to laugh, Charles, at the spectacle of my High Mightiness brought low by a woman. Now I am myself again, and by my faith, the best way to treat my lady wife will be to behave as though yesterday was a dream—which I did not share. More, I shall sort out her deception over the ruling of Atherington in such a way as will offer her no satisfaction, no chance to enjoy any more secret jests at my expense.'

'Oh, bravo! That is more like yourself, Drew. Come, let us to the feast.'

'Aye, Charles, where I shall behave like a grave and reverend *signor* who would never attempt to tumble a chance-met wench in the greenwood!'

Chapter Four

'Bess, my dear, I cannot understand how it was that your husband did not know of Sir Braithwaitte's illness! I distinctly remember that he was informed. You said that he might have forgotten—but how could he forget a matter of such importance? It would be most careless of him, and he does not appear to be a careless person. I was always surprised that he appointed no one in my husband's place, but allowed you to take over the governance of Atherington!'

Aunt Hamilton had been twittering away to Bess on this undesirable subject ever since Drew and Charles had left them. Walter Hampden, her Chief Comptroller, had also approached her, frowning heavily, as they awaited her husband's return to the Great Parlour. Bess had silenced him by immediately turning on her heel and ordering Gilbert to arrange for goblets of sack to be brought through to the company, ostensibly to help them while away the time until dinner, but actually to keep them from questioning her.

Even so, Walter, a neglected goblet of wine in his hand, had not taken this none-too-subtle hint, but began immediately to question her, saying, 'Madam, I would have a word with you. I remember that we wrote several times to Lord Exford informing him of Sir Braithwaite's sad mishap, so how was it that he knew nothing of it? Most strange, most strange.' He shook his old head in wonderment as he finished.

He had been Sir Braithwaite's trusted right-hand man, and had continued as Bess's after it was plain that Lord Exford, by his silence, seemed happy for matters to continue as they were, without sending his man to oversee Atherington's affairs.

Atherington, under his and Bess's guidance, with the help of the Council, had subsequently become so prosperous that after a time Walter had ceased to question this somewhat odd arrangement. As Bess had feared, however, Drew's apparent ignorance of the truth about Sir Braithwaite's condition was beginning to trouble him.

'Oh, I am sure that this is but a misunderstanding,' Bess proclaimed feverishly, wishing that Drew wuld return so that they could repair to the Great Hall and set about the banquet. Her husband could scarcely expect her to begin discussing matters of business whilst they were eating and drinking their way through Atherington's bounty.

His grim face, however, when he returned from Sir Braithwaite's tower room, gave her no reason to expect that she was going to receive much mercy from him, either at the banquet—or anywhere else. His cousin Charles, by contrast, had an expression on his face which showed that one person, at least, was deriving some amusement from the situation.

'I am at your service, madam,' Drew announced. 'Bid your Steward to escort us to the Hall.'

He held his hand out to take hers as though nothing was amiss, but his mouth, set in a hard straight line, was an indication that their private life, like their public one, was to be as coldly formal as his voice.

Gilbert the Steward, however, was delighted. If he had a complaint about Lady Bess's rule, it was that she was too easy in her conduct of it. All the heavily manned little ceremonies which Sir Braithwaite had insisted upon had been done away with. And, since they mostly centred around Gilbert's affairs, he had felt that his station in the Atherington household had been demeaned.

Plainly his new master thought differently, and so they all processed majestically into the Hall, where pages, at Gilbert's instructions, ran forward with napkins and bowls of water. The napkins were to protect the guests' fine clothing, and the water was for them to rinse their hands in after they had eaten of the roast beef, the chickens, the pigs' trotters and all the other delicacies carried in on great platters by another half-score of obedient pages. The napkins then found their further use in drying wet hands, although some still preferred the old custom of waving them in the air. Gilbert was beside himself with joy.

Not so Bess. She hated ceremony, considering it a waste of precious time. For her, informality was all. She wondered what Drew's preference was. The fact that he was being so correct in his conduct today was not necessarily a guide to his character if she remembered how lustily—and improperly—he had set about her yesterday!

She stole a look at his noble profile as he sat beside her. It was still grim, and his mouth was set in stern lines. She wondered if she dare try to soften it. She would have to go carefully, for seated as they were in the place of honour in the middle of the long table, all eyes were upon them, save for those few of their senior officers who shared their side of it.

She was about to speak when Drew forestalled her.

'I desire an explanation from you, madam my wife, as to why you did not see fit to inform me of your uncle's grave and disabling accident.'

So, war had been declared, had it? There was to be no peace over the dinner plates. The best form of defence, Bess had long ago concluded, was attack. She went on to it, keeping her voice low, but firm.

'Not so, m'lord husband. You were kept fully informed. Do try the chicken legs, I beg of you. They are tenderer than most because of the delicate foodstuffs Dame Margery insists on. Meat cannot be tender, she avows, if what is put in the animal to make it grow is tough.' The gaze she turned on Drew was a melting one.

Drew was not melted. 'To the devil with Dame Margery—and her chicken legs, too,' he said roughly. 'Do not seek to deceive me, wife. I am of the belief that you lied to your Council and to me.'

'Now why should you think that, husband? And it is unkind of you to curse Dame Margery. She is a very hard worker, and loyal to Atherington—as are all my servants.'

'And is she a liar, too? Does she also go running around. . .?' Drew stopped himself and cursed inwardly. He had not meant to refer to yesterday's contretemps, and here he was reminding her of it! Not a very clever ploy. In life, as in chess, one did not give the enemy an advantage. He swallowed his words and started again.

'You may be sure that I, and my advisers, will examine your books and documents with the utmost care, and if I find any maladministration, I shall know full well who is to blame.'

Attack! Attack! Trumpets were blowing in Bess's brain. 'And you will not blame yourself, husband—if you do find anything amiss, which I doubt—that for ten long years you have ignored Atherington and left us to our fate? I have been a woman for six full summers, ready to do a wife's duty, and bear your children. Address your reproaches to the one who deserves them, sir, which is not my good self, but one who is nearer home to you!'

Oh, sweet Lord! Now she had done it. She had lost her temper—as, by his expression, he was losing his. He leaned forward, food forgotten, and said between his teeth, 'Do you not fear a day of reckoning, my lady wife? For you should.'

'No more than you should,' returned Bess hardily.

How dare he reproach her, how dare he? Her eyes flashed at him, as they locked with his, stare for stare. Not only their food, but the spectators were forgotten.

'Oh, indeed,' he sneered. 'And that youth who was with you yesterday—is all seemly between you?' He had meant to save this for the privacy of their room, but the woman would tempt a saint to misbehave, for even as they wrangled he wanted to fall upon her and have his way with her; the way which he had been denied yestermorn.

For she was temptation itself. How could he be moved by one who was so unlike all the women whom he had favoured so far? She was black, not blonde, her eyes were dark, not blue, her complexion was pale, not rosy, she was not small, but was of a good height—and instead of being meek in speech she had a tongue like the Devil. Nor did she fail to use it at every turn.

By God, it would be a pleasure to master her, to ride her to the Devil who had blessed, nay, cursed her with that tongue. Aye, and beyond him to the lowest pit of

Hell where only the demons lurked, forgotten even by their unsavoury Lord! The very thought of using her so was doing cruel and untoward things to his body.

Drew tried to calm himself. He must not let her catch him on the raw every time she spoke.

'I think you mistake a woman's place, madam. It is to be quiet, to obey her lord, to be meek at all times. . .'

'I'd as lief be dead!' Bess could not help herself. The words flew out of her, interrupting him in his catalogue of what a good woman should be.

'I have no mind,' she exclaimed in ringing tones which the whole table could hear, 'to be like patient Griselda in Master Chaucer's poem, who pitifully thanks her husband for his mistreatment of her.'

'Nor am I minded to be the husband of a nagging wife, always determined to have the last word.' Drew roared this as though the demons he had conjured up were at his back, prodding him with their pitchforks.

Well, at least formality had flown out of the window and honesty had taken its place, thought Bess, stifling a smile at the sight of all the shocked faces around the table.

Worse, aunt Hamilton was quavering at her, 'Oh, my niece, my dear niece, remember that your husband stands in the place of your God—to be obeyed at all times. . . This is no fashion in which to conduct yourself. . .and in a public place, too.'

Little though she cared to admit it, Bess knew that aunt Hamilton was right—at least as regards the place in which her differences with her husband ought to be aired.

She gave an abrupt laugh, and put her hand out towards Drew's, saying, 'How now, my lord, let us cry quits for this meal, at least—and shake hands on it. We are not players on a stage, paid to entertain an audience.'

His wife had spoken as frankly and freely as any boy,

and her manner was smilingly confident as she did so. The moment—and the relationship between the pair of them—swung in the balance. Drew was aware that he could base his answer on his own masculinity and his consequent right to rule his wife, and thus reject her offer outright. All between them would then lie in ruins. Or, he could forget his husbandly rights, take her offered hand, cry truce—and let the game start again.

Even as he wavered Bess said, still frank and as though she had read his mind, 'Come, m'lord, let us set the board out for a new game and forget the old one.'

As though of its own will, and not his, Drew's hand thrust itself forward, and grasped her smaller one, enclosing it in his where it fitted so warm and sweetly, that he felt his anger leaching out of him.

'Quits,' he said. 'But I cannot promise what will happen on another day.'

'No,' shot back Bess. 'But then, no more can I!'

'A strange truce,' smiled Drew, determined not to lose his self-control again, 'when the two principals who have agreed it are still at war!'

'*I* am not at war,' announced Bess, picking up one of Dame Margery's chicken legs and throwing a sideways glance at Drew as she did so. 'On the contrary, I am enjoying my dinner, and am consequently at peace.'

Her sideways glance nearly undid Drew, it was so full of fun and mischief. He gave a little groan, and then leaned forward to take the half-eaten chicken leg from her hand and to begin to eat it himself, his eyes on hers. 'What does Dame Margery baste her meat with that it has one effect on you, madam, and quite another on me?'

Bess smiled crookedly at him. 'Why, you must to the kitchens, sir, and ask her. Though whether she will have an answer to satisfy you, is quite another thing.' Her smile, unknowing to her, was provocation itself.

A witch! A very witch! Had there been a potion in the goblet which the eager page boy had handed to him as he sat down? Only that could explain why she was keeping his hot blood on the boil. Used to meek women, determined to please him, to meet one who met him with defiance—and smiled so sweetly at him in the doing—was having the strongest effect on Drew. He could not wait for the evening, to have her in the Great Bed which was sure to be in the master bedroom above him.

His wife was suffering from the same fever. The beautiful boy who had despised her had turned into a man who stared at her with eager eyes even as he reproved her. He waved his stolen chicken leg at her before eating it slowly, his blue eyes on her face exactly as though it were she whom he was devouring.

Well, Bess knew a game worth two of that! She leaned forward to take his wine glass, lifted it to her lips and drank it as slowly and sensuously as she could, her eyes on his, so slowly that Drew could have sworn he could see the crimson liquid staining her skin as it slid down her throat.

And then, glass in hand, she took his bread and its attendant cheese from the pewter platter which lay between them, and ate that, too. 'Tit for tat, my lord,' she murmured. 'Your bread, cheese and wine for my leg. A fair exchange? Say Yea—or Nay.'

Aware that his cousin Charles, eyes wide, was avidly watching this little scene, Drew hooded his own eyes, clasped the wrist of the hand which held the wine glass, now half empty, and putting his lips where hers had been, drank from it until all the wine was gone.

'Neither Yea nor Yea, madam, but half and half, and somehere in between. You shall not best me!'

'Nay, sir, but I must try. I am not Griselda.'

Oh, Bess knew that it was unwise to tease him so. But yet she must, and knowing little of the game of love, as yet untouched by a man's hands or lips, for Tib and the others had worshipped her from afar, how was it that she knew how to drive a man to distraction?

For Bess had no doubt that that was what she was doing, and even as she led him on with one ploy her busy mind, obeying her body's urgings, was driving her on to another. Some time in the future he would force a reckoning on her, she knew that, and her body throbbed at the very thought. But he was answering her and she must attend.

'Now, that I already know,' Drew murmured, 'that you are not Griselda. But are you Mother Eve who has already tempted—and taken—a man to lie on your breast, so knowing are your arts?'

'I have no arts, husband, other than those which Mother Eve gave me when I was born. And no man has known me either. I am as untouched as Eve was when the Lord God took her from Adam's side.'

Could he believe her, so frank and free was she? He was not to know that all of the Atherington household was watching their lady with the deepest astonishment. They had never seen her behave like this before. But then, she had never sat beside her husband before. Drew, trying to maintain his self-control, shrugged. He would pursue the matter of Tib, and his wife's familiarity with him, in private.

'Leave that, wife,' he told her curtly. 'We have other, more pressing matters, to discuss. After this meal is over we must have an accounting, you, your Council and myself. I shall be most interested to hear an explanation from you all as to why I was never informed of Sir Braithwaite's incapacity.'

One thing was plain to Bess. For all his easy surface charm—and there was no denying it—her husband was like a determined terrier with a rat in his jaws who would never let go, however much he was distracted, when he had set his mind on obtaining an answer to something which puzzled him.

'Oh, I think that you are mistook over that, sir. These mistakes will happen, will they not?' And now it was Charles Breton, sitting on her left, who received her charming sidelong glance.

'Oh, aye, indeed,' returned Charles, with a humorous duck of his head. 'Most like the letter was lost, either on its way to us, or perhaps, after it was received.'

'Very helpful of you, Charles,' commented Drew, his voice dry. 'I scarcely think, though, that my wife needs your assistance in explaining away the odd circumstances which appear to surround Atherington's affairs.'

Thus rebuked, Charles smiled and changed the subject. It would not do to provoke Drew so hard that he lost his temper. Drew scarcely ever did so, but he had been a rare sight on the few occasions when he had lost control of himself. He wondered what it could be that was disturbing his cousin so strongly. Knowing of Atherington's stalwart Protestantism, he asked a question to which he thought Drew could make no objection.

'Are there are many gentry families around Charnwood, Lady Exford? I had heard in London that there were—and that a number of them held to the old Catholic faith.'

Even as Bess began to reply, Drew swung around sharply to watch her as she spoke. Charles, he was sure, had no knowledge of the real reason why he was visiting

Leicestershire, and was therefore, unknowingly, doing him a favour by raising the matter. It would save him from needing to ask such a question himself. He listened with interest as Bess agreed that there were a large number of gentry families in the county, some of whom were Catholic.

'But not so many, I believe,' she ended, 'as in Derbyshire, where the Babingtons, my distant relatives, who are settled at Dethick, still hold to the old Faith. Most living hereabouts, though, are Protestant.'

'And are those around Atherington mainly Protestant, and therefore loyal, madam?' asked Drew, apparently idly.

'Assuredly.' Bess answered him eagerly; she wanted him to know that there were no traitors in Leicestershire. 'We are all, Catholic and Protestant alike, loyal subjects of our Queen.'

Drew knew this to be true in the main. There had been many plots against the Queen designed to assassinate her, and replace her by her imprisoned cousin, Mary, the Catholic Queen of Scots, but few English Catholics had been involved in them. They had mostly been hatched abroad. This lay behind Walsingham's uneasiness over the reports he had received, for they seemed to hint at a purely English conspiracy—a most disturbing development.

Bess had, quite deliberately, spoken to be heard by all, not simply her husband, and as a result all heads had nodded in agreement when she had finished speaking. Her Comptroller, Walter Hampden, sitting not far from them, raised his goblet of wine and said, 'With your permission, my Lord of Exford, I beg that on this auspicious day of your arrival we may all rise to toast, not only our good Queen Elizabeth, but the Protestant Faith.'

Drew rose and held his goblet high. 'With all my heart, my good sir. I give you Good Queen Bess and the Protestant Faith. Drink up, I beg you.' He threw his handsome head back and drained his goblet to the lees.

The whole room echoed him, but Walter had not finished. He called on the servitor to refill his goblet, saying, 'Again with your permission, my lord, I ask that the company may now be allowed to toast both you and your good lady, who has guarded Atherington's interests so bravely on your behalf.'

Now, what could he say to that, but, 'Most excellent and all good cheer to you, sir. I will allow your toast— but only if you will omit any salutation to me so that I may be allowed to drink to my lady wife also.'

A hum of delight ran round the table. Some of Atherington's people, watching their new lord, had feared that he and his lady might be at odds, but such a statement cleared their minds of worry. As for Drew's followers, including Charles, they were noting with some amusement that their master was using his notorious charm to win over his new subjects.

Bess, somewhat nonplussed by Drew's apparent change of heart, smiled up at him as he bent down to kiss her on the cheek before he led the company in the toast to her. 'Is this reconciliation, my lord? Or have you some other aim in mind?'

Oh, she was a clever minx, his wife! She did not trust him in the least—as he did not trust her. He whispered in her ear as he sat down again, 'It is not to Atherington's benefit for your people to think that we are out of humour with one another—even if we are. Smile, my lady wife, as I do—and thus we make our world happy. We may pursue our real ends when we are alone together.'

Alone together! The mere thought of it had Bess

quailing inwardly. No doubt about it, he would be the terrier and she would be the rat. But if so, why, as well as fear, did she feel a strange exhilaration? It was as though she had never lived until she had met him. She was on fire—and knew not why. She only knew that her husband was looking at her strangely, his blue eyes growing larger and larger as they drew nearer and nearer to her.

Panic rose in Bess's breast. She was sailing into unknown waters, a mariner lost in the steep Atlantic stream of which the poets wrote. To break his spell, deliberately woven, she was sure, to snare her, she turned away from him to see her great hound, Pompey, sitting up before one of the arras, his liquid eyes begging her to feed him.

'Oh, Pompey,' Bess exclaimed, 'I have quite forgot you in this hubbub.' She snatched a gnawed beef bone from the great platter before her, turned and tossed it to him, anything to escape her husband's compelling eyes. Pompey, snarling, leapt upon it, and laying it before her, began to worry at it.

'The hound which licked me yesterday, I suppose,' offered Drew smoothly, showing no sign that he had been thwarted in his desire to bend his wilful wife to his will. A line fit for a poet to use, he thought—so many meanings were there in it.

'Aye, husband, and a faithful one. He honoured you, for until yesterday he chose to like none but myself.'

The moment she had spoken she wished she had not made such an admission, for he pounced on it immediately. 'An omen, think you, wife?'

Before Bess could answer him, Pompey picked up the bone, now meatless, and trotted over to lay it at Drew's feet.

'Oh, traitor hound,' sighed Bess softly, 'to transfer your affections with such speed.' As though he had understood what she said, Pompey rose, laid his head in her lap—and then promptly returned to worship at Drew's feet again.

'They say,' remarked Bess, as platters of sweetmeats and sweet wine to drink with them were laid on the table before them, 'that dogs can see into the true hearts of men and women. What does he see in yours, husband, I wonder? A pity he cannot tell me.' The eyes she turned on him were mirthful and artless.

Drew retaliated by plucking a small cake from the platter and popping it into her mouth, not his, so that she could not soon answer him.

'That for your silence, wife. He would say only that he approves of me—or that he knows his true master when he meets him. Nay, do not try to answer me with another witticism, for your well of wisdom will soon run dry if you draw on it too often!'

And now his eyes were mocking hers again, and the excitement which boiled inside Bess rose higher and higher. Did he know what he was doing to her? Of course, he did, and it was done with an end in view; to subdue her, to bend her to his mental as well as to his bodily will—for was not that seduction's aim?

Unable to speak, Bess stared at him. He stared back. She swallowed, and the action set her long white throat working after a fashion, which, had she but known it, was seducing *him*.

Bess shivered. Suddenly she was frightened of the powerful attraction he had for her. Unused to the company of young men, let alone handsome and powerful young men, she had never learned those arts which women used, either to attract them, or dissuade them. So far Mother Eve had helped her, but she was approaching dangerous territory where that alone would not be sufficient to save her from him.

Save her! Almost hysterical laughter bubbled up inside Bess. Nothing could save her, for was he not her husband who might do as he pleased with her?

And would.

Any hope that he might be repelled by her as he had been ten years ago, and might not wish to touch her, let alone make love to her, had disappeared. It was difficult to know what he really thought of her—except, of course, that yesterday, not knowing who she was, he had addressed her in most flattering terms—and then tried to seduce her! But what did he think of her now that he knew that she was his wife?

And what did she truly want from him?

Bess swallowed again, and Drew looked away. Against everything which he might have expected as he had thought of this day on the way to Atherington, the wife he had delayed meeting for so long was rousing him simply by sitting beside him—and defying him! What had Philip Sidney once said to him? 'There is more pleasure to be gained from a woman who can meet and match you, than in one who is meekly resigned to endure whatever you have to offer her.'

Drew grinned to himself. Philip should meet his wife. They would make a good pair. On second thoughts, perhaps not. He wanted this high-spirited termagant for himself to tame—and to test whether Philip was right in his assessment of the extra pleasure to be gained from mastering such a skittish filly. Except that Philip had not said mastering, he had said meeting.

'Silent, sir?' queried Bess who had just finished eating her extremely sticky sweetmeat. She was beginning to learn that in an untried maiden desire and fear went hand in hand. She had asked herself what she wanted from him, and the answer was, she did not yet know. But the desire to tease him, to see the blue eyes burn at her, was strong in her. For if she could provoke him, why, then she had power over him.

'I was thinking,' Drew announced, 'of my friend Philip Sidney, who is a courtier, a scholar and a poet.'

'A paragon, then,' quipped Bess naughtily.

'Indeed,' returned Drew, who was beginning to realise how much he was enjoying this lengthy sparring match with her, carried out, as it was, in public. 'He has a high regard for the capacities of women, which I assure you, is rare at the Court, or anywhere else in England for that matter.'

'No need to tell me *that*, sir. Although we here at Atherington are not so dismissive of women's understanding.'

'So I see, wife, for it is plain that you have your Council eating out of your hand. I am curious to know how you have accomplished that.'

Bess was airy. This interminable meal was nearly at an end, and she was flown with good food and wine, and the exhilarating sensation of danger which surrounded her husband.

'Why, sir, that is easily done. One treats them as one treats Pompey, you understand. A little petting, good food, flattery—and the will to show them who is master here whenever it is necessary.'

Bess was immediately aware that this frivolous answer was an unwise one, but it had slipped out of her, and his answer, she was later to understand, was typical of him— for he took her meaning and embroidered upon it—as a good fencer may turn his opponent's skill against him to secure a hit.

'Mistress,' he said softly, leaning forward to take her goblet of wine from her. 'You mean mistress, not master—but I take your meaning, and I promise you I shall be very wary of you if you attempt to pet me, feed me, or flatter me—and then try to prove to me who is master here—or is it the other way round, lady, and you wish to be mistress?'

'Any way which you wish,' said Bess, full of good food, good wine and magnanimity, 'for you have the right of it—seeing that Atherington now has a master, as well as a mistress. Be brief in your answer, sir, I see that the feast is over, and Gilbert is unsure which of us should rise to say so.'

Drew laughed, and the sound of it echoed in one of those strange silences which often fall in the company of men and women assembled together. He took her hand and urged her to her feet.

'My friends,' he announced. 'We have eaten well. My wife and I bid you adjourn to the Great Parlour where I am told that musicians are assembled to play to us as we recover from the pleasures of the feast. Lead on, Gilbert, and let the company follow us.'

Chapter Five

Be damned to it! Drew had spent the whole afternoon with his wife and her Council, he and his Comptrollers examining books, papers and accounts, and at the end of it none of them could discover anything untoward with which she and they might be reproached. On the contrary, it appeared that Atherington was being more efficiently run than any of Drew's other estates.

His lawyer and principal man of business, John Masters, had been particularly severe in his questioning, especially over the matter of Sir Braithwaite Hamilton, but he could not shake the men before him. They stoutly maintained that m'lord had been sent all proper and pertinent details of his illness and their response to it, and it was not their fault if matters had gone awry at the other end.

Bess had said little, Drew noted glumly, leaving her advisers to speak for her. She had intervened only on one occasion when Masters had complained that some vital accounts relating to the sinking of new coalpits near Bardon Hill had been lost.

Before Walter Hampden could answer she had said, 'Oh, I ordered that a new book should be opened in another name, so that what was going into and out of the pit in terms of money should be clearly distinct from our other affairs. I believe it to be in the small pile before you. It is the new one in the blue cover.'

So it was, and John Masters was left to retreat as gracefully as he could, to his own and Drew's annoyance. Was there no way in which he could turn the tables on the wench? He had hoped that all the food and drink which she had consumed at the banquet would have made her sleepy, but no such thing.

Instead, as at the feast, she seemed to have an answer for everything. Well, it would be interesting to find out what answer she would have for him this evening, in the Great Bed when they were at last alone.

His temper was not improved by John Masters saying to him in a resigned fashion after the meeting, 'Our fears that matters might be awry once we learned of Sir Braithwaite's incapacity and your lady taking over the reins were groundless. On the contrary, Atherington is a model of how an estate should be run.

'I would have thought that it might be all her Comptroller's doing, but he assured me at the feast that it was she who insisted on prospecting for coal after she had learned that the Willoughbys of Wollaton in Nottinghamshire were increasing their income mightily by exploiting their pits by selling coal both locally and as far away as the East Coast. And it was she who insisted on cutting the staff and running the House more economically.'

'A wise lady, my wife,' returned Drew, who did not know whether to be glad or sorry at the news. How would she take giving up the power which she had wielded for the past five years and having to become a mere wife and mother instead? Perhaps he ought to give over to her the running of all his estates, as Lord Shrewsbury was reputed to have done to his wife.

Well, he was not George Shrewsbury, to be a doormat for a woman, even a clever one, and he was now resigned to the fact that his wife was clever as well as beautiful. A paragon, she had said mockingly of his friend Philip Sidney, and he could say the same of he—but he would not say it *to* her. A wife must learn her place.

'Husband?' There she was, before him, looking as bright and eager as ever. Tiredness seemed to be unknown to her. 'Husband, you are silent. I trust that you are not dissatisfied with what you have learned this afternoon?'

'On the contrary, my man, John Masters, and I, are in agreement that Atherington, like yourself, appears to be in the best of health. Your Comptroller is an excellent man of business, and his mistress appears to have an old head on young shoulders.'

Bess dipped him a great curtsy. 'You flatter me over-much, husband.'

'No, indeed, no flattery is too great for the woman who so cunningly contrived to conceal the true governance of Atherington from me for so long. Tell me, madam wife, did you burn the letters which your Comptroller caused to be written to me relating to Sir Braithwaite, or did they find their way to the cesspit rather than to to my office?'

'Oh, husband—' Bess eyed him reproachfully, deciding yet again that attack was the best form of defence. '—how can you accuse me of such shameless double-dealing?'

'Easily, my wench, easily. For that is what I would have done in your case so that I was not subject to someone from outside lording it over me.'

She would not waste her time in useless denials. Instead, her eyes hard on him, she said merrily, 'And your advisers, husband, do they agree with you over this? I should like to know whether I am universally damned.'

'Wife, they do not yet know you as well as I. Your advisers—whom you have also tricked—were so patently honest that their explanations were believed. But I do not believe them, and I shall never believe in anything you tell me unless I have first checked and double-checked its truth.'

'And I, husband,' Bess riposted, 'will do you the same honour—if so it may be called.'

The expression on her face was so mischievous as she came out with this that Drew began to laugh. Bess watched him a little before primming her face and saying soberly, 'I have told Gilbert to set out cooling drinks and a light collation for the two of us on the roof leads. From them you may see Charnwood and the hills beyond, almost, they say, to Northamptonshire on a fine day. I trust you approve of my orders. I thought that you might like to look over your lands and be alone with me for a little.'

'Excellent, wife, although I must remind you that we shall be alone together for a long time this night, and I shall not be admiring the view *from* Atherington, but that *inside* Atherington!'

Bess blushed! She could not help herself. For all her self-command she was but maiden yet. She felt the blush spread over her whole body so strongly that for a moment she felt, as she stood before him, that her clothes had all flown off, and she was as naked as Mother Eve before the Fall.

She turned away from him; away from his burning blue eyes which looked so passionately into her dark ones. Oh, he lusted after her—he had not been deceiving the poor wench that he had thought she was yester morning—but that did not mean that he *felt* anything for her.

Drew knew that he had stared her down, and for the first time had, if only for a little, mastered her. Exhilaration filled him. He took her hand, 'You will lead me to the roof, wife, if you will, for I long to see your view.'

Again Bess took his double meaning, but this time did not let it trouble her. 'Through this door, then. Up a winding staircase, and so we gain the leads.'

The stair was narrow, as well as winding, and dark. At one of the landings Drew took advantage of the dark and their nearness to turn her into his arms and do what he had been longing to do all day.

He kissed her, not simply on the lips but on the mauve hollow just above her tight bodice which betrayed where the cleft between her breasts began. To Bess's surprise this last kiss was more exciting than the one on her lips. Her whole body dissolved under it—as snow melts beneath the sun.

'You are my sun,' she wanted to say, but that would mean that she had submitted to him, and she had long determined, even before she had met him again, that she would never do that.

Instead she mewed like a kitten, so that Drew, beginning to be fully roused, stepped away from her. 'Not here,' he said, his voice hoarse. 'Later, later, we shall have all the time in the world.'

Unsteadily, Bess resumed her climb, which was more difficult for her in her fine stiff clothing than in her usual informal dress which her aunt so deplored. Drew, in some discomfort as he followed her, willed his body to behave itself, only for it to turn mischievous again when they reached the top of the steps and walked into the full afternoon sun which streamed across the leads.

For the sun gilded his wife's face and body as, unknown to him, it gilded his, so that both held their breath a little in admiration as they turned to look at the other.

'Arcadia,' exclaimed Drew, looking away from her to break her spell and admiring the view which lay before him. 'Arcadia seen from the rooftop of a Midlands mansion.'

'Indeed, a splendid sight,' agreed Bess as they looked across fields, woods and hills into the pale blue distance. The only sign of the habitation of men was the sheep which dotted the distant fields as they turned around to look at the valleys of the north, the hilly land being all in the south.

'I must agree with you, wife,' smiled Drew, but the view that he was now admiring was the one of Bess as she stood, arm outstretched, pointing into the distance. 'But I think that I prefer the scenery nearer home.'

And he took her into his arms.

'We are alone, wife. Let us dally a little.'

Oh, but dallying with Drew was delightful, even if love was far away and lust very near. He was kissing and stroking her, and gently cursing the stiff bodice which denied him the glories of her breasts.

It was when he began to lift the heavy skirts of her dress to caress her other treasures that Bess sprang away from him.

'No,' she exclaimed breathlessly, her face flushed with arousal, her dark eyes seeming larger than ever. 'The servants will be here shortly to serve us. They must not find us. . .' She stopped.

Bess saw that Drew was not in full command of himself. He put out a hand to pull her back to him, then he, too, stopped. He was breathing as fast as she was, so fast that he turned away from her to brace his hands on the parapet which ran round this part of the roof.

'I had thought that you meant us to be truly alone—so that we might be husband and wife,' he ground out at last.

Seeing him thus, Bess thought to wreak a small revenge on him for his demeaning words about her on their wedding day. 'What, husband? Can you possibly be so impatient to bed me as not to wait for the night when you have allowed ten long years to pass without seeing me, or writing to me a word unconnected with the business of Atherington?'

She saw him stiffen, saw his hands leave the parapet to curl themselves into fists before he unclenched them and turned to face her.

'I did not know. . .' he began.

'Know what?' asked Bess coolly. 'That Arcadia, that golden rural paradise, and its nymphs awaited you here?' She would have been less than human, she thought later, if she did not try to hurt him a little as he had once hurt her. The memory of her wedding day still returned, if less frequently, to haunt her.

She saw him flinch, his pride wounded. Perhaps he had thought that he merely had to smile at her to win not only her acquiescence, but also her trust, if not her love. Was he accustomed to easy conquest? Bess though that perhaps he was. However much he attracted her, and he did, she would not surrender her essential self to him until he gave some sign that he was offering her more than the opportunity to be pleasured—and then forgotten again.

Would he depart for another ten years if once he gave her a child? If so, she must guard herself so that when he left her again their parting would not break her heart.

'There is no Arcadia,' he declared almost savagely. 'It does not exist on earth save in the minds of men and women. They make their own heaven—as they make their own hell.'

It was the very last thing which Bess expected him to say, and oddly enough, for all its savagery, it gave her hope. She began to answer him, to offer him perhaps, as the dove had offered Noah, an olive branch, but behold the servants were arriving, and they must be formal Lord and Lady Exford, taking their pleasure on the leads.

So the day wore on. They were never alone, which was the common fate, Bess was beginning to discover, of being a great one, a personage of power to whom servility was constantly offered. She had never lived her life so much in public before, for at Atherington there had been little need: her and her aunt's wants had been simple, and were simply served.

During their time on the roof she said as much to Drew. He smiled wryly before answering her. 'Ceremony,' he said, 'laps the life of such as we. It is expected. It is what earns us the respect of those whom we govern since they are never offered it themselves. And the ceremony my companions offer to me is small compared with that offered to the Queen at court. Surely, though, wife, you have experienced this before our arrival.' He waved a hand at those who surrounded them, adding, 'They exist but to please us.'

'It does not please me,' Bess returned.

'No?' His manner to her was courteous, but she saw that he was surprised. 'Very well then, wife. When we visit the stables I shall dismiss our train, and you alone will accompany me and introduce me to Tib—whom I thought your brother—and to the groom who also accompanied you yestermorn.'

Bess was suddenly fearful, made so by this seeming concession. 'You will not turn them away? After all, it was I who ordered them to accompany me so informally—as I am wont to do, seeing that we are peaceful here. No beggars or cutthroats populate our woods and fields.'

Drew made no answer to that, and later, when he had been as good as his word and sent his train away, he escorted her to the stables where, one by one, he was introduced to all who worked there, from the head groom down to the merest stable lad. He had a friendly word with each one, something which surprised Bess a little after his having said so firmly, 'They exist but to please us.'

To Roger he merely said, 'I trust you to guard my lady at all times, and in future you will ensure that she has a proper escort—unlike her habit in the past.' Roger made no attempt to answer him, merely offering his new master in the present as surly an acquiescent nod as he had offered his former mistress in the past.

Tib was the last in the long line to bow to the new lord. He and Roger had seen him arrive earlier in the day and to their dismay had recognised him as the young gallant whom they had assisted yestermorn! Of the two of them Tib was the more fearful of being turned away, since he had unwittingly aided his lady in the deception of her lord.

His lady he hardly recognised, so fine and fair was she. His silent worship of her turned into even greater adoration, but his knees knocked a little when the fine gentleman before him drawled, 'I see that you are not so forward in your speech, lad, as you were yestermorn.

Has the stable-yard cat got your tongue?' The cat of which he spoke was rubbing his black furry back and sides against Drew's fine silk stockinged legs, evidently liking the sensation.

'No, noble sir.' And then, inspired by his native wit, for Tib, unlike many of Atherington's staff, was lettered, he stammered, 'I am blinded by the sun of your presence, noble sir. Mine eyes are dazzled, and my tongue silenced.'

Unknown to Bess and those among whom he now lived, he was the only son of a ruined country gentleman who had hanged himself, leaving Tib penniless, alone in the world, and needing to find any work, however humble, in order to survive.

Bess gave a stifled groan. Pray God that her husband did not regard Tib's pretty speech as insolence, and turn him away at once as he had earlier half-threatened. For a moment Drew was of a mind to do exactly that, but something odd about the lad stopped him.

'Look at me, fellow,' he commanded curtly, for Tib, certain that he was about to be dismissed and waiting for the blow to fall, had dropped his head. 'Your speech is not that of a stable hand. What are you doing here? And what is your name? Besides Tib, that is.'

'I am called Jack Theobald, but my fellows always call me Tib. Because my father, who was a gentleman, died leaving me without any money or a family to care for me, I needed to find work lest I starve. I have always liked horses, and so I came here to work with them.' He dropped his head again.

'Hmm.' Drew regarded him for a long moment. 'You may remain as you are—for the present. I shall decide what to do with you later. Meantime, treat your mistress with the respect which she deserves, and all will be well with you.'

Scarlet mantled Tib's face. He swallowed, and seemed about to say something, but Drew had already turned away, taken his wife by the arm, and was gently walking her back towards the house.

'You were kind to him, husband, for which I thank you.' Bess was indeed grateful that Drew had not dismissed or punished Tib. In her limited experience, fine gentlemen were hard on those servants who might have seen them humbled, even though by chance. Drew made her no immediate answer. He frowned a little, and said, still curt, 'The fellow intrigued me. He speaks well, not like a peasant—or had you not noticed?'

Bess said slowly, 'I suppose I had. But so do some others whom I know to be of simple birth.'

'Lettered, too, most like,' continued Drew thoughtfully. 'He's wasted in the stables—even though he says that he loves horses.'

'Which I know to be true. He is very good with them. And Roger and Simon, my chief groom, both agree with me on that.'

'No matter. That is enough of him for now. Mind, though, that you do not rove the countryside again, alone with him.'

'I was not alone with him, husband, I had Roger with me, remember?'

'You know what I mean, wife—and see to it.' He released her arm, and was distant with her again. Goodness, thought Bess, what can be making him as crabby as an apple tree in the autumn? Surely he cannot be jealous of Tib?

But he was, for Drew did not care to think that a personable lad, nearer to his wife's age than he was, was

wont to spend much time with her on familiar terms. The
sooner he bedded his lively wife, curbed her roving ways,
saw that she was decently dressed at all times, and made
a suitably obedient woman of her, the better. She might
then not wish to pretend to be Atherington's lord rather
than its lady.

He gave her a sidelong glance. She looked thoughtful,
but not unhappy. It occurred to him that the best way to
break her in to her new life—he could find no more
gallant way of describing what he meant to do—was to
take her away from Atherington altogether, as far away
as possible from the officers and servants who were only
too willing to serve her.

And what better, then, than to begin to do
Walsingham's business for him by arranging for them to
visit Buxton as soon as possible as part of a bridal tour.
By what had been said during the day, she had never
been more than a few miles from Atherington. Thus he
would kill two lively birds with one stone, train his wife
in the way she should go, and find Walsingham's spy
for him! He would speak to her on the matter before
others so that she might be less inclined to begin arguing
with him.

'Go to Buxton to take the waters! But you have only just
arrived here, husband! I shall have no time to show you
your lands and tenants, or the new coalpits and the iron
works nearby.'

'I have not the lightest desire to visit coalpits,' returned
Drew testily to a wife who had, once again, disappointed
him by her refusal to agree immediately to his wishes.
'You may tell me about them, and that will be enough.
One pit looks very like another—and the same goes for
the ironworks. So long as they are well run, and bring

in the money to keep the estate solvent, I would be quite content never to see them at all. No, I am determined on a visit to Buxton where you may mix a little with your peers. You have spent too much of your life alone with servants—and thinking about coalpits.'

'Not alone surely, husband,' retorted Bess, 'You forget. I have always enjoyed aunt Hamilton's company— and she never thinks about coalpits, do you, Aunt?'

She waved a hand at her agitated aunt, who was scarcely able to conceal her distress at the sight of her unruly niece arguing once again with her husband. She said, her voice trembling, 'Oh, I take your husband's meaning to be that you have not mixed with those whom you may have to meet when he takes you to London, my dear. Your husband is but considering your happiness, I am sure. As for coalpits, I assure you, Lord Exford, that I have never thought about them once—nor encouraged my niece to do so.'

'That I can well believe.' Drew was sardonic. 'But I also believe that my wife does not need encouragement in her wilfulness. You may be certain, though, that I shall have my way in this.

'Charles,' he ordered, turning towards his cousin, who could barely suppress a grin at the spectacle of Drew being, for once, unable to charm a woman into instant submission, 'tell my household, as well as that of Atherington's, that all must be made ready for their lord and lady to leave for Buxton by a fortnight's end.'

So, it was a *fait accompli*, was it? Her wishes were to count for nothing. Charles was already speeding on his way to carry out his master's orders. Her husband watched him go, a grim smile on his face, before he said to her, 'It seems to me, wife, that to indulge yourself in Buxton's warm water might serve to soften your temper a little, and prevent me from losing mine.'

It was something of an olive branch and, a little ungraciously, Bess accepted it. 'Very well, husband. So long as my aunt may accompany me as my chief attendant.'

'Assuredly, wife, for I am certain that her choice of conversation will exactly accord with mine, rather than with yours.' A statement which proved that the olive branch had a few thorns attached to it.

Later alone, being prepared for bed, prepared for *him*, Bess was to ask herself with some bewilderment why she had been so resolutely opposed to visiting Buxton, for had she not frequently wished to do exactly that herself and had not done so because some problem at Atherington had always intervened? It was all *his* fault, of course, throwing orders at her and expecting her to jump eagerly to fulfil them every time he did so. Which had her contradicting him even when he was proposing something which she had always wanted to do!

And now, here she was, decked out like a boar's head being prepared for a feast, ready to be carried in on a platter for the lord to consume! Not an unlikely simile at all, for at aunt Hamilton's command her attendants had crowned her with a wreath of flowers, painted her face, plaited her hair, and dressed her in a nightgown so elaborate that she was sure that she could have gone to court in it. In short, they had done everything but stick an orange in her mouth and put *her* head on a platter.

It was only by brooding on this that Bess could prevent herself from worrying about what was going to happen in the Great Bedchamber when all this prinking and painting was over. First of all, of course, she would be led into the big anteroom at the end of the suite of rooms where Drew would be waiting for her. Were they dressing *him* as though he had no hands to help himself with? What would he be wearing? What would he think when he saw her dressed like this?

Well, she would know soon enough what it was to be Drew Exford's wife, for aunt Hamilton had handed her a posy of spring flowers and taken her by the hand to lead her through each room until they reached the anteroom.

And there he stood, so handsome that he made Bess feel quite faint. He was wearing a bedgown of such rich material that he glowed like the sun. Behind him stood his cousin Charles and his immediate entourage. Behind them stood a crowd of folk who overflowed the anteroom, the landing, and the great staircase which led to it.

All come to see her and Drew bedded.

Did they expect to remain until Drew had, in Aunt Hamilton's words, 'done his duty by her'? Years ago, they had done so, and ripped the sheet from the bed immediately afterwards to see whether or no the bride was virgin.

Surely Drew was too civilised for that? She would soon find out. With Charles on his right, and a handsome young page on his left, he advanced towards her, to take her hand so that she might stand beside him.

Charles and the page disappeared into the throng. And suddenly, from nowhere, Gilbert arrived, his white staff in his hand, to lead them to the bridal chamber. Hysteria threatened Bess. This was even more of a ceremony than when she had been married. But, of course, then she had been a child.

Hysteria had her muttering to her groom, 'I wonder that you did not employ a minstrel with a lute to go before us.'

Drew whispered back at her, 'Had I known that you

wished that, then I would have done so,' thus neatly turning the tables on her mockery.

'Ahem, ahem,' murmured Bess, her hand before her mouth, trying to stifle her laughter and, at the same time, look as grave as the ceremony demanded. Hand in hand they reached the bedchamber again, where the bedcovers had been thrown back, and steps had been put out for them to climb into the Great Bed's deep embrace. Which they did, and sat stiffly, side by side, as though they were already stone effigies on a tombstone while the company cheered them repeatedly and wished them a long life and many children.

At a signal from Gilbert, who was relishing all this unaccustomed ceremony, one by one, and in proper order, the humblest first and the greatest last, they all filed out. . .until she and Drew were finally alone. . .

For a moment neither of them moved or spoke. Bess was wondering what would come next and how soon Drew would turn to take her in his arms and do *that* to her. She knew perfectly well what *that* entailed, being a country girl who had lived among the animals and who had listened to the women servants laughing and tittering about the behaviour of the men with whom they worked.

What had always puzzled her was why any sensible young girl would wish to commit such an unlikely act so much that she risked being encumbered with an unwanted child and sent away from the protection which being on Atherington's staff gave them?

Whenever she had tried to broach the matter with her aunt Hamilton, her aunt had always told her firmly that such matters were not for young ladies of rank to discuss. 'Wait until you are married, my dear,' she had always replied, rolling her eyes to heaven to suggest to God that, once again, her niece was being a troublesome nuisance.

'But I am married, aunt, so that cock won't fight,' Bess once retorted, meaning that her aunt's explanation was faulty.

'Really, Bess, from where do you get such dreadful language? I would forbid you the stables only I know that you would disobey me. What I mean is—when your husband arrives, he will instruct you in what it is to be a wife.'

And that was always that. And tonight, presumably, Drew was going to instruct her. She had once asked Annis, who was a pretty girl and her personal maid, the question which her aunt had refused to answer. 'Shall I like it?'

Annis's reply had been robust. 'Oh, aye, though perhaps not the first time. That usually hurts.' She had said no more, for her aunt had come in suddenly, and heard Annis's answer. Shortly afterwards Annis had been sent to help in the kitchens, and a rather plain maiden lady had been promoted to be her maid.

So Drew would not only instruct her, he was likely to hurt her. The only thing which puzzled her was that whenever, during the day, he had touched her, she had found herself strangely excited and wanted him to continue doing so. Coupled with that had been an overwhelming desire to tease and provoke him. Life was really very strange if it gave rise to such contrary desires.

It grew odder still, for when Drew did move it was to jump out of the bed, to cross the room, untie his bedgown's sash and tear off the gown, throwing it on to the great chest which stood at the bottom of the bed.

Bess wondered whether she ought to avert her eyes from him, never having seen a naked man before, but she had no need to worry, for beneath the bedgown he was wearing a long shirt of thin linen which nearly reached the ground. It had a deep collar, with lace edging, so that now he looked like an archangel in the painting above the altar in Atherington's small chapel. His fair hair curled in waves and ringlets about his perfect face.

'That's better,' he exclaimed, and then he dived—it was the only word—into the bed again, to land beside her, and throw off the bedcovers to reveal her over-elaborate night rail.

'Come,' he said, laughing, 'you are as encumbered as I was. We were both attired ready for a masque at court, and not for the nuptial bed. But do not despair, we shall shortly be Mother Eve and Father Adam together before the Fall. Look, I have bought a painted apple for you, seeing that there are none ready to eat at this time of year!'

He turned away from her, leaving Bess to wonder what he meant, whilst he lifted from the small cupboard standing beside the bed something thin and square, wrapped in a blue cloth.

'Charles put it here for me this afternoon,' he told her, as he handed it to her. 'Open it, wife, your second present from me, the first being my picture in small. Here is another, by the same limner, and it is a little masterpiece, I assure you.'

Whatever Bess had expected from him, she had not expected this. She untied the ribbon which bound the packet, and opened the cloth covering it to reveal a tiny painting of Adam and Eve, quite naked. Eve was handing Adam a rosy apple, and a miniature serpent was leering at them from the tree around which it was entwined.

'Oh, it's beautiful,' Bess exclaimed reverently. No one had ever given her a present before. Her pleasure was so naked and so genuine that it quite overwhelmed Drew. Her eyes had widened, her lips had parted, and her whole face glowed in the candlelight. Desire roared through him.

'The woman tempted Adam and so he fell,' he whispered into Bess's ear, taking her chin into his hand as he did so. 'Will you tempt me, wife, that I may fall?'

Bess, still holding the little picture, whispered back, 'But the serpent hath not tempted me, husband, so how may I bring about your loss of Eden?'

'Let me be both serpent and Adam to you,' he told her, tipping her face so that they were looking into one another's eyes, 'since for men and women to love one another and to know carnal desire was worth the loss of Eden, for that was the price we had to pay for it.'

At the touch of his hand Bess began to tremble so that Drew dropped it from her chin, took the little picture and returned it to the cupboard's top. Her trembling grew the more when he took her chin in his hand again, and kissed the parted lips beneath the wondering eyes. 'Do not be frightened,' he said. 'I shall try not to hurt you.'

Which, Drew thought, might be difficult, for he had rarely, if ever, bedded a true virgin, and he did not know whether he was going to be able to restrain himself, if restraint were needed.

'Wife,' he began, at last, 'the father and the mother of us all went naked to their nuptials—'

Only for Bess to interrupt him with a little laugh, as he began to loosen her gown from her shoulders. 'Not so,' she said. 'They made themselves aprons—or so the Bible saith.'

Drew threw back his golden head and laughed, as much to break the tension which was beginning to build up in him, as to express his mirth. 'I see that you are learned as well as practical, wife. I also see that I shall have to be careful if I chop logic with you in future.'

'Is that what we are doing now?' queried Bess slyly.

'Indeed, no. This is instruction in Cupid's arts which I am about to offer you. The arts of the little god of love himself. Allow me, madam, and help me a little, I pray you. I prefer to see my wife, not the arts of her sempstress.'

So saying, Drew tugged at her nightgown, and shyly, Bess began to help him to undress her, her whole body aquiver with she knew not what. To have a man's hands stroke and caress her as he stripped her last piece of clothing from her was beginning to make her understand why so many of Atherington's maids had risked all in order to lie with their lovers. It was as though she had never lived before, never known that her body could begin to sing an age-old song under a lover's ministrations.

As once before she mewed like a kitten, expressing her pleasure so frankly and artlessly that Drew found himself trembling. He had meant to have her strip his nightshirt from him, but he found that he could not wait. He tugged it off himself, so that for the first time Bess saw the splendour of his naked torso, the blond whorls of hair on his strong chest, the muscles on his shoulders, back and arms which his elaborate clothing had hidden.

Her mewing turned into a strong cry as he took her in his arms, and began to stroke the length of her body. New to lovemaking, Bess lay passive whilst he pleasured her, his stroking and kissing growing ever more intimate, ever stronger, until she was writhing beneath him, her hands clutching at him until she clutched and stroked his rigid sex, so that he almost spilled himself into the bed, not into her.

The serpent himself, he thought afterwards, must have instructed her in what to do to bring a man low! 'No,' he whispered, his breath growing ever shorter, 'not now. Not this time, another. Give yourself to me, wife, let me make you mine,' and like the stallion, the stag and the other animals—both tame and wild—he made her his own.

And in the doing, as Annis had said might happen, he hurt her, even though he tried not to, tried to prepare her, to pace himself, but she was truly virgin and her body resisted him, so that she cried out.

But when he would have stopped, she clung to him the more, saying, 'No, what Eve could endure, I can,' until the age-old rhythm of love brought them both to climax.

Chapter Six

So this was marriage, Bess thought drowsily as she awoke in the Great Bed, secure in her husband's arms. For the moment whether she loved him, or he loved her, scarcely seemed to matter. Simple comfort was everything.

They were naked still—like Father Adam and Mother Eve—and whether their remote ancestors had loved one another in the poets' sense of the word was immaterial. Half sitting up, watching Drew as he lay quiet and sleeping as peacefully as a baby, she remembered how kind he had been on the previous night when, after their ecstasy was over, he had discovered that—as Annis had hinted—she had been hurt.

'Nay, wife!' he had exclaimed at the sight of her blood on his hands and on her body. 'I had not meant to be cruel to the virgin that you were—and to have hurt you so grievously was never my intent.'

Bess had smiled up at him. 'Oh, I am proud to show you that I *was* virgin, and the hurt was only for a short space, and was preceded and followed by such pleasure. . .' She stopped, and turned her head away, not liking to confess how great her pleasure had been, and how surprising.

Drew had found such charming modesty pleasing—it was so new to him. 'Nevertheless,' he had told her firmly, 'we must stanch your wound at once, and I must wait until you are healed before I pleasure you again.' He had sprung out of bed immediately, and Bess noticed once again how purposeful he was, how athletic in all his movement, how superb his naked body was.

'There are nightgowns and linen cloths in the big chest opposite to the bed,' she told him. 'We can make a bandage for me from one of them.'

'Not we,' he said, 'I must also help to bind up the wounded soldier in Cupid's wars.' He was astonished to discover how unhappy he was at having hurt her, particularly when she lay there looking at him with such soft eyes. She seemed very different from the argumentative puss with whom he had wrangled the day before.

He brought a large piece of linen over to the bed and began it to tear it into strips, one of which he gave to her, jumping back into bed to watch her at her work.

'And in the morning we shall ask for some healing salve from the physician whom I have brought with me,' he added when Bess had finished, smiling a little at the slow blush which spread over her face and body as he spoke.

'Come, my lady wife,' he said, kissing her, 'do not be ashamed. The whole world should know that the lord's lady came to him pure and whole—no need for shame there, but pride instead. And if we are blessed with a babe after this night's work then I shall know that it is truly mine—which is more than many men can claim of their children!'

He had, Bess remembered, sinking back on to her

pillow again, said no word of love. But what matter of that? He had given her of himself, and taken something from her, and if between them they had, indeed, made a child, then what more could she ask from him?

'A boy, husband? You wish me to give you a boy?'

Drew paused a moment. What answer would please her the most? This was a new thought for him, and a new action, too, for though he had always been kind to his bed-partners, that kindness had been impersonal, not deeply felt.

So when at last he spoke it was slowly and carefully, with no hint of the cavalier manner which he had used to her so far.

'For my first,' he told her, 'either boy or girl will do, but after that, I would wish an heir.'

He had his reward. Bess gave him a brilliant smile. She had feared that he would demand a boy from her— something which she could not influence, since only God knew whether a boy or a girl was created by the act of love, and poor human beings had no choice in the matter.

Thinking thus, she went to sleep again, to wake to find that her husband had gone, and that the bed was strangely empty without him. What had woken her was the arrival of her aunt Hamilton and a bevy of her ladies and ladies' maids. The maids were carrying basins and cans of hot water, soap and silk towels. Two footmen followed them carrying a large wooden tub for the hot water.

'Good morrow to you, niece,' exclaimed aunt Hamilton. 'Your husband said that he thought that you would be prepared to greet the new day.'

Bess sat up while aunt Hamilton came over to her and threw the bedcovers back, to reveal the bloodstained sheet. She helped Bess officiously down the steps, and out of the bed as though she were an invalid, before ordering the leading maid to strip the bed of the sheet and hold it up to the assembled company.

'Behold your lady's virtue,' she cried.

Bess had an insane desire to laugh, something not shared by all her staff who gazed at her reverently. Since everyone in the room must have been well aware how chaste her life had been since birth, their reaction seemed a little extreme to her. They surely could not have been surprised.

After that, the footmen having filled the bath and retired, she was washed and dressed and her hair was formally arranged. Finally she was led out of the room and down the stairs, the leading maid still carrying the stained sheet.

Bess would have liked to break her fast in the kitchens, something which she had frequently done in the past, but which she was dismally sure she would never be permitted to do again. And where was her husband? And why had he left her alone?

She was soon to find out.

He was waiting for her at the bottom of the Great Staircase, Gilbert in attendance, as usual; his white staff in his hand. The only surprising thing about the last ten hours or so was that Gilbert had not been present when her husband had finally pleasured her in order to announce his success to all the world!

This thought set Bess smiling: a sight which pleased her husband. Drew was finding that his visit to Leicestershire and the act of making his wife his own was vastly different from his forebodings before he had set out. Then he had been expecting to find a plain young woman who, when he came to bed her, he would have been unable to pleasure, because without desire for her he would have been unable to perform his husbandly duties.

That would have been the polite way of putting it! For Drew, like his friend, Philip Sidney, was fastidious and, unlike many men, they both needed a woman to attract them before they could pleasure her.

Instead, he had found a woman who was not only beautiful, but possessed an attraction for him so powerful that he wondered at himself and his strong reaction to her.

And from wanting at first to show her who was master he had discovered, once he was in bed with her, that it was her pleasure, not his, which was important.

'Welcome, wife,' he said, taking her hand. 'We are to eat in the small parlour. I told your Steward that I thought that you might wish to be private with me this morning, so he has arranged that we should eat only with our two Comptrollers—and your good aunt, of course, and leave the others to the Great Parlour. We may then discuss our setting out for Derbyshire, and a little of our future lives together.'

Bess's smile grew. She had not wanted to be surrounded by the stares of the curious who would watch her to guess how she had survived the night when she had ceased to be a maiden.

Breaking her fast with him, listening to him talk to Charles and to Walter Hampden, she was beginning to forget a little the long years of hurt after his dismissal of her on their wedding day as his monkey bride. Whether he loved her or no, he was plainly reconciled to having her for his wife, and by the manner of his speech he was prepared to take her not only to Buxton, but to London.

'You must send orders to London, Charles,' he was saying, 'causing Exford House to be made ready for a mistress, as well as a master. My wife will wish to live in a home, not a barracks fit only for the use of men. You will understand, Lady Exford,' he told her, 'that both my father and myself have lived there for long years without a woman's soft touch. All that must change in future. Perhaps, like Bess Shrewsbury, you will wish to oversee the ordering of the house yourself.'

He looked around the small and gracious room in which they were taking their ease. 'Yes, I am sure you will, seeing that Atherington is all a home should be. Full of warmth and comfort.'

'Such,' said Walter Hampden, 'is owing to your lady, my good lord. She has always insisted on the comfort of others, besides herself, being considered.'

'Then from now on she must consider mine,' said Drew, offering Bess his most dazzling smile, 'as I must consider hers.'

Oh, it was all so different from what Bess had feared, especially after her first unfortunate meeting with him. She had seldom in her short life felt so mindlessly happy as she did on this bright summer morning. Pompey, couched by the door, must have sensed her pleasure, for he came running to her to push his wet nose into her hand, and to receive a titbit from her plate. And when Drew bent to stroke him, traitor that he was, Pompey again transferred his affection to him immediately.

'So, you continue to charm my dog as well as me,' whispered Bess to her husband. 'Will you leave me aught of my own?'

Drew raised his pewter tankard of good Leicestershire ale. 'Husband and wife are one in the eyes of God and the law, but I trust that I shall not be an overbearing husband.'

Well, that was for her to find out in the future, was Bess's wry inward response. Aunt Hamilton had once said that the true test of a husband was not in the early days of marriage, but later, when custom and usage had begun to take their toll. Then a husband must become a friend as well as a lover—as poor Sir Braithwaite had been to her aunt before his accident had made him less than a man, and no kind of a companion.

Perhaps it might be a good thing for them to repair to Buxton, there to learn one another's ways in surroundings which would be new to both of them. Meantime, there was the present—particularly the nights, when Drew shouted himself a kind and inventive lover, and Bess roved the wide seas of passion in his company. At dusk all cats are grey, the proverb said, and in the dusk of the bedroom what mattered was not her and Drew's looks but the meeting of their minds as well as their bodies.

Bess was beginning to discover that passion had many dimensions, and in one of them she found that she had recovered the shock of delight which she had felt on that long-ago day when she had first seen her husband, before he had seen her, and said the unsayable.

And yet, always, even in her nightly joy and her daily happiness in his company, there still lurked at the back of Bess's mind a shadow, a dim memory of those unhappy words of his which could never be unsaid. She had once read that at Roman feasts and celebrations, the participants were always reminded by an acolyte whispering warning words into their ear, that life had its pains as well as its pleasures. Nothing was to be taken for granted: the present was to be enjoyed, and the future. . . would happen when it happened.

A strange thing was happening to Drew—something he had not foreseen. Beforehand, he had always thought his time at Atherington would be a boring rural interlude, something to struggle through before he went on to the real business of his life at Buxton, but, as time went on, everything changed. He fell easily into the natural rhythms of country life. Atherington, he discovered, was always busy—though not after the fashion of the Court or the Town.

He rode out into the countryside with Bess, even visiting the coalpits of which she had spoken so proudly and, despite what he had said earlier, he displayed an intelligent and informed interest in them.

And daily he jousted with Bess after a fashion that was quite different from his previous dealings with women. She was, by turns, exasperating, infuriating, and argumentative. She refused to pander to his every whim, and proved herself to be both brave and clever. And everything she did was informed with the greatest good humour and such smiling impudence that she attracted him so much that whenever he was with her, even in the day, he could scarce keeps his hands off her.

At night she had become his lusty and inventive lover so that with her he reached heights of passion such as he had never known before.

'They called your grandam "The Spanish Lady", wife,' he gasped at her once, as they lay entwined, their hair and their bodies moist with the force of their mutual passion. 'By what name shall I call you?'

'Call me no lady at all,' she replied sweetly. 'I am simply Drew Exford's wife!'

At which he took her in his arms again. . .

The two weeks to be spent at Atherington became three, and it was Drew who put off their departure, excusing his delay by claiming that letters of business had come from London and needed to be attended to properly and not in haste: Buxton could wait.

'Must we go at all?' Bess asked him in the dark watches of the night. 'We are so happy here.'

Drew sighed. His duty called him, if only feebly. He knew that he ought to arrive at Buxton before the Queen of Scots did, and he was risking that by his delay in leaving.

He turned and kissed her. 'I have promised you a holiday from care, wife, and a holiday you shall have.'

Bess sat up. 'Care? What care? For the last two weeks I have had no care at all.'

'Nevertheless, wife, you deserve to be waited on, to be truly idle. We must be away at the end of this sennight.'

Were it not for his mission he would have given way to her pleadings, for in these early days of marriage Drew had found his Arcadia and did not wish to lose it by engaging in the sordid intrigue to which he was committed. Nevertheless...as he himself had said... nevertheless...

He made a sudden decision. His roving and adventurous days were over, the days when nobody and nothing depended on him. This enterprise would be the last of its kind.

To Bess he simply said, 'Grant me this wish, wife, that we have our bridal tour together in the fair Peak District of which I have heard so much.' For the first time he felt himself a cur because he could not tell her the true reason for their visit to Buxton.

And then, at last, all was made ready. The long train of coaches, carts, wagons and horsemen set off for Buxton so that m'lord and his lady might take the waters in the company of their peers. Atherington, which Bess had never left, was left behind, and the future which she half-welcomed, half-feared, lay before her.

'Where do you think we are, Aunt? I thought that my lord said that we should not stop for another hour, and here we are, not ten minutes agone, and at rest again.'

Aunt Hamilton, seated in the coach with Bess, and one of her ladies, shook her head. 'I'm sure I don't know, child. I have not been so far this way before. I think that we have passed the Derbyshire borders, but have not yet reached the hills amongst which, I believe, Buxton lies.'

Impatient, and eager to be on their way, Bess put her head out of the crude unglazed window in the coach's door. The coach itself was little more than a simple enclosed box mounted on a farm cart's frame, unsprung, and consequently very uncomfortable. Since the day was fine Drew, together with most of the men, was on horse-back, and she put her head through the window to try to find him.

The road, now that they had left the main road north, was nothing more than a rough track between fields, and they had reached a sharp turn in it. A stand of trees sheltered it so that Bess could not see the track beyond it. Nor could she see Drew and Charles, or the outriders who preceded them to clear the way for the most noble the Lord and Lady Exford. She could, however, hear neighing horses, raised voices, and shouting, but could not distinguish anything which might reveal what all the commotion was about.

Bess opened the coach door and, ignoring aunt Hamilton's wailings, she began to walk along the track, picking her way through the horsemen who were patiently waiting for their orders to start off again. Tib, who had become Charles's page—the one whom he had brought with him from London having broken his leg before they left Atherington—was holding his master's horse. He saluted her with a raised hand, and a short, 'Mistress,' before turning his head away.

'What is it, Tib? Why have we stopped?'

Tib had been told by both Drew and Charles that
Bess was out of bounds to him, and that his future with
Atherington lay in remembering his own low station and
Bess's high one. Accordingly, instead of answering her,
he shook his head and shrugged indifferently.

So be it, thought Bess sadly, watching the easy days
of her youth disappearing with her former happy relationship with him. She was truly Lady Exford now, and she
would not make trouble for him, so she walked on until
she reached the trees. And there, beyond the bend, was
the reason for the sudden end to their rapid progress
towards Buxton.

Half across the muddy track—for it had rained on the
preceding day—a coach and a large covered wagon had,
by some accident, come together. The coach, being
smaller and of unsteady balance, had fared the worst,
and was lying on its side on the track, blocking the way.
The wagon was tilted askew against a tree.

Richly dressed men and women were sitting and standing in the shade of the trees. Charles and Drew, a little
way away, were talking to a large middle-aged man in
clothing as splendid as theirs. One motley crew of attendants from both parties was engaged in trying to right the
coach, another was pulling the wagon free, and a third
was trying to control the frightened horses which had
been pulling them.

Except that one horse lay still on the ground—its right
foreleg was twisted beneath its body, obviously broken;
the other foreleg was twitching. It was, Bess suspected,
the one which she had heard neighing its anguish,
although it had fallen silent now. A page was standing
miserably by it, and failed to see her until she dropped
on her knees by its head. She put out her hand to stroke

it, even as the page exclaimed, 'No, mistress. Do not put yourself in danger.'

To Bess it was suddenly as though an illuminated picture in a book which she had been reading had come to life. She had been outside the scene, but was now part of it. Drew, his attention drawn by the page's shrill shout, swung his head around to see that his wife had appeared, and, as was common with her, was about to make herself useful in a situation which was fraught with danger.

He strode over to lift her by the shoulders and drag her away from the horse. 'No, wife,' he ordered, his voice commanding, 'this is no place for you. If you wish to be of use, there are women here who would benefit from your sympathy. Although they are not injured, they were thrown down when the coach and the wagon collided, and are badly shaken. Fortunate it was that we were right behind them and may help them. They, too, are on their way to take the waters at Buxton.'

'But the poor horse is hurt,' Bess began, trying to look back. Drew caught her again, and made her look forward.

'It is no concern of yours, madam, and will be taken care of. Come, these are friends of mine from London, Sir Henry Gascoyne and the Lady Arbell, his wife, who is most distressed, having sprained her wrist.' So saying, he urged Bess gently along until they reached the shade of the largest tree where a splendidly dressed young woman was seated. She was leaning against its massive trunk, her eyes closed.

It gave Bess the strangest pang to discover that the Lady Arbell was the most beautiful woman she had ever seen, and that when she opened her lovely blue eyes it was to shine them on Drew, and speak to him, ignoring Bess on his arm, and his attempts to introduce her as his wife.

'Oh, Drew, dearest Drew, 'tis better than medicine to find you here in this savage wilderness.' She pressed a large lace handkerchief to her eyes to hide them for a moment, before withdrawing it to stare at Bess, looking her up and down as though she were a servant she was about to hire—or dismiss.

'Your wife, you say, Drew? How odd. I thought you unmarried.' She took in Bess's practical brown travelling dress with a contemptuous glance. 'Well, well, madam, I see that *you* are well equipped to survive in the wilderness.'

Then, petulantly, 'Will someone not silence that stupid animal? I vow that it was he who caused this dreadful accident by his refusal to respond to the whip,' for the injured horse had begun to complain again.

But not for long, since he was cut short in full cry by the crack of a horse pistol giving him the *coup de grâce*. At which the Lady Arbell gave a delicate shudder, and offered him a graceless epitaph by exclaiming, 'Thank God for that. I thought no one would ever silence the wretched creature. Why did it take you so long, Drew— and Henry—' for her husband had come up to them '—to dispose of it?'

She gave a great sigh and covered her face with her kerchief again. If, Bess thought, her wrist was damaged, it was but a slight hurt, seeing the extravagant play she was making with both her hands.

And it was Bess's turn to stare—at the Lady Arbell. She knew now why Drew had wanted her away from the horse, and that her commonsense should have warned her of what its fate must be. But it had been so beautiful lying there, and to think of one of God's own creatures coming to such a sad end, whilst its mistress wailed selfishly of her own minor discomforts, enraged her.

''Tis a good thing we humans are not so harshly treated as horses, madam, when we are wounded,' Bess told her bluntly, 'else a damaged wrist such as you sport might have your husband pistoling *you* down on the spot. . .'

'Wife! For shame,' exclaimed Drew savagely, as the Lady Arbell, giving a great cry, fell back against the tree trunk, her kerchief pressed to her eyes again.

'This is not fitting,' he told her. 'You forget yourself, particularly since I have offered a seat in your coach to the Lady Arbell on her journey to Buxton, seeing that her own is beyond immediate repair. Pray ask her forgiveness at once.'

He had grasped her right wrist in a grip of steel. The eyes which met hers were as darkly blue and sharp as a Damascene blade. He meant to be obeyed.

Bess wanted, oh, *so* desperately, to disobey him. Her anger at the languishing looks with which the lady had favoured—and was still favouring—her husband, whilst her own husband, whom she was ignoring, stood fatuously by, was overwhelming her. Commonsense prevailed. To defy him in public, over such a matter, would be foolish, even though her every sense revolted at having to apologise to the heartless trollop before her.

'Forgive me, madam, if I said aught to wound you. But it grieved me to see such a splendid creature destroyed, and in my grief, I forgot myself.'

There, it was out. The Lady Arbell waved her kerchief at Bess again. 'Oh, very well. I take you to be country bred, unschooled in the niceties of civilised life, and therefore must be forgiven. You must instruct your little wife, Drew, before you subject her to the scrutiny of the town, lest she bring mockery upon herself. And now pray lead me to the comfortable seat which you have promised me.'

Detaching Drew from Bess, she took his arm, leaving her husband and Bess watching them as Drew escorted her away until the bend in the road hid them from sight.

The expression on Sir Henry Gascoyne's broad and pleasant face was so rueful that Bess took pity on him, saying robustly, 'Why, sir, your wife and my husband were so distressed by her injury that they forgot to introduce us. Has my lord arranged a place for you in our cavalcade—or were you riding, as he is?'

'Riding? Why, yes, my lady. It was fortunate that I was ahead of the accident. The driver of our coach has broken his arm, and your husband has kindly lent us his physician, and promised the coachman a place in one of your carts, our remaining ones now being overfull.'

Well, at least Drew hadn't been so determined to make eyes at the Lady Arbell that he had forgotten to do his duty by her servants, was Bess's somewhat acid internal reaction to that. But it was his wife, not Drew, who would have to pay for his kindness by enduring the spiteful tongue of the lady all the way to Buxton.

She would try to persuade him to allow her to make one of the party which was travelling there on horseback!

Alas! It seemed that Drew was determined that she was to entertain the Lady Arbell all the way to Buxton, so that the pleasure which Bess had been taking in her first excursion into the wide world outside Atherington was quite dimmed. Lady Arbell's first demand had been that Bess and aunt Hamilton's attendant ladies should be banished from the coach so that she might take up the whole of the seat on one side of it. Aunt Hamilton and Bess, she graciously conceded, might have the other seat between them.

Bess had had no opportunity to defy her, for Drew

had told her in no uncertain terms that the Lady Arbell, being injured, must have all her wishes met. She thus, seething inside, was compelled to obey the Lady's slightest whim.

'For,' the Lady told Bess as majestically as though she were the Queen herself, 'I am not used to being cramped after such a fashion as to sit hugger-mugger with my inferiors. I wonder that you were happy to share your seat with your attendant lady—but, then, of course, I am forgetting that you are country bred and not accustomed to the finer manners of the town. Your good husband permitting, I shall be happy to instruct you— beginning with the task of reforming the manner in which you are dressed.'

So saying, she patted her own heavily brocaded and farthingaled gown, with its tight and low-cut bodice, below a cartwheel ruff of giant proportions which was held up with whalebobe stiffeners. All of which left, Bess admitted, little room in the small coach for anyone else but a dwarf to sit comfortably by her. The Lady Arbell was apparently ignoring the fact that the skirts of her gown, and her fine shoes, had become lavishly smeared with mud from the track. She had also lost the high heel from her right shoe whilst tottering through the muddy turf to the Exfords' coach. Drew had therefore carried her the last part of the way.

He had looked uncommonly happy whilst he was doing so, Bess had noted, although the lady, being fashionably plump, must have been a heavy armful!

'The roads and byways between Atherington and Buxton are muddy and sometimes impassable so that one occasionally needs to get out and walk whilst the coach and wagons are pushed uphill,' Bess said. 'I therefore thought it best to wear the simplest clothes and the stoutest shoes I possess. Indeed, I have a pair of boots ready under the seat lest I have occasion to walk through a watersplash!'

'Dear child,' said the Lady patronisingly, 'do not dwell so heavily on your country breeding. A true lady is known by her appearance, and so must dress accordingly. As for the mud—' and she lifted her skirts disdainfully '—why, I have a covey of attendant ladies, washer-women and sempstresses to care for my clothes—so I do not trouble myself over any mishap which may befall them. You speak of watersplashes—why, the footmen will carry me through them, if necessary. No, no, I see that you must be properly schooled and I will do my old friend Drew the favour of taking you on.'

She preened a little as she finished, and then, before Bess could so much as open her mouth, either to thank her or to refuse her supposedly kind offer, she added, 'No, do not thank me. I could not allow Drew's lady to bring on him the laughter of the mob.'

Thank her! For what? For her infernal rudeness, and her unkindness to aunt Hamilton, to whom she had not addressed a single word, and to their two attendant ladies whom she had turned out to be squeezed among the occupants of the following cart when there was still plenty of room for them in the coach?

As for her injury, Bess did not believe a word of it. She was using it as an excuse to get her own way, some-thing which she had doubtless been doing all her life. The sooner they arrived in Buxton, the better, when she could go her own way and cease to taunt Bess and make eyes at her husband—which she did every time Drew rode up to the coach and spoke to them through the opening in the coach door.

'You appear comfortable, ladies,' he remarked approvingly. 'It will not be long before we shall stop to eat at midday. In the meantime, continue to amuse yourselves. My wife will be pleased to have a new companion to talk to.'

Bess gave him a watery smile whilst inwardly thinking, No, I'm not. For she does not allow me to speak and all she wishes to do is to patronise me.

From what Drew was saying, he appeared to think that they were having a splendid time together whilst the Lady Arbell prattled on about how she intended to transform his wife into a simpering copy of her own stupid self.

Around noon, as he had promised, they stopped. The footmen helped them out of the coach and led them off the track into a woodland dell where the servants had set up trestle tables and covered them with food and drink. They were far from any inn or hostelry, Drew had told them, and would entertain themselves. In the evening they would sup at Tutbury where they hoped to stay overnight.

A carpet had been spread on the ground and cushions were placed on it on which the ladies sat, whilst the men arranged themselves on fallen tree trunks, benches lifted from the wagons, or on their cloaks spread on the ground.

Through the trees the wooded hills of Derbyshire were mauve against a pale blue sky. Bess declined ale and drank water, fetched for her from a nearby spring. The Lady Arbell kept up a litany of charming complaint at the same time as she spoke movingly of eating in Arcadia. Mrs Facing-Both-Ways was Bess's sour verdict on her.

The servants brought to them pewter plates laden with pieces of chicken pie, slices of cold spiced beef with its attendant mustard, and thick trenchers of buttered bread to be eaten later with wedges of red Leicestershire cheese

made in Atherington's dairy. Afterwards apple tart was
handed around——to all of which Lady Arbell took exception as being not sufficiently refined for her delicate
palate.

Drew, seated by her, opposite to Bess who was eating
heartily of everything, said quietly, 'Riding in the coach,
madam, does not create the appetite which being ahorse
in the open does.'

Lady Arbell shuddered. 'Oh, I would not wish to journey far on horseback——even if it made me able to eat
such coarse stuff as this.' She waved a fair white hand
at her neglected plate which lay on the grass beside her.

'I am,' Bess announced eagerly, through a mouthful
of Dame Margery's good bread, 'most willing to take
horse and ride with you, husband, thereby seeing more
of the fair Derbyshire countryside as well as making
myself ready for the next good meal we shall eat at
Tutbury.'

Drew looked across at her happy smiling face. His
wife was as different in appearance from the Lady Arbell
as she could possibly be. Her hair had come down a little
and the black velvet cap, which was supposed to cover
it, had fallen to one side. Her serviceable brown skirt
with its modest, highly laced bodice, was also askew,
showing the white linen petticoat underneath it. He was
surprised to discover that his wife's innocent disarray
pleased him more than the Lady Arbell's careful finery.

This overset him a little, for he had long been one of
Arbell's admirer's and had her husband not been his
father's friend he would have made her his mistress. She
had more than once hinted that she would not be averse
to having him for a lover. He also found that his wife's
hearty appetite both amused and pleased him——but he
could not allow her to snub the Lady.

He shook his head at her. 'Nay, wife. It seems to me that your appetite needs little encouragement, and I doubt whether your short excursions around Atherington have fitted you for a hard ride through difficult country. No, no, continue your pleasant gossip, and later, when we reach Buxton, allow me to arrange for some easier outings for you.'

Bess tried not to look as unhappy as she felt. Her spirits rose a little when, later, Drew took the opportunity to walk her to the coach, leaving the Lady Arbell to her husband's care.

'You do understand,' he told her, 'that politeness alone means that I cannot permit you to ride with us. It is your duty to entertain our guest, for that is what she is.'

'She seems to think that it is her duty to educate me, rather than mine to entertain her,' Bess grumbled at him. 'But I will do as you say. Do all fine ladies from the court resemble her? If so, I do not wish to be a fine lady!'

'She is very delicate, very much the young wife of an older man,' admitted Drew. 'She was the daughter of the last Earl of Frensham—hence she keeps the name of the Lady Arbell, being of a higher rank than a mere knight, rather than being called Lady Gascoyne. She was married to him against her will. More, she was of the Catholic faith and he is not, but her Protestant guardians insisted that she renounce her religion in order to marry him— that was the condition of her inheritance. You should feel pity for her.'

'She is so busy pitying *me* for my uncouth country manners,' retorted Bess sturdily, 'that she would resent me if I tried to pity *her*.'

'Nevertheless,' said Drew, handing her in to sit by aunt Hamilton, 'you will remember what my wishes are, I hope.'

He gave her such a winning smile that Bess's heart melted within her. She could forgive him anything if only he would look at her like that more often. Unfortunately the Lady Arbell had drawn level with them and saw the smile.

'What, still wooing your wife, Drew?' she mocked at them. 'I thought that it was not the fashion these days for husband and wife to care for one another, once married. It is not like you to be other than in the van! You will be writing sonnets to her next, instead of to your mistress.'

His mistress? Did he have a mistress? Had he left her behind in London? Or did the Lady mean that now that he was married he ought to acquire one? Preferably herself, no doubt! Unless, of course, she was already his mistress.

Sir Henry closed his eyes in a pained fashion, but made no effort to reprove his wife. He opened them again, and said gently, 'Remember how young Drew's wife is, my dear, and that he has but lately met her again. She needs your encouragement—which I am sure you will offer her.'

Bess could not resist temptation, and said, mischief in her eyes if not in her face. 'Oh, Sir Henry, you may rest assured that your wife is doing all that you might wish her to do. She has been offering me encouragement and advice ever since she became my companion on the journey!'

Sir Henry took this at face value and offered her a relieved smile, but Bess saw at once that she had not deceived Drew. He shook his head reprovingly at her behind Sir Henry's back, took him by the arm and walked him away before Bess could say anything more.

She had not deceived the Lady, either. 'I see that you have a shrewd, if rural, wit, madam,' she hissed at Bess, as she settled her elaborate skirts around her. 'You may have cozened your husband and mine, but I know very well what you are at. Do not think that you may trick me at will.'

Before Bess could speak, aunt Hamilton, who had sat silent ever since they had been compelled to share the coach wit their unwanted guest, exclaimed indignantly, 'My niece does not deserve your strictures, my lady. She has been the soul of politeness ever since we first offered you succour. You mock at her country manners, but I prefer them to the insolence of the town.'

'No doubt,' sneered the Lady, 'since you share them yourself! If you are both so determined to carry the smell of the pig sty around with you, then I will leave you to your unfortunate preference, and say no more.' She turned her head away from them, closed her eyes, and to Bess's great relief spoke no more until they reached Tutbury in the early evening.

Chapter Seven

'**W**ith so many great ones visiting it, and so much spoken and written of it, I had not expected to find Buxton so small,' was Bess's first remark to Drew when they rode into the village. Earlier that day he had relented a little, had given way to her pleas, and had allowed her to leave the coach so that she might ride into Buxton beside him.

Two nights ago whilst eating their supper at Tutbury before retiring to spend a blissful night in bed which went far, in Bess's estimation, towards making up for the disappointments of her day, Drew had told her of the book which a friend had lent him and which was full of the delights of the place—Buckstone, as he called it. It had been written by a physician, one Dr Jones. Drew did not tell her that Sir Francis Walsingham had passed it on to him so that he might know what to expect when he arrived there on his secret mission.

'Which is why I have brought a pair of musicians with us,' Drew said, drinking his soup, 'for the good doctor urged those who used the baths only to do so after they had spent several happy days listening to music. Music, he said, chases away melancholy.'

He cocked an enquiring and naughty eyebrow at her before adding, 'Can you think of another activity which might chase away melancholy, madam? And shall we engage in it when the meal is over? I vow I cannot wait until we have drunk Buxton water!'

Bess gave him a merry glance. One thing which she had not expected before his arrival was that she would enjoy Drew's lovemaking so much and join in it so heartily.

'And having read the book, and learned how popular Buxton has become amongst the nobility and gentry, I took the precaution of writing to the Earl of Shrewsbury to warn him that we should be arriving this week, and would require lodgings in his Great Hall. I had no mind to pleasure my wife in the barren wastes lost amongst the cold Derbyshire hills.'

So here they were, riding along a rough track by the River Wye into a large dale surrounded by the hills of the Peak. The hills were of a height such as Bess had never seen before. And in this dale was Buxton, a village so small that Atherington village seemed large beside it. It did not, Bess was to find, even possess a church.

What it did possess was George Shrewsbury's Great Hall of which Drew had told her. Four square, built of stone and four storeys high, it stood beside the spring which they had come to visit. Nearby were the Baths, and at the sight of them Bess shivered involuntarily. Even though it was summer, the Derbyshire wind was keen, and the Baths were open to the sky although one of them had a gallery around it, with seats and hearths in it, to warm the bathers and air their clothing when they had finished splashing in the waters.

Of course, the Lady Arbell, alighting from the coach which Bess had spurned that morning, allowing aunt

Hamilton's elderly attendant to have a more comfortable
seat than that in the cart to which the Lady Arbell had
consigned her, immediately set up another litany of complaint. She shuddered theatrically, and no wonder, Bess
thought, for she was wearing a low-cut bodice which
revealed most of her bosom, exclaiming, 'Is this what
we have ridden so far—and in such discomfort—to see?
We had been better advised to have remained at home.

'Husband,' she called to Sir Henry who had just
descended from his horse, 'have we not mistook our
destination? This surely cannot be the sacred well and
the divine water of which we have heard so much!'

'Now, now, my dear,' soothed her husband, slipping
the cloak from his own shoulders to drape it around his
wife's. 'You will feel better when we are indoors before
a warm fire.'

He had evidently been reading Dr Jones's treatise, too,
because he added, 'We are recommended to take our
ease for several days before we drink of the water. The
air of Derbyshire is keener than that which we are used
to, and we must grow accustomed to it.'

Arbell allowed herself to be led indoors, leaving Bess,
who was wearing a man's warm leather jacket over her
sensible brown stuff dress, to dismount from her horse,
and follow her in. Drew moved forward to take her hand.
'You are not too discommoded by the cold, wife?'

'A little, but not so much as the Lady Arbell. Her
courtier-like clothing is no match for the winds which
blow here.'

'No, indeed. I am pleased to see that you are dressed
for any weather, wife.'

Chatting together in such easy friendship enabled Bess
to forget the annoying Lady Arbell and the worrying
suspicion that Drew had been closer to her than he ought

to have been. Hand in hand they entered George Shrewsbury's fine new building, to be welcomed by Thomas Greves who ran the Hall for the Earl. It contained, he told them, thirty rooms where the nobility and gentry might lodge, 'As well,' he added, 'as those merchants and yeomen whom m'lord allows to stay here at reduced prices as an act of charity to those less fortunate than himself and his peers.'

'Large though these rooms are,' Bess whispered to Drew when they were at last left alone together in them, 'they will not accommodate all of our people.'

'Charles has arranged for half of them to lodge at the local inns,' Drew told her. 'Cease to trouble yourself, Lady Exford, about our arrangements. You are here to enjoy yourself, and forget the labour of running Atherington. You must be ready to break your fast, for Greves says that he is about to serve a midday meal in the Great Hall where all the lodgers eat together daily.'

So she would have to endure the Lady Arbell at mealtimes, would she? No matter. She would enjoy herself, as Drew bade her, and be at last a lady of leisure— something which so far she had never experienced. Perhaps, if she were lucky, she would be far removed from Sir Henry and his wife at table.

Her luck held. She and Drew found themselves among a clutch of Derbyshire and Leicestershire squires who were flattered to be thus seated among the great. The food was excellent. Timothy Blagg, who owned land not far from Atherington, advised her cheerfully, 'Try this excellent ale, m'lady. The Earl of Shrewsbury has it sent here especially from Chatsworth, as well as the splendid cheese which graces our table today. Yesterday we ate fowls and rabbits which m'lord's servants had delivered in quantity for us. We are as well fed as any in England.'

Drew smiled a little at this, but later acknowledged that Buxton fare was well worth the eating, and that the Earl had provided splendidly for his guests. 'Not that he loses by it,' he concluded shrewdly, 'seeing that we pay him handsomely for his pains.'

'Master Blagg said that they are expecting the Queen of Scots to arrive here any day now,' offered Bess. 'And since, like her, he is Catholic, he is longing to see her—although he drank to our present Queen right heartily at the end of the meal.'

Unknowingly, Bess destroyed a little of the pleasure which Drew was beginning to find in her company and in this visit to a county whose rough beauties he had often heard spoken of, but had never seen. She had reminded him of his duty and of the promise which he had made to Walsingham, and for a moment the bright day grew a little dark for him. He could wish that all that he had to do was to pay attention to his wife's pleasure and his own.

His one hope was that the Queen of Scot's visit might be a little delayed so as to give him more time to woo his wife. In the meantime he would not only enjoy himself but would listen carefully to what his companions at the table were saying. They might be indiscreet in his presence since they knew him only as an idle courtier, not as one of the intimates of those who ruled England for the Queen.

'And Master Blagg says that it would not be wise for us to visit the Baths *after* we have eaten,' Bess went on eagerly. 'On the contrary, we must always do so *before* we eat—preferably in the morning.'

'And again in the evening before supper,' Drew continued for her, smiling at his wife's enthusiasm for everything she did, so different from the Lady Arbell's bored haughtiness, 'and after that we shall be put to bed with bladders of hot water to make us sweat. I suspect that Master Blagg has also been reading the good Doctor's book!' He paused a little before whispering naughtily in her ear, 'I think that we know a better way than that to make us sweat, eh, wife?'

Bess sparked back at him immediately. 'You are a rogue, sir, to speak of such matters here. . .'

'But you agree with me, do you not?' Drew said wickedly. 'For, after all, are we not husband and wife, and does not the wedding ceremony say that marriage is for the procreation of children, and how shall we procreate unless we enjoy ourselves in the marriage bed?'

There was no answer to that which Bess could usefully make, other than a feeble assent. 'I suppose that if Buxton water improves both our bodies and our souls then the act of procreation may become more effective.'

'Well said, wife, and I will remind you of that this evening, never fear—even if we have not yet qualified for the bladders of hot water by dipping into the cold Bath water!'

Which he duly did, and that night the moon streamed through the windows of Lord Shrewbury's noble hall on a husband and wife sleeping the sleep of the well and truly satisfied. Drew's worries over spying for Walsingham, and Bess's jealousy of the Lady Arbell, and any other lady who trained her arts on Drew, were alike forgotten. . .

'I had not thought that Buxton water would be quite so cold,' Bess gasped several days later, as swathed in towels, she sat on a bench in the roofed colonnade surrounding the Bath, not far from one of the great hearths and its flaming fire.

'Rather you than me, m'lady,' muttered Jess, her tire-woman, as she vigorously rubbed her mistress down. 'I don't much like bathing—even when the water's warm. I wonder how m'lord is enjoying himself. They say that in wicked Italy men and women bathe together, but such rude manners have not reached here yet, praise be to God.'

Bess was not quite sure whether she agreed with her woman. She rather thought that she might have liked to watch Drew swimming in all his naked glory—although she was also sure that she didn't really wish to see Sir Henry Gascoyne or some of the fatter squires unclothed. Drew had told her that on his visit to Italy with Philip Sidney they had both learned to swim in the warm Mediterranean.

'And a very pleasant pastime it is, too. When I take you to my home I shall have the pleasure of swimming with you in the river which runs at the bottom of the Park. We shall be like the gods of old, madam, sporting in Arcadia.'

Take her to his home! Did that mean that he did not intend to leave her at Atherington, but would make her his true wife in every sense by keeping her by his side? Every one of Bess's newly awakened senses quivered at the very thought.

She had laughed her pleasure at Drew's enthusiasm, and told him, 'Alas, husband, I need no teacher, for my father taught me when I was a child. But I shall join you with pleasure.'

'There, m'lady. You are dry and your clothes are warmed. Do you wish me to dress you now?'

'Oh, yes, at once.' Bess's eagerness was created by the appearance of the Lady Arbell and one of her hangers-on, Marian, the young wife of Master Blagg. Marian was monstrously pleased by the Lady's patronage, she never having met anyone half so grand before. Arbell, indeed, was singularly gracious to her, in contrast to the half-mocking manner in which she always spoke to Bess.

'Greetings, madam,' she carolled in Bess's direction. 'I see that you have taken to the water before us. A pity, we could have pretended that we were the Three Graces, or the three goddesses who appeared before Paris.'

This parade of classical learning was obviously designed to put both Arbell's hearers down. Determined not to let Arbell patronise her, Bess asked, as Jess laced her into her overbodice, 'And, pray, whom ought we to nominate as Paris? And where shall we find a golden apple?'

It occurred to her that apples had played a large part in her conversation lately and, pondering why this should be so, she almost missed Arbell's sulky, 'Ah, I see you have read the classics, Lady Exford. Now, as to Paris, looking around our gentleman the choice must lie between dear Marian's husband—and your own. I wonder to which lady either of them might choose to give the apple?'

It had become plain to Bess that, by her slightly bewildered expression, Marian knew nothing of 'The Story of Paris of Troy and the Three Goddesses'. This belief was confirmed when, plucking up her courage, she asked hesitantly, 'And for what reason, pray, dear Lady Arbell, should my husband—or Lady Exford's—imitate Paris, whoever he was, by giving an apple to anyone?'

Before Arbell could answer Bess said rapidly, 'Why, Paris, the Trojan prince, was given a golden apple and told to hand it to whichever of the three Greek goddesses, Athene, Hera or Aphrodite, he thought the most beautiful. He chose Aphrodite, the goddess of love, and was rewarded with the beautiful Helen. But he also earned the undying hatred of the other two goddesses which, in the end, caused the Trojan War and the fall of Troy, and his own death.

'My advice to your husband—or mine—would be that he should take his golden apple to the nearest goldsmith and exchange it for some good English money. Thus we should all end up happy—and Buxton will not fall!'

The look with which the Lady Arbell rewarded Bess for this sublime piece of nonsense would have killed a man at ten paces! She had hoped that the obsequious Marian would have said that of the three of them the Lady Arbell must surely be the one to be rewarded with the apple. Instead, she was laughing at Bess's deflation of Arbell's mock heroics.

'Oh, I'm sure I should not like to bring about any such terrible thing,' she exclaimed. 'You agree, m'lady Arbell?' she added, unaware of that Lady's anger.

'How can I disagree? I see that your husband awaits you, Lady Exford.' Arbell could not wait to be rid of Bess so that she might regain Marian Blagg's innocent worship, which had, for a moment, been transferred to the woman whom she regarded as her rival. 'Does *he* admire your pedantry, Lady Exford? I had not thought him to be attracted by female learning.'

'Oh, I think that he prefers it to female ignorance,' was Bess's careless answer. 'Pray hand me my straw hat, Jess. The sun is strong today.'

'You have the air of the cat who has stolen the cream about you, wife,' remarked Drew thoughtfully when Bess joined him, all rosy and refreshed from her bath and her sparring with the Lady Arbell. He had not seen the Lady and her companion, but he was beginning to learn his wife's ways—and read her looks.

'Have I, husband? Why, as to that, the sun pleases me, you please me, and my late companions have afforded me pleasure, the Lady Arbell most of all.'

Drew thought it wise not to pursue the matter further, but was much entertained over the next few days by the spectacle of the Lady Arbell trying to put Bess down, and being constantly foiled by her quick wits. More than ever he wished that it had not taken him so long to become reacquainted with the pearl who was his wife.

Unaware of the undercurrents around her, and that below the surface of her pleasant life there lurked those who would destroy it, as the pike lurks to feed on the lesser fish in the rivers and streams beside which she daily walked, Bess continued to take her innocent pleasure. It was not diminished on the day that the Queen of Scots's party rode into Buxton to be received as nobly as a once-reigning monarch ought to be.

Those lodging at Shrewsbury's Great House were waiting in its Hall to receive her and to pay her their respects. Prisoner she might be, but she was also the Queen Elizabeth's cousin, and her heir—which was the motive, Drew knew, for the plots against Elizabeth and on her behalf.

'She is not as beautiful as I expected her to be,' Bess whispered to Drew. 'But she has a right royal presence, has she not?'

'She is no longer young,' Drew whispered back to her, 'being nigh on forty years old. I had not expected to find her so tall.' He had never seen her before, and although he had heard much of her beauty and her charm, no one had told him that she was as tall as he was, being all of six feet in height.

And here she was, being introduced to them—or rather

they were being introduced to her by a servile Greves—
as m'lord the Earl of Exford and his lady wife. They
were now face to face with her, and could see every
detail of her fading beauty and her unfading charm.

'Oh, but I have heard of you, my lord of Exford,' she
exclaimed in her pretty strangely accented voice in which
French and Scottish inflections fought for dominance.
'You are a friend of Sir Henry Sidney's son, Philip, are
you not, and play at tennis with him?'

Now this was a surprise, and not a welcome one for
Drew. He had thought himself almost anonymous, and
he wondered who had made the effort to inform the
Queen of his friendships. And what else had they told
her of him? Was there someone who knew what no one
ought to know—that Drew Exford was more than a
simple friend of those in Sir Francis Walsingham's
circle?

No matter. He bowed and smiled, saying, 'You do me
great honour, your Grace, to remember such idle details
of my life.' The Queen made him no answer but, serene
and cool, sailed by him in majesty to smile in her turn
at Bess, and say, her eyes kind, but shrewd, 'And a good
day to you, Lady Exford. I had not heard that you were
married, my lord,' she said, turning her head towards
him again.

'Long ago,' he replied easily, 'as children often are,
but only recently have we claimed each other, now that
the time for settling the future of the line has come.'

'Ah, so that is why you are here, and not gracing my
cousin's court.'

'Indeed, your Grace. To take the waters—and secure
the line.' Drew hoped that he was not overdoing things,
but no one appeared to see anything extraordinary in
what was being said. Bess, however, who had spoken

briefly to the Queen, praising the beauties of Buxton and the Peak, remarked to him afterwards, 'Now, what was all that about, husband? How should she know of you— and tennis with Philip Sidney? You had not told me of that.'

'Most remiss of me,' smiled Drew, who was thinking up something innocuous to say to his wife, who was far too shrewd for her own good. 'It is to be supposed that she was informed of who was lodging in Buxton and that one of her train knew of myself and Philip and took the trouble to mention it to her so that she might have something to say when she met us.'

Why did she not believe him? Bess only knew that, in the short time in which she and Drew had been husband and wife, she had come to learn the false notes in his voice; notes, she was coming to find, none other than she could hear. He was troubled, no doubt of it, by what the Queen had said, and why should that be?

A wise wife ought to say no more, and being a wise wife—for once—she fell silent. But, having been Bess Turville who had run Atherington by virtue of letting little pass her by, she put the matter at the back of her mind, not to be forgotten, but to be brought out again if a future ocasion warranted it. . .

At the time, though, she listened carefully to what the Queen was saying to Sir Henry and the Lady Arbell who were standing beside them, but could detect no false notes there. The Lady Arbell was as overblown as usual in all that she said and did, and Sir Henry was as apologetic. The Queen spoke only briefly to them, passing swiftly on to young Timothy Blagg, whose day, nay, his year, was made by the Queen's graciousness and the length of time she spent with him.

So long was she with the squires that the Lady Arbell

hissed her annoyance first at her husband and then at Bess. 'She behaves as though she were already our Queen, which, pray God, she may never be. Nor is she as beautiful as I was led to expect. Indeed, she is not beautiful at all!'

She preened herself as she spoke. And while Bess agreed with her, for she had heard much of the Queen of Scots's loveliness, and had not stopped to think that years of disappointment and imprisonment must have left their cruel marks on her, she also thought it tasteless of the Lady Arbell to make such a severe judgement on one so unfortunate.

And so she said to Drew later, when they were preparing to eat with the Queen and her companions. Drew hesitated a moment before answering her. At last, 'She has brought most of her misfortunes on herself,' he said slowly. 'She made a most unwise marriage to young Henry Darnley, involved herself in his murder, and then married a brutal adventurer, the Earl of Bothwell. Everything which she touched turned to lead, and when that happens one must ask whether a person is unfortunate or has brought it upon themselves by their own misjudgement.'

This, from Drew, was harsh. So far he had said little on matters of state, and when he had done so had spoken idly, as though little concerned. He must have read Bess's expression for he added, wryly for him, 'Come, wife, we are here to take the waters and enjoy ourselves. I have ordered Tib to tell the musicians to attend us this afternoon when we visit the Baths. The day is fair, the sun is shining, and it may shine on us, as well as the Queen of Scots.'

Something she had heard earlier struck Bess as he finished speaking. Something he had said. 'You told me that the Lady Arbell had once been Catholic.'

Drew stared at her, his eyebrows raised. 'Aye, wife, so I did. But what of it?'

'That being so, husband, I am a little, nay, more than a little, surprised to find her so hot against the Queen of Scots, and so much for our own Queen.'

'Hot against Queen Mary, was she, wife?' Drew was thoughtful. 'That may not be as surprising as you think. Recent converts are always the noisiest for their new faith, I have found.'

'Oh,' Bess was thoughtful in her turn. 'You are wiser in the ways of the wide world than I am. I had thought that perhaps she was jealous of the Queen's reputation for beauty—except that she denied that the Queen was beautiful.'

'Mayhap so. Let us forget them both. We have our own pleasures to follow—as they have theirs.' He offered Bess his arm and they walked together down the main staircase and into the great room where yet another splendid meal had been prepared for them, and this time, the Earl of Shrewsbury himself was there to eat it with them.

But despite what he had said to Bess, Drew did not dismiss what she had told him about the Lady Arbell from his mind. Warily he asked himself whether someone who wished to plot against England's Queen might not, as a blind, pretend to be hot for her, and hot against the person whom they really wished to serve.

Certainly the Lady Arbell would bear watching, and also the young Catholic squire Timothy Blagg, who could scarce eat his meal he was so busy staring worshipfully at the Queen. Bess, suddenly aware that Drew for some reason was distrait, saw that his eyes were on Arbell— and her heart sank.

Sat matters so? After only a few short weeks with his

newfound wife, was her husband ready to dally again with the Lady? It seemed so. Her temper was not improved when, after the meal, the Earl of Shrewsbury approached her and asked her whether she was satisfied with her lodgings.

'Indeed, m'lord, most satisfied,' she told him, turning to Drew for confirmation. But he was no longer at her elbow—in fact, was not visible at all. Charles had taken his place and it was to him that she appealed for support instead. It was not, sadly, the first time that it occurred to her that since they had come to Buxton her husband's cousin and Comptroller was more assiduous in his attendance on her than Drew was.

Bess pushed the thought away. It was disloyal. She chattered animatedly to Lord Shrewsbury, who found that Lady Exford was a far more attractive young woman than report had said. Most attractive, but he would not tell his redoubtable wife so.

'And you are comfortable at Buxton, my lady? You find the waters agreeable?'

'When the weather is warm, yes.' A reply which had him laughing before he released her to pay further attention to his prisoner, the Queen of Scots, who was seated in a corner of the room holding court, a bevy of young men and women about her. He had, he acknowledged to himself, a heavy burden to carry in making sure that she did not use these few weeks of relative freedom to instigate plots and treachery against his mistress, Queen Elizabeth of England.

Bess looked about her. Drew was not one of the party about the Queen, although Sir Henry Gascoyne was— but the Lady Arbell was not with him. She decided to go in search of him.

She walked through the double doors at the far end of

the room. They opened on to a corridor which ran the length of the house. Tall windows, each with its enclosed seat, were set into its length, offering a view of Buxton and its surrounding hills. And there, in one of them, sat the Lady Arbell with Drew Exford by her side, his hand on hers. They were talking intimately, heads together.

What a cosy pair they made! A pity to disturb them was Bess's acid—and dismayed—thought. It was one thing to suspect her husband of marital treachery, quite another to find him at it.

She advanced on them, making no effort to keep her footsteps muted on the highly polished wooden floor. No matter! They were so engrossed in each other that they did not hear her coming. And when they did they sprang apart to face her, each of them smiling at her as though she were the dearest creature they knew.

'My dear,' Drew said, rising to greet her. 'The Lady has been giving me messages from my London friends. Master Sidney, she tells me, has not yet left for Wilton. The Queen, alas, is still not best pleased with him, and he intends to fly from her shade where once he lived in her full sun.'

'I wonder,' replied Bess, 'that any of you can bring yourselves to leave her neighbourhood! And you, Lady Arbell? Is it her shade you fear, or her sun you enjoy?'

'Oh, her sun,' smiled the Lady. 'But, as I was telling your husband, my physician has recommended me to take the waters to restore my health, which too long a stay in London always impairs. My husband being so much older than I am, he requires an annual visit to a spa, and this year he decided to try what Buxton has to offer.'

She turned her great eyes on Drew—needlessly— since he was already busily engaged in drinking in her manifold charms, and added, 'To find old friends here is one of the delights of the place. It quite makes up for the grim hills which surround us.'

Somehow her hand strayed on to Drew's silken thigh and patted it absently. She gave a great start, appeared to recall that she was in the presence of his wife, and removed it, saying, 'Pray forgive me, I quite forgot that we are not at court and must adhere to country manners.'

Yes, I might as well be a milkmaid, fumed Bess, from the manner in which she speaks to me, and Drew has apparently nothing better to do than behave as though she has bewitched him! Aloud she said, as sweetly as she could, for she would not let the Lady score any points off her by appearing openly jealous. 'I thought, husband, that you were of a mind to make an early visit to the Baths—'

Before she could continue further, Drew said, also smiling at her, 'Oh, my dear, the Lady Arbell has asked us to accompany Sir Henry, herself, and Master Blagg to St Ann's Well where we may drink the holy water. Tomorrow we may then all repair to the Baths.'

'But the weather might change,' protested Bess.

'Very unlikely, we are told,' put in Arbell. 'The old man who advises us on it hath said that it will be passing warm for the next week. Besides, the Queen of Scots will be going, and it would, Sir Henry says, only be civil for us to accompany her on her first outing. After that we may please ourselves.'

So it was settled. Instead of a pleasant and quiet excursion to the Baths for the two of them, Bess found that they were to form part of a crowd attendant on the newly arrived Queen.

'It is always the same,' Charles told her as he escorted her to where Drew—and the Lady and her husband—

were waiting for them, since Bess had decided that she wished to change into stout shoes for the walk. 'Whenever the Queen of Scots visits Buxton she becomes the centre of attraction. Even Lord Burghley, and the Earl of Leicester when they came here, danced attendance on her. So where the great and powerful of our world are content to lead, we must follow.'

Bess could not tell him that her quarrel was not with the Queen, but with Arbell and her husband. It would sound too petty.

'You are not happy, wife,' Drew whispered to her as they walked to the well together. Sir Henry had recovered his wife, and she had bade an unwilling farewell to Drew. 'What ails you?'

'Nothing,' lied Bess. 'Except that I thought that we were going to visit the Baths privately this afternoon, not form part of the Queen's cortège.'

'Oh, we must do our duty,' returned Drew, who was well aware that it was his dalliance with the Lady which had disturbed his wife. But he had his other duty to do; that which consisted of trying to discover whether or no Arbell's visit to Buxton was wholly innocent. He wished that he might enlighten Bess as to what he was doing, but he was too old a hand to want to say anything to anyone about his mission. Even to his wife.

Particularly to his wife. He wanted to protect her, not put her at risk.

Bess was still complaining gently to him about their ruined afternoon. 'I wonder that, being good Protestants, we are all so eager to visit a Holy Well which the late Thomas Cromwell ordered to be closed because it was an incitement to Papistry. I can understand the Queen of Scots wishing to go there, but for the rest. . .' She allowed her voice to die away.

Drew, well aware of the true reason for Bess's unhappiness, replied gently, 'But the Well has been re-opened and our present Queen puts no obstacles in the way of those who seek to find a cure by drinking of its sacred water. You may see the abandoned crutches of the lame who were healed hanging beside it.'

He gave her a sly sideways look, adding, 'And those who have difficulty in conceiving a child also come here to ask the Saint's blessing—as do the newly married who wish to bear their husband a child without delay.'

'Oh, in that case,' replied Bess, 'I suppose I must drink of the water myself,' and she returned his sly look with interest so that, forgetting himself, the Lady Arbell and all etiquette, Drew could not resist leaning towards her and kissing her on the corner of her mouth.

'Do not fret, sweeting,' he told her. 'There will be other days for us to sport in the water.

By now the whole party had reached the Well, and their lackeys were handing them small pewter cups to drink from. A group of villagers stood at a distance watching the great ones who had favoured these remote hills with their dazzling presence. The lads of the village ran forward to hold the horses of yet more visitors, come from Chatsworth, where they had been the guests of Lord Shrewsbury overnight before travelling on to Buxton.

Drew, on examining them with the benefit of his good long sight, exclaimed delightedly, 'No, it cannot be! I vow and declare there is my good friend Philip Sidney.'

He took Bess by the hand and walked her over to where a tall man with a high-nosed face, pale blonde hair and a delicate colour had just dismounted from his horse and was handing the reins to his groom.

'Philip! What fair wind blew you here? I had thought you long gone to Wilton and that if you were taking the waters, you were taking them at Bath.'

Philip Sidney seemed to be as pleased at seeing Drew as Drew was at seeing him. 'Good friend, my uncle Leicester recently rebuked me for never having visited Buxton. He swears that the waters are superior to those at Bath, so I thought that I would follow his example and discover whether he has the right of it. Had I known that you were here I should have speeded up my visit even further. As usual, you have forgot your manners and have not introduced me to your good lady. She *is* your good lady, I trust?'

This last came out in a serio-comic manner with much raising of fine eyebrows. Drew took the question in good part. 'Of course. We have come on from Atherington to take the cure together. May I introduce my dear wife, Bess Exford, to my oldest friend, Philip Sidney? He invariably beats me at tennis, the dog, but I have been refining my skills in the bowling alley where I soon hope to gain my long-delayed revenge.'

Philip was offering Bess his most courtier-like bow, all waving arms, bent right leg and down-hung head— much as though she were the Queen. 'Ah, yet another Bess,' he rallied her. 'And are you as imperious as our divine majesty, or do you practise God's mercy on such poor mortals as myself?'

No doubt about it, he rivalled Drew in charm, but there was something melancholy about him. Now, whatever else he was, Drew was never melancholy. He possessed an effervescence of spirit which was never overwrought, always under control, and which served to inspire those he was with to believe that they, too, shared his ability to meet life head on and challenge it to do its worst, knowing that they would do their best.

He was effervescing now, but gently. 'You have

arrived just in time, my dear Pythias, to drink the water with her Grace of Scotland. A moment later would have been too late. Tib,' he called to that young man who was offering him yet another cup of holy water, 'pray give of Derbyshire's nectar to Master Sidney here, that we may convince him that Arcadia and its joys are not confined to the Southern counties, but may also be found in the Midland Shires.'

Philip grimaced as he took the pewter cup which Tib held out and raised it high. 'A toast to you, my Lady Exford,' he offered. 'I have drunk enough spa water in my journeyings to know that it seldom tastes like nectar! As for Derbyshire being Arcadia—well, as uncle Leicester says of most things, "We shall see what we shall see." '

He drank the water down with a flourish, saying as he finished. 'Not so bad, nor so well, either, if I may be allowed to pun, my dear Damon. And if we are using our Greek nicknames, then pray tell me under what divine pseudonym your fair wife passes.'

'Oh, he has not yet so baptised me,' replied Bess, who had been staring in wonderment at the pair of them. 'You call yourself Damon and Pythias, I suppose, because you are firm friends, as they were. But seeing that I am tall and brown-eyed and far from fair, being brown instead, I cannot be a goddess, but an alien sprite named—' and she hesitated '—Cleopatra.'

Philip Sidney gave a great shout of laughter, all melancholy fled. 'So, she does not need you, my Damon, for she can speak for herself, your lady. And she is learned in the classics, and subtle too. For, in the same breath she names herself plain and yet awards herself the name of the beautiful Egyptian temptress who conquered both the great Julius Caesar and Marc Antony.'

He dropped on to one knee, took Bess's hand and kissed it. 'I salute you, Cleopatra, and one day you must show me your barge.'

Bess laughed down at him, enjoying the jest. But suddenly she heard Drew give a short indrawn breath, and looked at him to discover, as Philip was doing, that the expression on her husband's face was not totally one of pleasure at his friend's jesting. For a fleeting moment jealousy rode there—and then was gone.

Bess's first response was one of a strange delight. For Drew to be jealous, even of his old and greatest friend, could only mean that he felt for her more than the tepid passion of mere friendship between man and woman. But she did not want her existence to mar what had obviously meant so much to him before he had met her.

She withdrew her hand from Philip's, saying, 'Oh, I promise to tempt no one—except my husband, of course.'

The awkward moment was gone. All three of them were laughing, and were presently joined by new friends, and old ones, who demanded to know what the jest was but were fobbed off by Drew announcing that it was one of Philip's learned ones which needed so much explanation that the jest disappeared in its unravelling.

'Then,' drawled the Lady Arbell, no fool she, 'why was it amusing you so greatly? If the jest had disappeared?'

'Oh,' smiled Philip Sidney, 'the fact that the jest needed explanation was the jest itself!'

The laughter this provoked ended their private conversation and talk became general. Most of the company had drunk of the well water and were beginning to make their way back to the Great Hall. Bess found herself one of a group of wives whose husbands were making much of their new companions. Philip had already told them that he was taking lodgings at the Hall.

He took advantage of a break in the gaiety to slip an arm through Drew's and say, as though still jesting with him, 'Remind me to pass on immediately a letter which I have for you in my saddlebags. It is from Walsingham; once he knew that I was making for Buxton, he was urgent that I deliver it to you as soon as possible. Which I will do. I had not known that you were so friendly with the old Fox.'

'Oh, matters of business,' responded Drew airily. He had no intention of telling Philip the truth of his relationship with Walsingham, the less people knew of it the better.

Besides, he was protecting Philip as much as himself by keeping mum. Which was all a great nuisance, for now he had two hostages to fortune instead of only one.

Chapter Eight

Walsingham's letter was written in a double tongue—but was to the point.

'Know, dear friend,' he wrote, 'that my good wishes go with you and your lady to Buckstone. I have, unlike my lords of Burghley and Leicester, never visited there, but I am told that the waters are powerful and conducive to good health. That you should remain in command of yours is the wish of your old mentor and adviser. I fear that there is something in Buckstone's air which might bring on your melancholy.

'Know that all that glisters is not gold, and that there are many who affect a military stance who have never seen a battlefield. Know, too, that women make even better plotters than men, since to make up for their lack of bodily strength they frequently emulate the duplicity of Master Reynard the Fox himself.

'Know also that I have news of the greatest lady of all whom you have never pursued, but may be doing so by now. She is pursued by many for their own advantage—and for hers. My Lord of Leicester was hot for her once, but his common sense prevailed in the end and he fled the field. Others are neither so wise nor so expedient, and rumour hath it that more than one of the young squires at Buckstone may have drunk from tainted wells rather than the pure springs blessed by Saint Ann.

'This being so, take urgent care of your own health, and that of your good lady—to whom I hope that you are now reconciled. Do not yet stray from the straight path of marital virtue is the advice of your mentor. As with men, so with women, all that glisters is not gold. For your assistance I am despatching you a messenger, who will prove his allegiance to me by showing you the token of which we spoke in London.

'I send this by the hand of Master Philip Sidney, whose interest in Buckstone is confined to his friendship with you and his desire to compare its waters with those of Bath. Fail not to write me a loving letter in return. News from you always delights my old heart.'

'Does it, indeed?' was Drew's sardonic comment, made aloud. He had waited until he was alone before opening the old Fox's missive, which he was now trying to decode. Someone pretending to be a soldier had arrived, or was going to arrive at Buxton and was, per-haps, involved in plotting for the Scots Queen, who was, he supposed, the lady whom he had never pursued but was pursuing now. He was to watch this man and his friends.

As for the squires—Drew could wish that his master in London had been more explicit, but he guessed that until the supposed military gentleman made contact with his target, or targets, he was not in possession of their names. He wondered who Walsingham's messenger might be: he doubted that he was already acquainted with him.

It was only when he was refolding the letter that he saw that there was a hasty *postscriptum* scrawled on the back. '*Nota bene*, young friend, that every camp has its traitor. . .'

Now what did he mean by that? Drew puzzled. Was he saying that one of Drew's own entourage was to be suspected? And if so, if he knew his name, then why not give it to him, straightway, to act upon? Or was this simply one of the rumours that his other agents had picked up and passed on, which he thought that Drew ought to know of?

Reynard the Fox, indeed! Who should know better about foxes than the master of them all, sitting in his lair in London. He was waiting and hoping that Drew would discover who the conspirators were so that all their correspondence might be intercepted, read and passed on until the moment when, full details of the plot being known they, the hunters, became the hunted and Reynard would make the kill, instead of being killed himself.

Tickled by this fancy, Drew called for Charles, who was working on his books in the next room. He had been to the Well, but had left early. Drew had decided to begin his work for Walsingham without further shilly-shallying.

'Have you met any military gents in Buxton, Charles?' he asked. 'I have a mind to talk tactics again. I have been re-reading Vegetius on the "Art of War", and trying to reconcile what he says with my journeyings as a seafaring adventurer.'

Charles looked up from his work. 'Strange that you should ask that, Drew. A military man was in Philip Sidney's party, Captain Ralph Goreham by name. I spoke to him at the Well. He had drunk water at Spa, he said, and compared Buxton unfavourably with it.'

''True, there is no comparison,' remarked Drew absently, 'Spa being a bustling civilised centre, not a small village lost among hills. But Buxton has its own attractions, for all that. I suppose that Goreham practised his trade in Europe.'

'In the Habsburg Empire, he said. Against the Turks.'

'Ah, yes, the Turks. Odd how each country has its own favourite enemies. Now we scarce know how to choose between the Spanish and the French, but for the Habsburgs the Turks take the prize every time.'

Charles thought that these comments were quintessential Drew. He had an imaginative turn of phrase and thought, rarely met. It was sometimes difficult to remember that he was more than a mere lightweight courtier, but was someone who had lived the rough life of a sailor aboard a man-of-war. His easy charm meant that one tended to underrate him.

Before Charles could answer his cousin, Bess entered. She had changed out of the sturdy clothing she had worn to visit the Well and, though she by no means rivalled the Lady Arbell in splendour, she was more like one's expectations of Lady Exford than usual.

Her bodice was tight-laced and thrust her breasts upward. Between them rested a black pearl on a silver chain. Her ruff was more of a cartwheel than it usually was, and her brocaded skirts were fuller. Her tiring woman had dressed her lustrous black hair high and had adorned it with another silver chain from which yet another black pearl depended onto her forehead.

She was even painted a little, although her creamy complexion, Drew considered, did not require paint— nor her cherry-red lips.

Forgetting Charles, Drew moved over to take her by the hand and kiss her on the cheek. 'I shall,' he murmured into her ear, 'ask Philip to give me some much-needed lessons in the art of writing poetry so that I may hymn the praise of brown eyes and black hair, since all the poets I know of sing the praises only of blue orbs and blonde tresses!'

Bess raised the peacock-feathered fan which depended from her waist by yet another silver chain, to look at him over it. 'You flatter me, sir. I know full well that I do not possess that blonde magnificence which men commonly call beauty—but if I please you, then I am content.'

'Oh, you do more than please me,' Drew muttered, and would have continued only Charles gave a loud 'ahem'— which brought him down to earth again.

He moved away from the temptation which his wife presented to him, and recalled, a little wryly, the anger which he had felt when he had seen his friend admiring her. That he could not even allow Philip Sidney to jest with her so frankly had surprised Drew. Philip had called her beautiful, but her attraction depended on more than that. A better word for her would be charming, and charming in the deepest sense of the word, for there was a witchcraft about a woman whose looks were so unlike those which the world admired, yet who could draw the soul out of a man's eyes simply by looking at him.

Drew blinked at this unexpected revelation. And, of course, it was why the Lady Arbell paled beside her, which explained the Lady's antagonism to Bess. For she knew instinctively what Drew had just discovered by an act of reason. That her arts were exactly that, arts and artificial, whereas Bess's behaviour was artless, and therefore its effect was all the more powerful. Hence her constant scornful railing at what she was pleased to call Bess's 'country ways'.

He surfaced to discover that Bess had picked up one of the papers relating to Atherington on which Charles had been working, and was questioning him about it. Which reminded Drew that he ought to be questioning Charles. It was a moment's work to join his wife in inspecting the ledger which Charles was now holding out to her.

'You have absolute trust in your officers, madam wife?' he asked.

Bess nodded. 'Most of my staff have worked for Atherington since before I was born, and I am sure that their loyalty is not in doubt.'

Drew gave a careless laugh. 'Well spoken, wife. Can you say as much, Charles? Is Exford's household equally exemplary in its loyalty?'

He was thinking of Walsingham's postscriptum as he spoke. Charles answered him equally lightly. 'I wonder that you need to ask! Your officers also are notable for the long years during which they have served you.'

It was an answer which Drew had expected, yet it disturbed him. If Walsingham were right, then someone around him owed allegiance to a faith and a cause to which the Earls of Exford had not subscribed since well before the present Queen had come to the throne. Like his predecessors, Drew valued the stability which the Protestant succession under Elizabeth had brought to England. And some one of his friends and servants was glistering like false gold—and he had no idea who it might be.

No point in questioning Charles further, however lightly, for his wife's shrewd eye was on him, and he marvelled again at how easily she read him when he was being false.

Part of her witchcraft, no doubt.

No, he must not even think that. For a woman to be suspected to be a witch was always dangerous, and he must not put her at risk—even in his thoughts. And besides, was he not reading her? And what did that make him?

A double knock sounded on the door behind him. It was Philip Sidney come to ask them to walk to supper with him. Charles closed his ledger at Drew's command and all talk of business matters ceased. Like Drew and Bess, Philip was all magnificence. His huge cartwheel ruff was only held in place by wires, and its pale glory showed his fine-boned face to the fullest advantage.

Oddly, Bess thought, as the two friends stood side by side, Drew's Apollo-like good looks were enhanced, not degraded, by Philip's austerity. They were fire and ice, sun and moon, two sides of a valuable coin. For the second time that day she surprised jealousy on a man's face. This time it was Charles, whose normally good-humoured countenance fleetingly bore an expression which could only be described as malign.

So fleeting was it that Bess doubted her own senses. She even doubted that she had seen what she thought that she had seen. Charles's expression had not really changed—she had been in the sun too long, and the light had begun to play tricks on her.

She was more certain of this than ever when Drew began teasing both Charles and Philip, demanding that they play bowls against him before they ate. His two friends joked back at him, exchanging cheerful insults as was the habit of men when playing together.

'And you, wife,' laughed Drew, turning to her as she walked, forgotten, between them, 'must challenge the Lady Arbell to a game of *Troule in Madame*. You have a fine way with the ball.'

'Oh,' said Charles, 'then I may wish for my lady to win—which is a favour I will not extend to my lord!'

More male laughter greeted this sally. Bess, who had no wish to challenge the Lady Arbell to anything, was compelled to smile when they met Sir Henry and his wife in the antechamber to the Great Hall, where Drew and Philip rapidly involved them both in their mutual folly. Bess had not seen her husband so light-hearted since they had reached Buxton.

Again, she sensed that there was something odd, something wild in his gaiety, but said nothing, smiling dutifully when Drew committed her to the childish game which was one of Buxton's specialities. Rolling litle lead balls into holes at the end of a bench scarcely seemed a sensible occupation for grown-up women, so naturally the Lady Arbell was devoted to it.

On the other hand, if her Drew was determined to have her play with litle lead balls, she might as well defeat the Lady Arbell at this silly game as not.

Which she duly did.

To that lady's great annoyance.

'I am glad that we had no money riding on this game,' she exclaimed pettishly. 'Although I find that I always play better when I wager something on it.'

'Then I shall be sure to come prepared with my purse to challenge you, using the same odds as my husband used when challenging your husband and his friends in the bowling alley.'

The Lady shrugged her elegant shoulders. 'As you wish.'

Bess uncharitably thought that her comprehensive defeat of Arbell had dimmed Arbell's enthusiasm for the game more than a little. She said nothing, however, other than, 'I would wish to see my husband play bowls. I had not known that he was a skilled performer.'

'Oh, I have often watched him when we were at court

together,' said the Lady, staking her claim to have known Bess's husband longer than Bess had. 'I will come with you.'

Which was not at all what Bess wanted, but she surrendered with a good grace, walking over to where the men stood, watching Drew demolish Charles on the bowling green as he had already demolished Philip and Sir Henry. There was another man standing with them, and ready to play, whom Bess had not seen before. He must have been one of the small party of gentlemen who had ridden over from Chatsworth. She wondered who he was.

As Drew had earlier done, when he and Charles had arrived at the green to find a stranger lounging on a bench, watching the squires who were engaged in an impromptu archery contest in the field nearby. He rose at the sight of Drew and his party.

'Ah, Master Sidney,' he drawled, 'you will do me the honour of introducing your friends to me, I hope.'

'Assuredly,' Philip returned, bowing, 'May I present to you, my most noble Lord of Exford, one Captain Ralph Goreham. My other friend, Lord Exford's cousin, Master Charles Breton, was, I believe, made known to you earlier this afternoon.'

Both men bowed most formally. Captain Goreham murmuring, 'Honoured, I'm sure, my lord.'

So this was Captain Goreham. Could he be the soldier of whom Walsingham had warned him to be suspicious? He was like every roving semi-mercenary captain whom Drew had ever met. He was over-dressed, over-mannered and full of himself. A man who, if Drew were being unkind, he would call a bully boy. Even the plume in the hat he was sweeping to the ground was over-large and shouted to the world, 'Pray look at me.'

Was it simply Walsingham's warning which was

making him suspicious, or merely his own dislike of the parasites who attached themselves like leeches to those who frequented Elizabeth's court and thus might offer some kind of rich pickings?

Best to say nothing, to use his charm—as Bess was learning to use hers—and play a waiting game. Meantime there was a game of bowls to be won—in fact, a number of games of bowls, and he had a mind to win them all. Whether to prove himself to himself, or simply himself to Bess, Drew was not quite sure. He had the absurd notion that, like the knights of old, he ought to have asked her for some favour to carry with him when he went into battle—a handkerchief, perhaps.

This untoward fancy had him laughing to himself so hard that he missed a sally from the Captain which set Charles and Philip laughing out loud.

No matter, it was probably as empty as the bombastic Captain who had perpetrated it, and who now invited himself to become part of their game. For some reason, whether it was Walsingham's letter, or fear that Bess might find Philip—or even the Captain, the Lord forbid—more attractive than her husband, Drew played with a savagery foreign to him.

Bess's arrival, and the friendly arm she slipped through his, lightened his burden a little. 'You won?' he asked her without taking his attention from Captain Goreham, who was the last person to play against him.

'Narrowly,' she returned, not wishing to crow over her defeated opponent, however little she liked the Lady Arbell. Besides, Sir Henry was standing by and she did not wish to offend him. He gave her an approving—and somewhat surprised—smile. 'You must be a good player to defeat my lady wife.'

'I was lucky,' said Bess untruthfully.

'Your husband, madam,' said Captain Goreham 'needs no luck. He carries all before him by his skill.'

'This is Captain Ralph Goreham, to whom I now formally introduce you, wife,' said Drew coldly for him. 'He flatters me, but does not flatter you. My wife, sir, has a keen eye and a strong wrist and needs no luck to enable her to win a game.'

The Captain bowed low. 'My pardon, m'lady. I stand corrected. And now your husband has defeated me, as he has defeated the rest. See where his last wood lies against the jack, undoing me, for I have no more shots left. His eye is as true as he says yours is.'

So, the mercenary Captain was bound and determined to flatter my wife, thought Drew, gritting his teeth. It seemed that all the world, after ignoring Bess Exford these many years, was suddenly bent on falling in love— or lust—with her. Perforce he was compelled to smile on the Captain, for, if he were the spy of whom Walsingham wrote, he had come to seduce more people than Bess.

The game over, they all strolled back to eat their supper. They had been provided, for once, with a meal of which Dr Jones would have approved: wheaten and leavened bread, and the flesh of goats and chickens boiled, not roasted. There was a great dish of pike, a platter piled high with boiled rabbit joints, and a quantity of fine ale. Wine had been banished, and more than one gentleman or lady's mouth was puckered as they ate fare which seemed exceedingly tasteless after the spicy roast meats to which they were accustomed.

'I had expected,' Philip muttered somewhat morosely to Drew, 'something better than this at Shrewbury's table. Uncle Leicester always spoke highly of it, but I am sure that he would not have approved of this gutless fare.'

'You are unlucky tonight, my friend,' Drew whispered

back. 'One day a week we eat that which the great doctor says will not excite our stomachs. Tomorrow will be better. Greves has told Charles that m'lord has given orders that we are to have a pig roasted, and chickens, too—to make up for today's Lenten offerings. And there will be good wine on the table, as well as ale.'

'Amen to that,' Captain Goreham called across to them, raising his tankard in a general toast.

Bess, watching Drew, was suddenly aware that for some reason, the gallant Captain was not at all to his taste. Usually he was hail-fellow-well-met with everyone, however lowly in rank: it was one of his charms. She wondered briefly what ailed him.

No time to think of that, though, for Philip, who sat on her left, was asking her about Atherington. 'You live on the edge of the forest, do you not?'

Master Blagg, on her other side, chipped in in his usual eager fashion. Decidedly he had country manners as the Lady Arbell had frequently complained.

'Charnwood is beginning to be called a forest by courtesy only, sir. Is not that so, Lady Exford? My friend, Jack Bown, tells me that less charcoal is burned there every year, and that the deer grow smaller in numbers and leaner.'

'Master Bown exaggerates, I fear,' said Bess. 'That is his habit. He constantly complains that the world is going to the devil.' She did not add that this was partly because he was of the Catholic persuasion and he considered that all matters had gone ill since Elizabeth came to the throne.

'But it cannot rival Sherwood,' smiled young Blagg. 'Which is much as it was in the days of Robin Hood.'

'That I do not dispute,' said Bess.

*   *   *

Later, when she and Drew were alone again in their bedroom, Drew said to her, apparently idly, 'This Bown, of whom Master Blagg spoke, who thinks that the world is going to the devil—of what persuasion is he?'

Bess, sitting up in bed, eager for the night's entertainment to begin, shrugged her shoulders. 'Oh, it is not surprising that he thinks thus. He is staunchly Catholic, you see.'

'Is he so? And he is Blagg's friend. But the Blaggs are Protestant I think someone said.'

'They are now,' explained Bess, 'but only since Queen Elizabeth came in. Master Blagg's father knew on which side his bread was buttered, my father said. Are you coming to bed, husband, or would you prefer me to offer you instead a roll call of the religious persuasion of all the esquires and manorial lords in the East Midlands?'

'Hussy,' said Drew amiably as he jumped into bed to land on top of her. 'I shall think up a suitable punishment for your impudence, Lady Exford.'

And so he did. And it was one which had Bess squealing with pleasure for, whether Drew loved her or not, he was able to take her with him into those fields of delight which she had never visited until the day he had ridden through Atherington's main gates for the second time in his life. . .

So, Blagg was a lapsed Catholic, was he? Like the Lady Arbell and one or two others whom he knew were frequenting Buxton in order—ostensibly—to enjoy its waters. And this Bown of whom Blagg had spoken— would he suddenly appear to join this happy little nest of possible traitors? Stupid, perhaps, to suspect that everyone he met might be a traitor, but, on the other hand, perhaps not. And then there was the problem of

Captain Goreham, of whom Walsingham had warned him—although he had warned him of no one else by direct inference.

These gloomy thoughts ran through Drew's head as he was being shaved for the day. Together with another one, which had only occurred to him recently. Why had Walsingham recruited him for this mission at all? He was not one of his inner circle of spies and agents, that was for sure, and his previous experience had been purely diplomatic.

Over breakfast, which today, at Drew's orders, had been commissioned from a nearby inn and brought from thence to his private room, he was rather quieter than usual, so much so that both his cousin Charles and Bess privately remarked on it, and were disturbed for quite different reasons.

It was only when there was a knock on the door which heralded the arrival of the Queen of Scots's private secretary, Claude Nau, who was apparently inviting himself to break fast with Drew's party, that Drew came to life.

'Sit! Sit,' he exclaimed. 'Tib, a stool for Monsieur Nau, and see that he is provided with food and ale.'

Claude Nau, a talkative man, devoted to his mistress, immediately launched into a lengthy explanation of his presence so early in the morning.

'Her Grace, the Queen of Scots, would count it an honour if you, m'lord Exford, and your lady, would consent to sup with her this evening in her rooms. She has already asked Master Sidney to join her and he has given his consent. At six thirty of the clock, after you have bathed, if that is agreeable to you.' He rose and bowed as he finished his message, and then sat down again to drink the ale which Tib had poured for him.

Bess, watching Drew, knew that he was troubled by

his invitation—but why should that be so? Even though he had treated Nau with perfect courtesy, she knew that he was ill at ease. Nothing, however, showed on his perfect face as he said all the right things to Nau, emphasising the honour which was being done to him by a woman who had once been a reigning Queen.

No one else seemed to notice anything untoward. Charles passed Nau a platter of cold meat, and a large slice of bread, which he seized and ate greedily. 'My mistress has a strong mind to see more of your lady, my lord Exford,' Nau offered through a mouthful of food. 'She misses the young company which she enjoyed when she lived with Lord and Lady Shrewsbury.'

Following her husband's lead, Bess too, murmured of the honour being done her: an honour which she could have done without.

She said as much to Drew later, when they were alone, adding, apparently innocently, 'I thought that you were none too pleased to be so singled out.'

Drew offered her a half-truthful explanation. 'Why, as to that, if her Majesty, my Queen, saw fit to treat her favourite, my Lord of Leicester, to a harangue about his lack of loyalty because he chose to favour the Queen of Scots with his presence at supper, what do you think that she will say to m'lord of Exford, one of her humbler servants, when she hears of this night's work?'

'Why, how should she hear of it, Buxton and London being so far apart?'

Her husband gave a short laugh. 'My dear wife, before you go to London with me you must learn the ways of the wicked world you will be living in. Someone, somehow, will pass this news on to the Court—and thence to the Queen in order to gain favour. As one courtier goes up, another goes down.'

Bess was not to know that, although there was truth in this, it was not the real reason for Drew's wariness, and for the moment his answer sufficed to reassure her. She worried later when she saw Drew single out the Lady Arbell for special attention, walking with her and Captain Goreham to the field where the men were engaged in an impromptu archery contest.

Philip Sidney, observing that her eyes followed Drew and his companions wistfully, said in his usual courtly manner, 'I, too, have a wish to engage in some field sports, and would ask you to accompany me——if it so pleases you.'

'It does.' Bess was frank, and as Philip gallantly took her arm and walked her along, she asked him, 'Tell me, sir, are all men the same? Do they all engage in competitions in which they seek to beat everyone against whom they strive? Is it a condition of being a man, as a tendency to sit and watch is that of a woman?'

'A grave question,' was Philip's equally grave answer. 'Except for one thing, my lady of Exford. I have been watching you as you watched us and by your expression I would have sworn that you would like to pull the longbow yourself. And if you do so, in competition, would you not wish to win? When you played at backgammon with me the other evening, your delight in winning was extreme, although courteously expressed.'

Like Drew, then, he saw more into the hearts of men and women than he usually spoke of. She rewarded him with a smile. 'To pull the longbow, yes. I have often wished to do that——but the pull may be too heavy for me, I fear.'

'Nothing to that,' replied Philip, smiling. 'I have a

light bow which pleases me, and which has come in my luggage. My man shall fetch it, and you may try your skill against me—for he shall also bring me my heavier one.'

What a surprise for Drew, thought Bess gleefully—if he can bring himself to neglect the Lady Arbell long enough to know that I am even here!

While Philip's man ran off to do his master's bidding, she and Philip sat on one of the benches and watched Drew and the Captain practise. Before they began to shoot against one another in earnest, the Lady Arbell, smiling prettily, handed Drew her fine lace-edged handkerchief which hung from her belt as an ornament rather than for practical use.

'You must be my knight,' she commanded him, ignoring her husband who hovered in her rear, and who seemed to be quite happy to have his wife admired by other women's husbands.

'My pleasure,' replied Drew, the faithless brute, hanging over her hand, and placing the handkerchief in his belt. Yes, he was quite unaware that his wife was watching him, her teeth clenched.

Bess unclenched them, rose and, moved by she knew not what, walked over to where Captain Goreham stood watching this pretty pantomine, and handed him her own fair kerchief, saying, 'Come, Captain, you must not be left out of this exchange of tokens. Here is my handkerchief, and for this round of arrows you must be my knight.'

'Willingly, m'lady, most willingly.'

It was Drew's teeth which were now clenched. But he could say nothing. He consigned both the Lady Arbell and his wife to the lowest pit of Hell. Was it not bad enough that he had to pretend to admire a woman whom he disliked and to be compelled in return to watch his

wife favouring a fly-by-night mercenary who could conceivably be a traitor of the deepest die?

He was so distracted that his ability to find not only
the gold, but the higher of the lesser colours on the target,
deserted him, and he fell an easy victim to the gallant
Captain in their first round. His temper was not assisted
by having to watch Bess be instructed in the art of using
the longbow by Philip Sidney. An art which consisted
mainly of Philip putting his arms around his willing wife,
meticulously aligning her posture as she was about
to shoot!

'You are off the mark today, sir,' remarked the observ-
ant Captain, who had a good idea of what was wrong
with his opponent. He plucked Bess's handkerchief from
his belt and waved it airily. 'My lady's favour has a deal
of magic in it today,' he remarked with consummate
impudence.

Bess, meantime, was beginning to enjoy herself, particularly when she overheard the Captain's baiting of
Drew. She found Philip's light bow easy to use, and that
she had, as he admiringly told her, a natural eye. The
only thing which prevented her from achieving an even
greater skill was her tendency to dissolve into giggles as
she—correctly—read Drew's face and grasped the
reason why *his* skill had also deserted him.

He deserved it, did he not? As the Lady Arbell
deserved to pout as her champion failed so dismally
where he had always succeeded before. If Philip noticed
this by-play he made no comment on it, only challenged
Bess to a contest. A contest which they both noisily
enjoyed, adding to Drew's inward fury.

Except that, just when the Captain thought that he was
about to overcome the known winner of all the male
sports available at Buxton, Drew suddenly saw the funny

side of the whole brouhaha. Who would have thought that he, the inconstant lover, should be so besotted with his wife that he fell the victim of a berserker rage when she became the object of the attention of others? It was a subject fit for the pen of Messer Boccaccio, no less, and this comic thought relieved him of his pain.

Furthermore, waiting his turn, he caught her eye—and the naughty minx winked at him! Oh, yes, she was winding him up, and he was fool enough to succumb to her cantrips. Chuckling to himself, he took his turn and started to shoot his arrows with such deadly grace that the Lady Arbell began to jump up and down and to squeak her approval. At which Drew, passing Bess on his way back to his mark, not only winked back at her, but also blessed her with a surreptitious kiss whilst pretending to frighten off a stray bee.

The Captain, unaware—or was he?—that his mockery of Drew over Bess's kerchief had almost certainly triggered off Drew's revival, watched helplessly as he was led to the slaughter.

Mournfully trying to hand her kerchief back to Bess, he sighed, 'Alas, your favour was not sufficient to help me to overcome your husband's skill. Had he not shot so poorly at the beginning of the contest he would have overcome me in quick march time, no doubt of it.'

'But you must keep my handkerchief,' commanded Arbell of Drew when he tried to hand it back to her, 'seeing that it brought you luck in the end.'

Ever the gentleman, he bowed and took it from her, kissing it as he did so. Oddly, Bess watching him, felt no jealousy at the sight, for she was remembering both his wink and his kiss for her. She could not guess for what reason Drew was pursuing the Lady Arbell, but she was suddenly sure that his doing so was no threat to her.

For was it not plain that he had been unable to shoot properly until she had shown that she had forgiven him?

Chapter Nine

'**A**nd exactly what game were you playing this morning with my so-called friend, Philip Sidney, wife?' Drew asked Bess once they were alone together in their rooms.

'Why, he was but teaching me archery, husband.'

'Was he so, then, wife? From where I was standing, it seemed that he was teaching you quite a different game!'

Bess's eyes were as innocent as her voice as she answered him.

'Seeing that you were at some distance from us, husband, I wonder that you could tell whether we were playing at any game at all, let alone a particular one.'

'Oh, a particular game, was it?' Drew's voice was half-joking and half-savage. 'Let me see whether I can play it, too.'

He strode over to where she stood, not far from the Great Bed, and put his arms about her, exactly as Philip had done when Bess had been encouraging him to tease Drew. He made as though to help her pull an imaginary bow, whispering in her ear as he half-turned her towards him, 'Allow me to hold you so, dear madam, for I must raise your elbow a little so that you may better control the strength of your pull.'

Bess made no effort to resist him, saying as she lookd into the blue eyes so near to her own, 'Like so, husband?'

'Nay, not so strong, wife, gently, gently. A subtle touch is best with the bow as in life,' and he allowed his left hand to slip down from her shoulder where he had been caressing her neck so that he might caress her breast instead.

'Was this the game that you were playing, wife?'

Bess's first response was to shiver with delight, and then to spring away from him, her cheeks scarlet as the import of his words struck her.

'Nay, sir! You wrong both me and Master Sidney to think that we would play those games reserved only for husband and wife.'

'Oh, but we all know that that last statement is not true, do we not? Many other than husband and wives play them,' whispered Drew softly as he took her face in his hands and began to rain butterfly kisses on it, abandoning the pretence that they engaged in mock archery, and engaging in the sport of love instead.

'It is true for me,' faltered Bess, pulling her mouth away from his. 'I could not bear for another man to touch me as you are doing now,' for Drew's hand had strayed beneath the skirts of her gown and was stroking her in such a fashion that she groaned and shuddered beneath his touch.

'Shall we play the game of husband and wife here and now, wife? Before we join the busy world again?'

'Oh, but they are expecting us downstairs, husband.'

'Then they must go unsatisfied rather than that I should, wife.' He had manoeuvred the pair of them on to the Great Bed where he set about satisfying them both to such effect that Bess's protestations were lost in her cries of joy as he brought them to consummation.

Silence reigned for a time until Bess sat up, all her clothing awry, and her hair tumbled about her shoulders.

'How may I send for my woman now that I am in such disarray?' she lamented, trying to restore her crumpled ruff and her disordered hair at the same time. Drew, lazily lying on one elbow, his clothes in similar state, squinted up at her.

'Why, how should she object, seeing that we *are* husband and wife and may pleasure each other at any time. But if your modesty forbids, then I will restore you to order, and you, if you please, will restore me until we both look like a pair of Master Holbein's paintings rather than flesh-and-blood human beings.'

Bess nodded her agreement, but she soon found that being dressed by Drew was nearly as arousing as being undressed by him! His hands seemed to be everywhere, and her hair became more, rather than less, unbound.

'I wonder how either of us is ever ready for the day,' murmured Drew as he restored her bodice to its proper place and, as he said, 'hid her treasures there from the sight of other men'.

Straightening her ruff took some tedious time, and had him sighing. 'Such a deal of calico, whalebone, wire and stiffening goes into our dress that we are nearly as constrained as the marionettes whom the Italians entertain us with. There, m'lady Exford, you are ready to dine—a little late in the day, mayhap. Now you may set me to rights.'

Setting Drew to rights was almost as teasing and tormenting and delightful as setting him to wrongs had been. And so Bess told him, which set him laughing and kissing her again, which began to undo all his earlier careful work, as well as hers.

Bess finally pushed him away. 'I, sir, am hungry. A

morning spent first at the butts and then on the bed has
served to whet my appetite nearly as much as a good
early morning gallop.'

'There's nothing better than a good early morning gallop on the bed,' proclaimed Drew. 'We must try it again
soon. And now to break fast, but seeing that we are to
dine with the Scots Queen tonight we must not overdo our
eating, for it will be ill seen if we have no appetite then.'

'In that case,' retorted Bess naughtily, 'a good early
evening gallop on the bed might ensure our good manners
in the Queen's rooms. We must not let it be seen that
we are not mindful of the honour which she is doing us.'

'The honour which the Queen hath done us is none so
great,' Drew whispered to Bess after they had been
received by Her Grace at supper that evening, 'for I note
that Captain Goreham is also an honoured guest, as well
as the Catholic half of the local gentry. We and Philip
are Protestant fish out of water.'

'Perchance,' Bess whispered back, 'she thinks that
though we may not be Catholic, we may be sympathisers.
But, look, we are not alone for here come Sir Henry and
his wife.'

She offered the Lady Arbell a false smile even as she
spoke—and received one back. Her greeting from Sir
Henry was bluff and sincere, the more so since Arbell
immediately attached herself to Drew, and pouted her
discontent on finding that when the meal was served she
was compelled to sit by her husband at some distance
from Drew and Bess, who were also seated side by side.

Bess had Captain Goreham on her left-hand side. He
made a dead set at her during the lengthy meal, the chief
subject of which was a dish of peacocks roasted in their
feathers, to which Bess took great exception, seeing that

the result was not only unpalatable, but unlovely.

Wisely, she kept her opinion to herself and concentrated on not encouraging the Captain to court her, which he seemed bent on doing. Unfortunately, what the Captain had seen at the archery butts had persuaded him that Bess, as a neglected wife, would be only too happy to receive his attentions instead of her husband's.

Fortunately, though, as the senior peer there, Drew was the focus of the Queen of Scots's interest, and she questioned him and Philip eagerly about their life at court, and their relationship with her cousin and captor, the Queen Elizabeth.

'If only I could meet her,' Mary sighed, 'I could perhaps convince her that I mean her no ill. These plots which are aimed at her person have nothing to do with me, you must understand. I neither initiate them, nor encourage them.'

She turned all of her celebrated charm on Drew. 'I am told that you are in favour with Her Grace, and I hope that when next you are at court you will convey that message to her. I have enthusiastic, but unwise, supporters who, because I am prisoner here, I am unable to restrain. You could perhaps pass that message on to her, too. And to Sir Francis Walsingham, who is her adviser on these matters.'

Did she know that he was Walsingham's friend and agent? Drew asked himself. Or was this idle conversation which was in truth not in the least idle, but was designed to convince him of her innocence—in which he did not believe at all.

The gallant Captain jumped into the small silence which followed before Drew could answer her. 'Oh, your Grace,' he exclaimed, rising and bowing in her direction, his table napkin at his lips, 'no one who meets you could be other than convinced of your goodwill towards your cousin. Were I fortunate enough to be able to have an audience with the Queen's Grace, I would be only too happy to pass on your message!'

Would he, indeed? And what importance would Elizabeth place on the word of a hireling soldier who would be happy to say whatever anyone would pay him to say? Perhaps he was hopeful that the Queen of Scots would offer him a fee to speak on her behalf. If so, he would be disappointed since the Queen had virtually no money of her own, and was dependent on George Shrewsbury for the very bread which she was eating at table.

But his intervention had saved Drew from having to commit himself in any way to the Queen who was entertaining him. He gave a half-smile in the Captain's direction and left it at that.

His right-hand side companion, Marian Blagg, announced, her innocent voice louder than she had intended it to be, 'Only a person without a heart, Lord Exford, could be content to see a good woman held prisoner, and not sympathise with the motives of those who seek to free her. Indeed, I have heard tell that Master Sidney's uncle, my lord of Leicester, not only wished to speak to the Queen on her Scottish Majesty's behalf, but was also wishful to marry her!'

This was to say the unsayable, and uttered in certain quarters the speaker might have felt her head loose upon her shoulders. Leicester had earned the Queen's displeasure for his temerity—and he was the Queen's favourite! What might Elizabeth not do to the powerless wife of a lowly country squire?

Marian's husband, Master Blagg, his face scarlet, murmured gently to her, 'Not here, my dear. This is no occasion for such a declaration, and might serve to place our hostess in peril should what you have said be repeated to her.'

'Oh!' His wife flushed, and said apologetically, 'Pray forgive me, your Grace, if I have spoken out of turn. I meant no harm.'

'Of that I am sure,' said Queen Mary, trying to comfort her. 'And I welcome the kindness with which you have spoken of me. But there are ill-wishers everywhere who might use your words not only against me, but against yourself. The path of virtue in my case is a narrow path indeed. We tread on eggshells—as I have cause to know.'

Silence fell. Everyone present knew of the Queen of Scots's sad story. Guilty or innocent of all of which she had been accused, she was paying a sad price for her unfortunate life.

Drew wondered whether Marian Blagg was betraying more than she knew. He also wondered whether her husband, in silencing her, was trying to retrieve what he thought that she might have given away: that there was a current plot on Mary's behalf, and that he was part of it. He would want no breath of suspicion cast on his loyalty. It was more than likely that his wife knew nothing of any conspiracy, but did know that her husband was sympathetic to Mary's cause.

The other question was: Did the Queen of Scots know of the plot? Her declaration of innocence was worthless. Neither could he take the word of anyone around the table—other than Bess's and Philip's—at face value. All present had an axe to grind and their attendance at this supper party might mean that their axe was a Catholic one!

Which begged the question as to why he and Bess and Philip had been invited. He sighed. He had always felt distaste at acting as Walsingham's amateur intelligencer, but as his feelings for Bess had begun to change so dramatically, his distaste for his task had grown too.

Had he known beforehand that he would come to care for his long-deserted wife he might have refused to play Walsingham's game. Common sense and loyalty to his mistress, the Queen Elizabeth, had him admitting that it was a task which he could not refuse—but that did not mean that he liked it. Ever since he had met Bess he had begun to change from the carefree young man who rarely questioned what he did—and how he did it. He remembered wryly what Philip had said to him recently about growing up, and no longer being a heedless boy.

And, of course, Walsingham had hinted at the same thing when he had told him, that last evening in London, that he was one of those who would carry on the responsibility of ruling England when he and Burghley and his fellow elder statesmen had gone to their last rest.

He shivered. Time was passing, and the easy Arcadia in which Philip and he had spent their early lives was passing, too. On the other hand, the life which he and Bess would spend together when this task was over had its own, different, attractions which were beginning to beckon to him.

Such as having sons and daughters to care for.

'You are silent tonight, my lord.' This was Goreham, his sly face as probing as his voice, accosting Drew when the meal was over, and they were standing about the room, with the Queen seated on a small dais at one end of it.

'Aye, well, sir,' returned Drew. 'For one reason or another I have suffered a tiring day—not least when I took you on at archery.'

Goreham took this as Drew intended, as a compliment.

His smile was insufferable. 'I must compliment you on your lady wife, m'lord. She is such a pearl as must soon grace her Majesty's court.' He even had the effrontery to wink at Drew as though he were aware of the early evening gallop on the bed with which Drew and Bess had celebrated their return from the Baths.

Only Philip's hand on his arm prevented Drew from telling the Captain exactly what he thought of him and his innuendos.

'Her Grace would speak with you, as well as your wife, Drew,' Philip said coolly—he had been surprised by Drew's quick show of anger at the Captain's impudence, and the Queen's rooms were not a fit place for his friend to lose his temper and provoke an unpleasant scene.

Drew recollected himself, stared dourly at the gallant Captain and went to join his wife who was admiring the tapestry on which the Queen had been working—a portrayal of the Babylonians in captivity—a referral to her own captivity, no doubt.

'I have my canvaswork with me,' Bess was saying in reply to a question from Mary, to have the Queen answer,

'Then you must accept my invitation to work with me on those afternoons on which you do not go to the Baths.'

Bess curtsied her agreement, saying as she rose, 'I thank you for your kindness, your Grace, and will be happy to join you at your invitation. In return, may I bring my husband's musicians with me to play for us? I am sure that he would wish them to entertain you.'

'Indeed, wife.' Drew had arrived in time to hear Bess's last sentence. 'You may have my blessing for that.'

Mary's face betrayed her pleasure. Whether Drew felt any at his wife being singled out was quite another matter. But he allowed the Queen to question him about his life at court and also to confess to her that he had only recently met his wife again after ten years.

'Ah, a subject fit for a poem by Master Sidney,' said the Queen, 'seeing that you and she are now two love-birds together.'

Bess glowed and blushed at this, whilst Drew bemusedly wondered how much of their mutual pleasure must be showing, seeing that he had been compelled to listen to several knowing references to it already during the evening.

There was no doubt that they did not please everybody. Mary's patronage of Bess annoyed the Lady Arbell, who said shrilly to Drew as the Queen invited Bess to sit on a stool by her feet—a rare favour—'Her Grace is in a charitable mood this evening—she extends her patronage to all the world.'

Drew chose to take this piece of nastiness in the wrong way, retorting with a smile, 'I will pass your compliment on to my Countess, my dear Lady Arbell. She will be flattered to be compared with all the world.'

This was not at all what Arbell had meant. She tossed her head and rewarded Drew's naughtiness with one of her own. 'I suppose that, after all this graciousness from her Scots Majesty, you will be turning Catholic yourself and raising her banner in the Queen's court.'

'Then you suppose wrongly, m'lady.' Drew's voice was cold and grew colder as he continued to speak. 'I do but use the occasion to practise my good manners as Messer Castiglione advises in his treatise, *The Book of the Courtier*. May I recommend it to you as useful reading.'

Never before had he made his displeasure known so plainly. His easy charm, his refusal to be offended, had been a byword at Elizabeth's court. But he would not lightly suffer anyone to suggest that he might commit treason. Especially when that suggestion had been made before others, and even though he might make further cultivation of the Lady Arbell difficult by rebuking her.

Philip took him by the arm again to walk him away. It was strange, Drew reflected, that a man as high-tempered as Philip was so determined to act as a peacemaker for others.

'You grow short, dear friend, when your wife is criticised,' Philip told him once they were away from the crowd and they were standing alone in a window embrasure. 'The fair Arbell cannot forgive you for resisting her charms, and the gallant Captain is bent on troublemaking—for what reason I know not.'

Drew suspected what the reason might be, but could not say so to Philip. He shrugged. 'I had not thought that I would ever be a jealous husband,' he confessed, 'but this morning I could even have cut *your* throat cheerfully when you sported with Bess at the butts.'

'Aye, so I saw.' Philip was dry. 'But it will not do. She is a good creature and will not betray you, so you have no need to show the world the temper that no one knew you possessed.'

Well, that was true enough, Drew thought wryly. He was even surprising himself, so it was no wonder that he was surprising everyone else.

There, in the window embrasure, alone because Philip had left him, he faced a truth which he had been trying to evade ever since he had first opened his eyes to see the forest nymph above him: he was passionately in love with the wife whom he had deserted for so many long years, and could only grieve for what he had lost by that desertion.

He had mocked Philip gently for writing of love, claiming that it did not exist, was simply a poet's invention—and here he was, love's prisoner!

The Queen had at last let Bess go. She was walking towards him. She reached him. Drew put out a hand, took hers, looked into her eyes, and oblivious of the room, of anyone who might be watching, he kissed the hand he had taken.

'Come, wife,' he said, still holding her hand and turning her towards the door. 'Let's to bed, and the rest of the world may wag as it will.'

Chapter Ten

Drew had left Bess peacefully sleeping in the Great Bed in order to go riding on his own so that, far away from all distractions, he might think clearly about what dark plots were being hatched in Buxton—if any were, that was.

Early though he was, others were up before him. Or, at least, his cousin Charles was. Fully dressed, he was yawning and stretching himself in the corridor which led to the door to the stables. He stared at the sight of Drew in his riding clothes and boots.

'What? Abroad already? I thought that you were still enjoying the pleasures of the bridal bed.' His tone was slightly mocking.

Drew ignored it. 'I decided that an early morning ride would clear away the cobwebs of last night's supper.'

Charles looked about him. 'And Master Sidney? He is not to go with you? Would you care for me to act as your groom?'

'No, cousin. I have a mind for my own company this fine morning. Cicero's will do for me, and none other.'

Charles shrugged. 'No matter. I shall walk instead to the Baths and pleasure myself there—if ducking myself in cold water may be called a pleasure. I doubt me that I shall be more of a man afterwards than I was before!'

Drew left his striding away. All Buxton except himself and Charles, seemed to be in the arms of Morpheus, the god of sleep. No matter, he needed peace and quiet.

He found it by riding to the River Wye, travelling along it for a little time and then taking a narrow track which led up into the hills. He was quite alone, and on reaching a grassy plateau from whence he could see Buxton lying below him, small and unconsidered, he dismounted, tethered Cicero to a tree which he then sat beneath, and pondered on the puzzle which the little town, nay, village, presented.

His thinking was unproductive. He decided that the sooner the someone to whom Walsingham had referred in his letter arrived and presented him with the token which would prove that he was truly Walsingham's man, the better. They could discuss, in the light of the knowledge that he would bring with him, who might be the traitor.

All that sitting in the bright morning was doing for him was to cause him to admire the beauties of the wooded hills and the sound of birds calling. It was a pity that Philip was not with him. He would have been writing a sonnet to the day, for sure.

Laughing at himself, Drew swung into the saddle again to start for home. He had barely travelled a hundred yards when he heard a whirring noise. Immediately Cicero threw back his head...and slowly crumpled to the ground...taking Drew with him in such a fashion that he was thrown over Cicero's head to land, winded but uninjured, near him. Rising only to kneel and to shake his spinning head, Drew saw that poor Cicero had been struck in the neck by an arrow—which had surely not been meant for him, but for his master.

He had sufficient presence of mind to crawl around his mortally wounded horse and take shelter behind him, away from the direction from which the arrow had come.

His left wrist and shoulder ached abominably where they had hit the ground in his unexpected fall. He listened for any sound which might tell him where the archer was hidden, but could hear nothing. He dare not stand up and look around him for fear of presenting an easy target.

He flattened himself as much as possible and lay still, scarcely breathing. The birds were singing, the sun shone and the faint breeze blew as though there was no one on the hill who wished to murder Drew Exford. It was his own fault, he conceded ruefully, his head against Cicero's flank, for riding out alone and lightly armed.

His poor horse was lying quite still, possibly mortally wounded, for a stream of blood was flowing from his neck. He cursed his own folly that was killing, or had killed, his faithful friend.

The silence of the early day was suddenly broken. He could hear hoofbeats coming from the direction of the river. Someone was approaching him on horseback.

The murderer—or not?

There was nothing he could do, nowhere to hide. He dare not run towards the wood for if the horseman had a bow, or a pistol, he was a dead man. He had a horse pistol on his saddle but Cicero had fallen on to it. He only had the dagger at his belt.

The hoofbeats grew nearer.

Drew loosened his dagger and began to draw it.

The hoofbeats stopped.

The newcomer dismounted. A man's voice, familiar to Drew, called out, 'Hola! Is anyone there?'

It was Captain Goreham. Was he friend—or foe? Had

he a sword in his hand—or a bow ready drawn in order to deal Drew the *coup de grâce*?

'Yes,' called Drew without rising. 'It is I, Drew Exford. Come no nearer, until I know whether you mean me any harm.'

The Captain took no note of him. He walked forward, stooped to look at Cicero—and saw the arrow in his neck.

'Ah, m'lord. I see why you are cautious. Shot at from ambush, were you?'

He said this as though it were the most natural thing in the world to find a young nobleman seated on the ground beside his stricken horse. Either he was innocent—or he was the most plausible sounding would-be murderer Drew could hope to meet.

Cautiously he raised his head. The Captain stood there, legs apart, unarmed, grinning down at him.

'Well, it was not I who shot at you, m'lord. I am a better marksman than your unseen enemy seems to have been—as you well know. And I have no reason to wish to kill you—but someone might think that he has.'

Feeling a little foolish, and caught at complete disadvantage, Drew stood up.

'And how,' he asked bluntly, 'am I to know whether you did take a shot at me, and when it failed, decide to try again another day?'

The Captain grinned, and spread his arms wide. 'Why, you may plainly see that I have no bow with me.'

'That makes nothing. You could have thrown it away when you saw that you had failed.'

'Oh, but I am an old soldier, sir. I would have made little of riding up and despatching you whilst you were still dazed. Someone who suspects that you are on the watch for traitors was doubtless your man, I dare hazard.'

Now how did he know that? But was not the Captain

one of those whom Drew had suspected might be either
the leader of the plot, or the go-between who was taking
messages from the Scots Queen to the Spanish or French
Embassy for forwarding to their masters at home? It still
did not tell him whether Goreham was friend or foe.

The Captain saw him hesitate, saw that Drew had made
no move to walk forward, but instead had drawn his
dagger and was holding it at the ready in his hand.

'You do well to be cautious, young sir. I confess that
I read you wrongly. I thought you a hothead, but you
did, I suspect by instinct, the correct thing when you hid
behind your horse, offering the bowman no target. And
now, suspecting me, you hold on to your dagger. My
apologies for doubting either your courage or your
wisdom.'

Drew made a sudden decision. He sheathed his dagger
and walked around poor Cicero.

'Whether or not you meant me harm a few moments
ago, it is plain that you mean me none now.' He deliberately turned his back on the Captain in order to kneel by
Cicero who was bleeding to death.

'A pity,' the Captain offered to Drew. 'By all I ever
saw, he was your faithful friend.'

'Whom I killed,' returned Drew bitterly.

The Captain shook his head. 'When you are as old as
I am, young sir, you will neither think nor say such
things. But it does you credit. I will give you a ride
home, but not yet.'

Drew could not decide whether he disliked the Captain
more when he was being greasily ingratiating or greasily
patronising. On the other hand, it was possible that his
arrival had scared off his attacker, and if so he owed him
a debt of gratitude.

But before he could begin to pay it the Captain smiled

benignly at him, and fumbled in the purse he wore at his belt, saying, 'It is a doubly good chance that we have arrived here together where no man may see us. Not only have I put your assassin to flight, but I had need to speak to you privately.'

The fumbling ended, he produced something from his purse, and handed it to Drew. 'I think that you might recognise this, m'lord.' Well, at least he had dropped the demeaning 'young sir', was Drew's inward acid response as he took what the Captain proffered.

It was a small gold button with the letter *M* engraved on it, and it was the token of which Walsingham had spoken on his last night in London before he had left for Atherington. The *M* was short for the nickname which the Queen had given her faithful servant, 'The Moor'.

So, the Captain was Walsingham's agent and not the Catholic plotter whom Drew had supposed he might be.

'My master said that you would recognise it,' the Captain offered. 'I have found no occasion for private speech with you before, and I am not wishful for my true allegiance to be known, you understand me, I'm sure.'

Yes, Drew understood him. The Captain was doubtless pretending to be a Catholic sympathiser and by doing so hoped to gain access to the secret councils of possible plotters.

'And now, m'lord, with that in your hand, you may tell me what you have found, or think that you might have found, about the traitors in our midst.'

Drew tossed the button into the air and caught it. 'Little enough,' he said. 'I suspect Master Blagg, of course, and the friend Jack Bown with whom he keeps company, but whether they are active traitors or mere wordy sympathisers of the Queen I know not.'

'Small fry!' The Captain was dismissive.

'So I supposed. But who is the Behemoth—the king of fish—who organises them? I suspect that the Lady Arbell is not innocent in this matter, but Sir Henry? Can one suspect him?'

'Oh, one suspects anyone,' grinned the Captain. 'That is a matter of course in this game.'

Drew decided that a frontal attack might be useful. 'And you, Captain, and your master. Do you know more—or less—than I do?'

'Oh, as to that, we know that there *is* a Behemoth, a leader, but who, we know not. Shortly after you left for the Midlands a letter destined for the French Embassy was found on the body of a go-between who was knifed in a London tavern—for quite other reasons than treason. It came from Buxton. It named no names, even the writer used a pseudonym. He called himself Leander. It said that a number of Leicestershire and Derbyshire gentlemen, led by Nemo, a man from outside the Midlands, were about to mount a plan to spring the Scots Queen from her prison and raise her standard. Help from both their Majesties of France and Spain was required for the plot to succeed. An invasion was suggested.'

'Nemo, eh?' Drew frowned. 'A nameless gentleman? And that is all?'

'Aye, we are at sea here, with no sight of land. My master has known of Nemo for some time, but knows not his true name.'

Drew suspected that Sir Francis Walsingham knew more than the old Fox was prepared to tell at this moment. He trusted no one, it seemed. Not even Captain Goreham—or the son of his old friend, Andrew, Lord Exford.

One last thing Drew had to find out before he said goodbye to his old friend who lay quiet on the ground. 'Your master told me in the most cryptic fashion that every camp has its traitor. I am supposing that he suspects someone near me. You have no notion of who it might be?'

'None.' The Captain's answer was unhesitating. 'And now, m'lord, it is time I gave you a lift home; you have been absent for so long that your servants must soon become anxious. But before we leave we must destroy the evidence.'

He bent down and wrenched the arrow from Cicero's neck. He looked up at Drew. 'If we are to make this look like an accident and not an attempt at murder, we must cut your steed's throat, seeing that his leg was broken in the fall—but really to conceal the mark of the arrow. If you wish, I will perform the *coup de grâce*.'

'No!' Drew moved forward, his dagger in his hand. 'He was my good horse, my old friend. It is I who must perform the last rites for him, you understand—hard though that may be. Leave me for a moment, and then you may take me back to report that Cicero has had an accident which cost him his life, but spared mine.'

The Captain made no answer other than to move away. He heard Drew say as he knelt to perform his unwelcome task, 'Oh, Cicero, before this is over you may be sure that I shall claim a life in exchange for yours. May you carry me again when we meet in the Shades.'

'But you are not hurt, Drew? Only Cicero? Nay, not *only Cicero*, that sounds unfeeling, for Cicero was your friend, was he not?'

Bess was watching Master Todd, Drew's physician, examine his left wrist.

'He was, indeed, and I shall miss him. Never mind that he was growing old, I would not have had him leave me before his time.'

Drew had given orders to Thomas, his head groom, to travel into the hills to recover Cicero's saddle—if that were possible. 'Take Tib with you, and no one else,' he had ordered, for Thomas and Tib were two of his men whom he was sure would be faithful to him and to Bess and who would not gossip if anything seemed out of the ordinary. Only the assassin must know the true reason for his horse's death.

Charles had met him as he left Thomas and Tib to carry out his orders.

'What's this I hear, Drew? That Cicero had an accident whilst you were riding in the hills above the town? How did that come about?'

'Quite simply,' Drew lied. 'As you know, Cicero was growing old. He stumbled and fell, breaking a blood vessel as he did so, as well as his right foreleg. I was lucky not to break mine, but I have hurt my wrist somewhat and bruised my shoulder. Master Todd is about to see to me.'

'You should not have gone out without a groom,' Charles scolded him. 'Captain Goreham says that he came across you, quite by chance, and that you rode pillion with him back to Buxton. Had he not found you, you might have still been walking home. You had ridden a long way into the hills, he said.'

'Yes, I owe him a debt of gratitude. Do not berate me, Charles, I have learned my lesson. I promise that I shall not ride out again without having half the grooms in Buxton in my train! Will that do?'

'Better that than fearing that you might have been lying one knows not where with a broken leg. Is not that so, Philip?'

Philip Sidney smiled agreement, thrust his arm through

Drew's uninjured one, and asked to be allowed to escort him to his rooms.

'By the Lord God, Philip,' retorted Drew testily, 'I have but a small sprain of the wrist, my life is not in danger, and a fellow likes to be on his own occasionally without all England dancing attendance on him! Confess, Philip, you often feel the same.'

'So I do. But you must remember that you are a married man now. Bess was beginning to fret over your non-return, and the news that you were seen riding pillion behind Captain Goreham did not relieve her of her fears until she found out that you had suffered but a minor hurt.'

What an unseemly pother, thought the disgusted Drew. And what would they all say if they knew the true reason for poor Cicero's death? And—more to the point— which one of the many who will offer me kind words of sympathy this afternoon is the person who tried to murder me this morning?

It was difficult to decide who might have wished to kill him since everyone whom he met expressed their distress at his untoward accident after such a fashion that it was difficult to believe that they were not sincere.

Even the Queen of Scots sent him a message through Nau, hoping that his injury was not so great that it would spoil his pleasure during his visit to Buxton.

Something which he had said to Captain Goreham on the ride back to Buxton stayed with him. 'You claim to be a man experienced in such matters, sir. Do you believe it possible that the arrow which killed Cicero this morning was meant to kill him, rather than me—a warning shot across my bows as my naval friends would say— to discourage me from further action?'

'Oh, aye, m'lord. Very like—although we have no

means of proving the matter either way.' So that was that—and altogether it left him in a most unsatisfactory situation. Particularly when Bess, in her usual thoughtful way, remarked to him as they prepared for supper that evening, 'Was there something odd about Cicero's death, husband?'

'Why do you ask?' Drew made his reply as lightly as he could.

'Nothing which I can put into words—except. . .' and Bess paused before continuing '. . .promise not to laugh at me if I explain why I might think so.'

'I promise.' Drew's tone was still light although he was inwardly cursing either Tib or Thomas if either of them had said anything to Bess which might have started her worrying about his safety

'It's this. I have come to know you very well, Drew, and your manner since you returned with Captain Goreham leads me to believe that Cicero's death was not quite what it seemed.'

So, neither Tib nor Thomas had talked—which was as well for them. 'And that is all, wife?' He smiled as he spoke.

'There! I said that you would laugh at me! And you have!'

'No, no, I am not laughing. But I am pleased that you should worry about me and poor Cicero. No need, my heart. Cicero is at rest—or perhaps galloping in the fields of heaven; and I am in perfect fig—except for a slightly damaged wrist. On the whole, matters went well for me, if not for my horse.'

It was the first time Drew had experienced that strange phenomenon which can occur between lovers: that sixth sense which picks up the true feelings of the other rather than the ones which they are claiming to experience.

He realised at once that he was also beginning to read Bess's thoughts—although not as strongly as she was reading his. He did not think that he had deceived her and, although he disliked lying to her, he had done so as much to protect her as to keep her in the dark for no reason at all.

So when they sat down beside the Lady Arbell and Sir Henry at supper and they began their litany of commiseration over Cicero and his fall, nothing which Bess said revealed that she, for one, doubted that he had told the whole truth of what had happened on the hills above Buxton.

He would have to be careful in future, although he ruefully acknowledged that there was little which he could do to prevent his wife from being so sensitive to all his moods.

Looking around the table he tried to work out who his would-be assassin might have been. Which of his kind friends was it who wished to see him dead because of what he might uncover? All of them looked singularly innocent, and the one person whom he might have suspected by his manner was Captain Goreham—who had turned out to be the one person who wished to keep him alive—if only as a useful informant who could guide him to a larger payday. For Drew had not the slightest doubt why the Captain was such a keen patriot!

Drew's appetite had quite deserted him. A matter of comment for Arbell, who managed to inform the whole table of its disappearance.

'Small wonder,' she said, with Sir Henry echoing her every word, 'when you have endured such a harrowing experience!'

Much though he would have wished to retort that he was not harrowed at all, Drew desisted if only in honour

of Cicro's memory. He tried to guide the conversation
into other channels, but so little which was exciting ever
happened at Buxton that the company would not lightly
surrender such a juicy bone.

'I am beginning to wish that I *had* broken my neck
this morning,' he whispered savagely to Bess, 'and then
I should not have had to endure listening to all this
twaddle. One might think that a man had never fallen
off a horse before.'

'Do not say so, Drew! Not even in jest. The unkind
gods who might fulfil such a dreadful wish could be
listening to you.'

'Exactly,' said Charles, who had overheard him, 'You
must not frighten your wife—and the other ladies, Drew.
Their feelings are more delicate than ours.'

'Then I would wish that their delicacy would extend
itself to another topic,' Drew ground out. He saw Philip
reward him with an odd stare for his strange behaviour,
and tried to control himself. He had to admit that what
had happened earlier had shaken him. It was not only
his fall and Cicero's death which perturbed him. The
knowledge that he was as hunted an animal as the stag
or the fox whom he had often pursued on Cicero's back
was a strange and daunting thought.

But it behoved him to pull himself together and play
the man, and not act like the spoiled darling of the court
which Captain Goreham obviously thought that he was.

He saw the Captain's eye on him, and shouted manner-
lessly down the table in his direction, 'I have a mind to
draw a bow against you tomorrow forenoon, Captain
Goreham. Never mind that my wrist is damaged, it will
need more than an unhappy fall to deter me from doing
what I have a mind to do.'

And if that was not a direct challenge to the unknown

swine who had tried to kill him, then nothing was.

Bess stared at him—and his odd uncourteous behaviour. Philip leaned towards him and said, 'Now, Drew, you should rest, rather than exercise, your wrist.' A comment which Charles and Sir Henry both echoed.

'As an old soldier, I must advise you otherwise,' boomed Sir Henry jovially, 'and no more riding for a few days. You should not court another accident until you have recovered from the first.'

With everyone so exasperatingly concerned for his welfare it seemed a miracle that anyone should wish to kill him! Even the squires joined in when the meal was over and they were standing about, drinking the last of the ale, the ladies disporting themselves on large settles before a blazing fire—the day having been cool and the evening cooler.

The only exception was the Captain, who followed him when he strode away from the company and out through the main doorway to stand on the steps in the open, watching the rising moon.

'Should you be showing yourself so partial to me?' Drew half-snarled at him. 'Is it wise, considering everything?'

'Perhaps not. But that was a rare old challenge you flung at me and the rest of the company, and I told your crony Sidney that I was following you to make arrangements for the morning's match.'

'Forgive my ill temper,' Drew said. 'You do not deserve it. If you must know, it is the inability to discover who my enemy is which is galling me. I had not half so ill a temper when I was engaged in a sea-fight against the Spaniards and we boarded their ship so as to make it our prize.'

It was the Captain's turn to be surprised. 'Ah, you have seen action, then, m'lord?'

'When I was nineteen I financed a ship to prey on the Spaniards' galleon run in the South Seas and persuaded my guardian to allow me to be an officer in the crew. So, yes, I have seen action. But at least I was face to face with my enemy then, and did not suspect that a friend might be stabbing me in the back.'

'Exactly so. I understand that you sent your grooms to recover the furniture on your horse. Did they suspect that anything untoward had happened?'

'If they did, they knew better than to say so,' grinned Drew. 'They had orders to be as quiet as possible at what they found at the scene of the accident. I can only hope that they put it down to my wounded pride over being thrown.'

'And your good lady? She is not troubled, I trust?'

Drew was not sure whether he disliked the Captain more as a friend than as an enemy. His good lady, indeed! It made his young and pretty Bess sound as old and stale as her namesake of Hardwick. Nevertheless, he reassured the Captain that he had not told Bess of the true cause of his accident, so that consquently she was not too overset.

A fact borne out a few moments later when she joined them to admire the crescent moon, the surrounding stars and the clear sky.

'So this is where you vanished to, husband. Am I to suppose that you found the silence and peace of a summer's night more to your liking than the noisy fuss which your morning's accident has created? I hope, Captain Goreham, that you have been discussing anything other than poor Cicero's misfortune with him. I have no mind to retire with a husband who is as sore as though he had spent the day as a bear being baited.'

The Captain's smile for her was one of admiration. 'Exactly so, m'lady. We have been talking of sweet nothings, I do assure you; furthermore, it will be my pleasure to leave you alone to enjoy the moonlight.'

He bowed and was gone.

'I find that I like the Capain more than I did,' remarked Bess thoughtfully. 'Now why should that be so?'

Well, not because he is given to telling the truth, was Drew's inward reaction to that. Instead he said, his voice grave and considering, 'I suppose it is because he has the good sense, like yourself, to speak of other things to me. Tomorrow morning's archery match, for instance. We were mulling over the niceties of it.'

A statement which made him as big a liar as the Captain! It suddenly occurred to Drew all over again that one of the drawbacks of being a spy—or even a humble intelligencer, which he was—was that one rarely spoke the truth, even to one's wife. He also thought that, his own attitude to the Captain having changed somewhat, Bess's intuititive understanding of his moods had resulted in changing hers, too.

He took her by the arm, 'We had best return, I think. I would not have it thought that I was engaging in a lengthy fit of the sullens.'

'No, husband. But you are allowed, I hope, to enjoy the evening with your wife.'

The face Bess turned on him was so artlessly mischievous that Drew found himself giving a little groan and taking her into his arms. The sweet scent of her filled his nostrils. A passionate few minutes followed—until Drew released her from his demanding arms and stepped away from her.

'Not here, wife. Not here. It would not be seemly for

us to be discovered enjoying ourselves in the open like a pair of country lovers.'

Laughing, despite being full of the frustration of joy denied, Bess shook her head at him gravely. 'Oh, you are right, Drew. Think what the Lady Arbell would say of you—that your wife, the milkmaid, had corrupted the finest flower of Her Majesty's Court. What can the world be coming to?'

He was so enchanted by her charming impudence that he took her in his arms again, and whispered into her ear, 'You must not be jealous of her, wife. Think rather that she is jealous of you.'

Bess pulled away from him a little. 'But she is so beautiful in the way which our world accounts beautiful.' The words were wrenched from her.

'Her face, yes. But her soul, Bess—what colour is that?'

Bess hid her face in Drew's hard chest—and his scent was now all about her. Horse, the open air, and the lavender in which his shirt and doublet had been packed in his trunk, were all mixed together with the characteristic musky aroma of a roused man.

Blindfolded, she would know him anywhere. Not to be united with him here, in the clean air, away from the gossip and the knowing eyes which followed them everywhere, was sweet torture indeed.

Nevertheless, she walked indoors with him, to endure for a little space the company of others until, alone together, they could end what the fair night outside had begun.

Chapter Eleven

'**W**ho would have thought that the gallant Captain would be late for this rendezvous?' complained Charles to Drew the following morning. 'He was full of it last night. Swore that he would have his revenge on you. A strange revenge, not to turn up at all.'

'Mayhap he is unwell,' returned Drew, who had seated himself on a small stool placed behind the mark from which the archers shot. A number of other men were busily engaged in shooting against one another before they retired to the baths. Tib stood by, guarding Drew's bow and his quiver full of arrows. Philip Sidney, present to watch the match, was saying nothing, but his expression showed that he agreed with Charles.

Charles, indeed, was in a bad mood. He had just had word that morning that a courier carrying a satchelful of accounts, letters and instructions whom he had sent to the Comptroller at Drew's London house had been attacked at an inn on the London road, just north of the capital. The courier had been robbed of the small amount of money he was carrying, but the satchel had not been stolen, even though its contents had been strewn about the road outside the inn. The robber, or robbers, had not thought that they were worth making off with.

Drew, listening with half an ear to his lamentations, was looking towards the house, waiting for Captain Goreham to appear. Instead, he saw a page whom he recognised running in the direction of the butts.

'Ah, Charles,' he said, 'cease your pacing and your cursing. I believe that a Mercury is coming haste post-haste towards us with a budget of excuses from the good Captain, I believe.'

Drew's Mercury was the Captain's youthful page, now advancing on them, an important look on his face.

'My master, Captain Goreham,' he piped at Drew, bowing low before he spoke, 'presents his apologies to you, my Lord of Exford, but he has awoken with the recurrence of an old leg injury which makes walking and standing difficult. He trusts that you will forgive him and, knowing that you may not have broken your fast, he asks you to do him the honour of breaking it with him in his room.'

'Well done,' said Drew. 'To remember all that is a great feat, young sir. Tell your master that I will be pleased both to eat with him and to offer him my commiserations on his injury. We shall shoot against one another on a future day, I am sure.'

'And if you believe that tale, Drew,' grunted Charles, who had taken the Captain in acute dislike, 'you are greener than I thought that you were. He is obviously regretting his challenge and taking the opportunity to avoid being beaten.' Philip was nodding agreement with him.

'No matter.' Drew stood up as the page ran off. 'Civility demands that I wait upon him as he asks. To do otherwise would be too cruel a snub. You will both present my excuses to my wife, who has already gone with Sir Henry and his wife to break her fast.'

He could only wonder what game the Captain was playing now. Like Philip and Charles, he doubted the truth of the tale the page had told them, but not for the same reason as they did. No, the Captain wished to speak to him as soon as possible, and alone, and this was as easy a way of doing so without drawing suspicion on them that he could contrive.

The Captain was lying upon a settle, his leg stretched before him, and cushions behind his back. 'Which,' he told Drew while pages and footmen finished setting out a meal for them, 'is also exceeding painful. So painful that I could scarce rise from my bed this morning. Was not that so, Tom?' he asked the sturdiest footman of all.

'Oh, aye, master. In great pain you were. A-moaning and a-groaning. Should have stayed there.'

'Not I,' said the Captain, looking manful. 'An old soldier such as I am must needs be out of bed, not lying in it like a foolish milksop. True, my lord?'

'Oh, very true,' agreed Drew, wondering what was coming next when the Captain dismissed all his servants on the pretext that 'old soldier as I am, I do not need coddling. That will ruin me sooner than aught else.'

They were alone. Drew watched the Captain leap briskly out off the settle and begin to pile his plate with bread, butter, meat and cheese from the groaning table. No sign was left of his troublesome injury.

'Happy to see,' Drew could not help remarking, 'that my mere presence seems to have brought about a remission of your agony.'

'Exactly so,' agreed the Captain, his mouth full. 'Eat up, my lord. You will need your strength for what I am going to tell you.'

Hardly a way to encourage a man's appetite; nevertheless Drew, too, filled his plate with the excellent victuals which Shrewsbury's kitchen provided, and drank his good ale.

'Now, m'lord,' intoned the Captain, putting down his plate. 'Attend to what I have to tell you. We—that is, Sir Francis and I—had no notion of how messages were being sent to the French Embassy by the plotters here. It was quite by accident that we discovered that there was a plot at all, but we could not find its conduit to the Continent. I have today received definite proof that a letter was secretly sent from Buxton to London during the last week.'

He paused, before saying, 'You will not like it when I tell you where it was discovered and who was carrying it, although we believe the courier to be innocent.'

'Go on,' Drew's voice was steady, though he knew that he was about to hear some bad news.

'We had word that the courier left Buxton on Monday, a week ago. One of my men knocked him on the head at an inn in Barnet, and found the letter in a secret pocket in the satchel carrying papers bound for your home in London. Yes, m'lord—' for he saw Drew's face change colour '—that is the right of it. And I am supposing that this is as great a surprise to you as it was to me.'

'Then you suppose correctly, Captain. Although I find this news both unwelcome and difficult to believe.'

'Nevertheless,' said the Captain, 'that is the truth of it.'

'And did this letter give away who wrote it—and who the plotters were?'

The Captain shook his head. 'Alas, no, my lord. False names were used. The letter was read, copied—so that those versed in codes might try to decipher it further—and then was sent on its way again when the courier recovered.'

Drew knew who the courier was. A young gentleman of his household, Robert Nash by name. He was relieved to learn that the Captain thought him to be innocent. Except that two other persons were guilty—the man who had smuggled the letter into the satchel and the man who would remove it from its hiding place and send it on its way to the French Embassy.

And both men must be his retainers, his trusted servants.

'So, I am harbouring the traitors, Captain.'

'Not all of them. Others are involved, but your men are the conduit through which the treacherous post to the Continent is directed.'

This did not make Drew any happier. For it now seemed that it might be someone whom he trusted who had tried to kill him. He was aware of the Captain watching him as he stuffed bread, cheese, and sliced, spiced beef into his mouth.

He must say something, something full of common sense and determination as befitted his position. It came to him that what he would have liked most of all to do before he answered the Captain was to talk the whole thing over with his wife! Which was indeed a strange thought to have, except that she was level-headed after a fashion which he had never expected a woman to be.

'What then,' he said at last, as the remainder of the cheese disappeared down the Captain's throat, 'ought we to do?'

'What we have been doing. Be patient and wait to see whether our men in London can uncover anything. Your home in London will be watched to try to find out who carries the letter to the Embassy. If and when we do so, then we can perhaps lean on him, and thus discover who else is involved. On the other hand, more might be gained by leaving him free so that we might learn who his associates are.'

Lean on him! It would be Topcliffe, the torturer at the Tower of London, who would do the leaning—which was only what a traitor deserved when all was said and done. Still, he had to believe that the Captain knew his murky business.

Drew had small appetite for the food before him. Nevertheless, he ate as though he were hungry, the food ashes in his mouth. Who was it whom he trusted who was betraying him?

Later, in the evening as they talked after their meal, Bess was asking herself the same question. She was not concerned with spies and plotting but whether her husband was betraying her. She had come, thanks to his loving attentions to her, to believe that her suspicion of him over the matter of Lady Arbell was foolish, based on unfounded jealousy. In the last few days Drew had seemed indifferent to the Lady Arbell's attractions. His manner to her had become cool and indifferent.

But today he had changed again. Bess was not to know that Drew, driven by the need to discover exactly who was betraying whom at Buxton, had decided to encourage Arbell in her pursuit of him, in the hope that if she were involved in a Catholic plot, she would by some means give herself away when talking to him.

More wounding than that, Bess, who had spent the afternoon at the Holy Well with Marian Blagg, had walked back to her room up the great staircase and along the corridor which led through some of the bedrooms. She had heard voices; the voices of a man and a woman laughing together.

It was Drew and Arbell, standing before a window,

talking intimately. Arbell was facing towards Bess, when she saw Bess coming, she flung her arms around Drew and kissed him on the cheek. From where Bess stood it seemed that Drew was encouraging her. In reality, Arbell, desperate to seduce him, thought that to make trouble between Drew and his wife was the best way to win him.

Drew heard someone coming. He detached himself—with some difficulty—from the clinging Arbell and turned to face his wife.

'Ah, there you are, my lady. You left the Well early?'

Bess was acid. 'No earlier than I intended, my lord. Was there some reason why you wished me to be late?'

Arbell, who had now backed away from Drew, smiled sweetly at Bess. 'I will give him back to you, Lady Exford, so that he may prepare himself for the evening meal.'

I had not thought that she had me to hand back, was Drew's glum reaction, but judging by Bess's face, she believes what the lying bitch has just suggested.

His bow to Arbell before they left was as gallant as he could make it, although the moment that they were out of the Lady's hearing he said to Bess, without any apology, 'Although appearances might seem otherwise, you are not to suspect that there is anything between the Lady Arbell and myself, wife.'

'No?' Bess raised her eyebrows without raising her voice. 'I wonder what you would say if I behaved as lovingly to your friend Philip—or Charles—or even Captain Goreham?'

Drew gritted his teeth. 'I should say a great deal, believe me, but—'

'But I am not to say anything because I am a wife, not a husband. No, Drew, do not gloss over your behaviour. I would rather you were honest with me. I do not like deceit.'

'Damnation, I am being honest with you, woman! I mean what I say, but. . .'

'But what? Do you mean what you do? And the Lady, does she mean what she says and does? That kiss she gave you, for example?'

'That kiss meant nothing. She forced it on me.'

Bess began to laugh, genuine laughter, no bitterness in it. 'Poor Drew, to be so assaulted by a woman. Shall I force a kiss on you, husband? Like this?'

And in a mocking imitation of Arbell she turned towards him, flung her arms around him and kissed him vigorously on the lips.

They had reached the privacy of their inner chamber. Drew's response was to take her in his arms, bear her down on to a fine Turkish carpet, and give her not one kiss, but many, before pleasuring her so vigorously that they both lay spent on the floor when their lovemaking had ended.

Panting, half-naked, his lips scarlet—as were Bess's with the force of their passion—Drew looked down at her, as she gazed up at him. 'Now, woman, will you believe me? Do you think I could have treated you so lustily if I had spent the afternoon making love to *her*? I'd as soon make love to a. . .a. . .'

Words failed him. He couldn't think what it was that he didn't want to make love to. . . Instead, he began to stroke and pet Bess again, until she whispered into his almost unhearing ear, 'I think that the word you could not find for the Lady Arbell was "pillow". And if we are going to make the beast with two backs again, husband, do you think that I could lie on something soft whilst we do so? The floor, even with a carpet on it, makes a hard bed.'

'Assuredly.' Drew picked her up again and carried her to the bed where they enjoyed themselves so heartily that they scarcely had time to clamber into their elaborate clothing before repairing to supper.

Even so, for the next few days, like Drew, Bess could not quite recapture the mindless happiness which she had enjoyed before she had seen Arbell kiss him so intimately. A shadow lay over her.

Drew's shadow was the knowledge of his household's involvement in the plot against the Queen. He saw and heard nothing to give him any clues which might help him to solve the mystery. By the end of the week, both Charles and Philip separately asked him what was troubling him. Was it so obvious? Plainly he would not make an agent if being a simple intelligencer was so hard to carry off!

And then a further blow fell. Captain Goreham challenged him to an archery match to replace the one which had been cancelled because of his supposed injury.

'But we must meet privately, you understand,' the Captain said, looking solemn. 'We need to be alone.'

The next morning an early hour found them at the butts. They went through the pretence of a match, although neither man's mind was on the game. They spent the time between the rounds talking of what was paramount on both their minds, although a watcher from the windows of the Great Hall would merely have seen two men enjoying themselves in the cool of the early morning.

'I have news for you,' the Captain said. They were

standing at some distance from their two pages, whom
they had encouraged to engage in a match of their own.
'I have had a despatch from London which informs
me that they have discovered the member of your household who is passing letters from Buxton to the French
Embassy.

'One of your maidservants has a lover there, a man
who poses as a senior footman, but is someone quite
other. They are lovers, and she has been suborned into
helping him by the promise of marriage. She does not
understand quite what she is doing, but she takes charge
of the satchel with the secret pocket after its legitimate
papers have been removed and takes the letter from the
pocket to give to her lover. Later he gives her a letter to
Buxton which she must slip into the satchel before it
goes north again.'

Drew contained himself with some difficulty. He was
astonished to find, after the Captain had passed on this
bad news, that he could shoot at all, let alone shoot well.

'Can I believe you?' he asked, after he had shot into
the gold again. 'You are telling me that it is someone
from my *own* retinue who is sending the letters from
Buxton?'

Captain Goreham shot again before replying. 'Indeed,
m'lord. As you plainly see, it must be so.'

'And have you any evidence of who the spy at the
Buxton end might be?'

The Captain pulled an arrow from his quiver. 'None
at all, except. . .' and he paused before looking quizzic-
ally at Drew '. . .except that on the face of it, the traitor
can be none other than yourself!'

The heavens reeled around Drew. So this accounted
for Walsingham's odd treatment of him. That he thought
Drew to be the traitor, and Goreham was obviously here

to keep watch on him, rather than on anyone else.

He shot again. And hit the gold again.

From a great distance he heard the Captain behind him murmur, 'Well shot, m'lord.'

He was surprised by his own coolness when Tower Hill, hanging, drawing and quartering loomed before him. He stepped away to allow the Captain to take his turn, saying, 'I suppose that denial is useless, but deny it I must.'

'Failing any other evidence.' The Captain was almost negligent in the manner of his reply.

Drew wanted to throttle him, and Walsingham, too. The Captain said, his own arrow having found the gold, 'The main plot here began after you arrived. Earlier we know that it was being run from London. And your grandfather was a Catholic.'

'Oh, rare, sir, rare,' mocked Drew. 'Seeing that he was a young man in the old King's time when everyone was a Catholic. On that evidence you had better attaint and execute all the males in the kingdom.'

'I did not say that you are a conspirator, or even the chief one. Simply that the burden of the evidence lies in that direction. Convince me otherwise. Such are my orders.'

'Since my unsupported word of honour is not enough, only by unmasking the true traitor can I prove my innocence. Simply to shriek denials at you, and play the offended fool, would not have you believing otherwise.'

Without waiting for an answer Drew shot again—and struck the gold again. It seemed that his cold hauteur in the face of such a dreadful accusation disturbed the Captain more than it disturbed him, for from then on the match was downhill all the way for his opponent. Drew continued to find the gold whilst the Captain was doomed to the outer colours.

On his last hopeless shot the Captain put down his bow and turned to face Drew. His manner had changed completely. All its greasy unction had disappeared and the real man, hidden beneath it, appeared: the mercenary soldier completely sure of himself.

'The match is yours, m'lord. And I must confess that I have misread you again. True or traitor, you are not the soft, courtly creature I took you for. Your hand did not shake even at the moment of accusation. Rather than causing you to lose the match, from that moment on, your skill improved.'

'And what,' asked Drew, 'am I to make of that? That you think me a cold-blooded plotter—or simply cold-blooded—or that you said what you did to make me shoot badly?'

The Captain shook his head, 'Why, as to being a conspirator, sir, I know not. Only time will tell.'

Drew turned on his heel. 'And now it is time to break fast. Forgive me if I do not accompany you back to the Hall. I have much to think of, and would prefer to do so alone.'

He walked away in the direction of the Holy Well. His first thought was that he must keep watch for the courier returning with the satchel so that he might stop him and examine it before any one else did. What he found would determine his next action.

He also asked himself how serious the Captain's accusation had been. He thought that it might not be totally so, but the fact that it had been made at all explained Walsingham's odd behaviour towards him—and why he had been chosen to go to Derbyshire. Lacking evidence of any kind either about the Captain, who was conceivably a double agent, or who exactly the true conspirators might be, he could come to no real conclusion until he found some.

He only knew that he had grown hungry and that Bess might wonder where he had gone without telling her of his destination. She might even suspect that he had a secret tryst with Arbell—which would never do.

On reaching the Hall, he found Charles and Philip talking together in the entrance. About him, apparently, for Charles said, somewhat reproachfully, 'Ah, there you are, cousin. A pity that you did not care to tell us that you and Captain Goreham had decided to engage in your postponed match this morning. Master Sidney and I would have enjoyed watching it.'

'We met on a whim,' Drew replied shortly, 'and were bent on our own pleasure, not on that of others.'

He was aware that he sounded surly, but he felt surly, and in no mood to humour anyone. One thing he had decided on his walk: that he would treat all the members of his household as though they were the traitor—even Charles. He excluded Philip from suspicion, knowing that his hatred of Catholics was so strong that he had even lost favour with the Queen because of his opposition to her marrying the French Catholic, the Duc d'Alençon.

And Bess. He excluded Bess because he would have staked his life on her honesty.

'Forgive me,' he said, brushing by them both. 'I am hungry. I will talk to you both later when breaking my fast has improved my humour.'

Charles said nothing. Nor Philip neither; he raised his fine brows and wondered what flea had occupied Drew's ear and spoiled his usual calm temper. He felt constrained to ask, his voice light to take the sting out of his words, 'You lost the match, then?'

Drew, already on his way, turned back, and shook his head before he answered him. 'On the contrary, cousin and friend both, I won it easily. May all such meetings for me end in victory.'

Chapter Twelve

Was he, or was he not, dallying with Arbell? If so, it wasn't making him very happy. On the contrary her husband, who had been in the best of humour when they had arrived at Buxton, was now in the worst of one.

Bess was preoccupied by this sad thought whilst she was being dressed for the day. Her maid was tying her sleeves on to her bodice and carefully arranging the little rolls which concealed the joins. Bess had refused to wear the huge ruff which her maid—and fashion—demanded, and had chosen a small one instead.

'But the Lady Arbell will be sure to be wearing hers,' the maid wailed.

'All the more reason for me not to do so.' Bess was crisp—and, for her, a little demanding. What she really wanted to do was put on her old coarse, brown dress and go riding with Drew across Charnwood Forest. She was growing tired of idleness at Buxton, of being pushed in and out of stiff clothes and being expected by her waiting women to rival the other ladies in the excesses of her dress.

Drew put his head around the door. 'You are beautfied enough to allow me in, I hope.'

'Far too beautified.' Bess was aware that she was being pettish but she could not help herself. 'I have enjoyed my visit to Buxton, husband. It has been a happy change to be idle, but I am growing wishful to see my home again and go riding with you in something more comfortable than this.'

'Ah, I suppose you mean that old piece of sacking you were wearing when I first met you,' riposted Drew, kissing the cheek which Bess's maid had just treated with some sweet-smelling oil designed to make its user stay young for ever—or so the herbalist had said. 'Couldn't you consider something between the two?'

'Only if it were comfortable.'

'The Lady Arbell—' began the maid.

'No,' ordered Bess. 'Do not speak of her again. I have not the slightest wish to look like her. What are you laughing at, husband?'

'Anyone less like the Lady Arbell than my dear wife, I have yet to meet. Pray leave us,' he told the maid.

'Now,' he asked, 'what has brought this fit on, wife?'

'Jealousy,' said Bess bluntly, 'and the fact that I wish to go home. We have been here long enough. Yes, I have enjoyed myself, but I find that I am growing homesick.'

Drew would dearly have loved to accede to her wishes, but what he was unable to tell her restrained him. He could not leave Buxton until he had cleared his name and uncovered the real traitor. After a week of waiting and watching, he was still no nearer to doing that, for the courier from London had not yet returned. He did not wish to tell Bess the unhappy truth. He could only hope that the Captain's suspicions of him would be cleared up without her having to know of them.

Instead he remarked blandly, 'I think that you deserve a little longer holiday, dear wife.'

Bess was blunt again. 'What keeps you here, Drew? Me, or the Lady Arbell?'

He took her in his arms, and said fiercely. 'No, do not believe that. We must stay a little longer. I have my reasons for asking you to agree to this. Believe me, like you, I am wishful to be back at Atherington again.'

This came out after a fashion which Bess could only believe was heartfelt.

But could she believe him?

'And your reasons are?'

'I cannot tell you—not yet, at least.'

He only wanted to protect her, but by doing so he was in danger of losing her trust. He was going to lose it a little more when he made his next request.

'Sir Henry has asked that we make up a party of men to go riding along the Wye. He hopes to find deer, and we shall take our bows with us. He has permission to shoot from Lord Shrewsbury. He has asked that you keep company with the Lady Arbell whilst we are gone. We are like to be away until evening.'

'Men, only men? Why cannot I accompany you? I can ride a horse as well as any man. And I do not wish to spend the day with the Lady Arbell. You may tell Sir Henry that I have a megrim and beg to be excused.' Bess was unhappily aware that she sounded both unreasonable and petulant.

'Not all the men. Charles will not be going. He has accounts to do, he says, and Master Blagg is expecting his Steward today, and will only accompany us if the man arrives before we are due to leave. Nor will the Captain go. Like you, he has a megrim.'

Which, seeing that he knew that she hadn't a megrim, thought Bess dolefully, could be taken any way you liked.

'Don't look at me like that,' Drew told her. 'I have

no wish to go, either, but I have no real excuse to offer.' Which was not the true reason why he wished to join the expedition. There was always the possibility that someone might say, or do, something incriminating whilst they were at ease. A slight possibility, but still a possibility.

'Very well, then. Go—I will entertain myself.' She accompanied this with a kiss on his warm cheek to show that she forgave him for deserting her. 'Do your duty— for I understand that you do not wish to snub Sir Henry by refusing his invitation.'

Relieved, and after a kiss in return, Drew left her to sink down on a settle in her useless finery—for who was there to see it now? Except that Drew came back to put his head round the door again to say, 'Do not sit indoors, dear wife. Tib may escort you should you wish to ride.'

'But you know I must pretend that I have a megrim,' Bess wailed.

'Then think of a better excuse,' and Drew was gone.

I shall offer no excuse at all, thought Bess grimly. The kitchen shall pack us a picnic, and Tib and I shall pretend that we are quartering Charnwood Forest again. The maid must take off my fancy clothing and I shall borrow some of Tib's, ride astride and pretend that I am virgin again and may do as I please! And what I please is to be as far away from the Lady Arbell as possible.

For Tib it had been like old times come back again. He and Walter, one of Lord Shrewsbury's grooms, had accompanied his lady on a ride into the hills. They had broken their fast on a grassy knoll among the trees, eating bread, butter and cheese with gusto. Once they had stopped to drink pure, fresh water from a stream. Bess was, for a brief space, the very young lady whom he had dared to love from afar.

They arrived back at Buxton in the middle of the afternoon, their small idyll over. For all her happiness that carefree afternoon, Bess could not truly wish herself maiden again; she had come to love her husband and would not have the old days return.

Tib cared for their horses, helped by Walter, after watching his mistress walk cautiously back into the Hall lest anyone see her in her boy's garb. Walter wanted to talk about the day, and the girl he hoped to marry who lived and worked at Chatsworth, being part of Lord Shrewsbury's immense household, but Tib did not want to hear of the happiness of others.

He excused himself, and decided to look for one of m'lord's dogs which had wandered off that morning and had not been seen since. It was as good an excuse as any to be alone. He set off whistling to keep his spirits up and occasionally calling Ranter's name.

After a time Tib no longer needed to whistle to be happy. He had become resigned to the fact that, now that Bess was married to m'lord Exford, she was forever out of his reach. He had come to the edge of the Great Hall's demesne, where a wall separated it from the scrub and brambles which surrounded it. Near a rude gate which opened on to the wilderness stood a small stone building in the shape of a classical temple, which overlooked the view towards the distant hills.

Was it possible that naughty Ranter had hidden himself away there again as he had done a few days ago? Tib walked over to it and up the steps which led to a small verandah and a doorway which gave access to an inner room. The door stood slightly ajar.

He was about to shout Ranter's name when he heard

voices and muted laughter. Someone was using the little temple for a secret tryst, no doubt about it—the voices were both male and female, and their tone was loving and confidential.

Tib smiled to himself, and turned to leave—and then stopped. One of the voices, the woman's, was speaking his mistress's name after the most derisory fashion, and he recognised it as that of the Lady Arbell.

Now, who could she be with? Stableyard gossip held that she and m'lord Exford were lovers, but Tib had never believed that, and she could not be with m'lord now, for he was far away on a deer hunt with the Lady Arbell's husband.

And then he heard the man's voice—and the sound of it shocked him, not only because it told him who the Lady Arbell's lover was, but even more because of what he was saying.

'Oh,' he laughed, 'we have foxed them properly, my love. And, the cream of the jest is that, with any luck, we shall have the whole world believing that Exford and his wife are conspiring to set Queen Mary on the throne of England, something which will bring great profit to us both, whether we succeed in our enterprise or not!' The woman's laughter which followed was hard and cruel.

No! Tib was almost beside himself on hearing this, for no less was being joked about than a conspiracy to condemn his master and mistress to a cruel death on Tower Hill!

His shock on hearing such treachery—and who was planning it—was so great that he forgot to be cautious as he ran from the temple to find Lady Exford immediately to tell her of what he had overheard. Alas, someone had left a pail in the lee of the steps and his foot caught it and sent it clattering.

The man's voice called, 'Hola, who's there?' and on receiving no answer, there was the sound of following footsteps. Tib realised too late that he must not be discovered and began to run as fast as he could, but his pursuer was fleeter of foot and was upon him before he had gone many yards. He spun Tib round so that they stood face to face.

They were quite alone; Tib was unarmed and the other man held a dagger in his hand. He laughed at the sight of Tib, standing there with no saviour, no one in sight to whom he might call for help.

'Oh, the faithful servant,' he jeered. 'Not someone to bribe to keep quiet, I fear,' and before Tib could comprehend that his doom was upon him, he drove the dagger into Tib's breast.

Tib fell and lay still. His murderer bent down and dragged him to the edge of the undergrowth where, with luck, he might not be found for some time. He wrenched Tib's small medallion of St Christopher from around his neck, and cut his half-empty purse away to suggest that the man who had shot at Lord Exford might have found easier pickings.

And then he returned to the Lady Arbell to tell her that they were safe, but that they must, separately, return to the house at all speed so that no one might suspect that they had aught to do with the murdered man outside.

Behind them, Tib, half-conscious and not quite dead, pressed a lax hand to his wound to stem the flow of blood and began to drag himself free in the direction of the Great House. . .

Bess, dressed in her finery again, visited the Baths, something which she had not done for several days. Afterwards, refreshed, and feeling the need for exercise, she decided to take a turn in the grounds which surrounded the Hall. Hardly had she done so before she saw Philip Sidney coming towards her across the grass, a book in his hand. He greeted her with a smile.

'I had thought that you were with the deer hunters,' she rallied him.

'Well, so I was, but I grew weary of the chase after we had eaten, and the poetic fit being on me, I stayed behind to indulge it—I always carry a small notebook with me, you understand. Then, the Muse being satisfied, I decided to return early to Buxton, only to find that the others were home some time before me, having gone by a shorter route! On learning that you had gone to the Baths, Drew decided to walk there.'

Beth gave a little groan. 'Alas, we must have crossed with each other. I returned by the longer path. We could have met and taken a walk together.'

Ever gallant, Philip sought to console her. 'In his absence, will you do me the honour of walking with me a little instead, madam?'

'Only if you promise to read me your latest sonnet when we have done so,' returned Bess gaily. Despite missing Drew, she was feeling at peace with all the world, and could even have been civil to the Lady Arbell if she had suddenly appeared.

'To the temple then, that haven of peace away from the noise of the Hall,' Philip said, 'and there I may read you my new sonnet, and after that talk philosophy—if it so pleases you.'

'Oh, everything pleases me this afternoon, Master Sidney. Yes, I will walk with you.'

Afterwards, Bess was to think glumly that every time she thought that she might have found Arcadia, something dreadful happened to ruin it, and to remind her of the cruel harshness of the real world in which she lived.

They were almost at the little temple when they saw something lying on the ground before it. It appeared to be a heap of discarded clothes, but no, it could not be that, for it was moving. Nearer to, the pathetic heap turned out to be a man stretched on the ground, who tried to lift his head a little as they approached him.

'Stand back, Bess,' Philip ordered her, for like Bess he had seen the trail of blood behind the fallen man. 'I do not think that this is a sight for you.'

'No,' exclaimed Bess feverishly, disobeying him and running forward. 'Oh, sweet Jesu, I do believe that it's Tib,' and before Philip could stop her, she was on her knees beside her poor servant who was covered in blood and plainly dying.

He was trying to speak to her, but when he did so his voice was so faint that she could not hear him properly, nor could Philip, who knelt on his other side.

She took his hand. 'Oh, Tib, who has done this to you?' Her voice broke as she spoke.

Tib only knew one thing: that he had found his beloved mistress again and that he must warn her before death claimed him. 'Betrayed,' he managed to choke out. 'You are betrayed by the Lady Arbell and—' and even as he began to choke out her lover's name there came a gush of blood from his mouth and he fell headlong into the darkness of oblivion and death.

'No!' Bess could not believe it. Tib had been her playmate and later her friend and protector and now he was gone.

'Come,' said Philip, rising gently after closing Tib's eyes. 'We can do no more for him. We must return to the House and make arrangements for—'

'No, I shall stay with him until those arrive who will

carry him to his last resting place before he is decently buried.'

'It might not be safe,' Philip began, to have Bess say passionately,

'I have known him all my life, and this is the least that I can do for a faithful servant.'

She was not to be moved, and Philip, respecting her wishes, left her there alone, to wonder numbly who it might be who wished to betray her and why. She was sure that the Lady Arbell had not murdered Tib, but the man who must have been with her in the temple and whom Tib must have unfortunately surprised.

But she would speak of his last words to no one for she knew that Philip had not heard them. Besides, how could she accuse Arbell—whom everyone must know she disliked—lacking any evidence to support her, without appearing stupidly spiteful? Nor could she yet speak of this matter to Drew, for, things being as they were, it might be him of whom Tib was trying to speak.

No, that could not be! Drew was no murderer, she was sure of that. And, after he had overcome his first anger with Tib because he had been a witness of his behaviour to Bess, he had been consistently kind to him.

It was all too much. Bess dropped her head and, still holding Tib's hand, began to weep for him and for the happy days which were gone.

Chapter Thirteen

Tib's murder did not create quite as much commotion as the attempt on Drew's life, for as the Lady Arbell tastelessly remarked, 'He was only a servant, after all.'

It was as well that she did not say that in Bess's hearing—or in that of the Queen of Scots, who had once seen a faithful servant, her Italian musician Rizzio, murdered in front of her.

Bess had never liked the Queen so much as on the first occasion when they met after Tib's death when she commiserated with her on it. 'Such a terrible thing to happen, and here in the depths of the country where we are alone, and where we must fear that someone we know might have done such a dreadful deed.

This unhappy thought was on a number of minds, Drew's and Captain Goreham's among them. The Captain found occasion to whisper to him, 'Do you suppose that your man was in league with the traitors, m'lord?'

'Unlikely, I would have thought. Unless he was recruited after he had arrived here—either by someone in my retinue, or another's.'

Drew would have expected Bess to have been distressed by Tib's awful end and the fact that she had witnessed it, but the depth of it surprised him. He was not to know that Bess's unhappiness was magnified by her lonely worries over who Tib's murderer might be, since she had told no one of his last words. One other thing which kept her silent was that if she reported them, the finger of suspicion would be sure to point at Drew, who was thought to be attracted to the Lady Arbell more than he should be.

Her fears haunted her for the next two days, until, quite suddenly whilst reading her Bible, she had a revelation. She did not compare it with St Paul's on the road to Damascus, for that would have been blasphemous, but it was a revelation all the same.

Why was she doubting Drew? Nothing he had ever said or done to her—or to others—gave her any reason to believe that he might do anything as dreadful as kill Tib. And certainly not just to stop him from revealing that he was enjoying a secret tryst with Arbell in the little temple.

She loved Drew, and love, they said, or as poets like Philip said, was blind, but she was not so blind as to allow love to destroy her better judgment. And another thing had begun to trouble her. Tib had coupled Arbell's name with betrayal and her first thought had been that Drew might have been betraying her by trysting with Arbell—to put it politely.

But suppose that Tib had meant something quite different from that? Something which might explain why Drew had been shot at—that he was being betrayed, as well as herself? The thought seemed fanciful. . .and yet. . . and yet. . . Were they not in the neighbourhood of a woman for whom many men had plotted, might be plotting even now, and would surely do sure in the future?

But how could she and Drew be involved in this? Devious plotters might wish to kill the Queen of England on behalf of the Queen of Scots, but why should they wish to kill Drew?

One thing she must do, and at once, as soon as they were safely alone. She must tell him of Tib's last words.

So it was that later that night, once their servants had left them and they were alone in the Great Bed, Bess gently put aside Drew's attempts to make love to her and said, as composedly as she could, for she did not wish to sound like a hysterical fool, 'Drew, there is something of great importance which I must tell you and no one else.'

He leaned back on his pillows, his arms crossed above his head, laughing up at her as she sat there so still and so solemn.

'Come, wife, what is it that has you putting on such a Friday face? I know Tib's death has disturbed you, but life goes on and, knowing him, I do not believe that he would have you grieving endlessly for him.'

Bess said, still calm and reserved, 'Three days is hardly endless, Drew, but yes, it is of Tib's death that I wish to speak. That afternoon, when Philip and I found him lying on the ground in his blood and trying to crawl to the house, he spoke to me.'

Drew sat up, his face changing from a comic mask to a tragic one like an actor in buskins interpreting a Greek play and lifting one mask from his face to replace it with another.

'He spoke to you? Philip said nothing of this, nor have you—until now. Why, wife, why? For what he said might be of such import that we might be able to identify his murderer.'

Bess closed her eyes, and then opened them again as she took his right hand which lay lax on the counterpane.

'Listen to me, my lord of Exford, and you will know why I have said nothing—not even to you until this secret moment. Philip could not hear him. I was bent over him, and it was to me to whom he spoke, and to none other. He said, and you must believe that I heard him aright, although his voice was choked with blood. . .'

Her own voice faltered and died, as Tib's had done. Drew pressed her hand lovingly, and she found strength to continue.

'He said, "You are betrayed. By the Lady Arbell and. . ." And then he spoke no more, for blood gushed from his mouth, and so he died before he named a name. I have thought long and hard. I do not believe that Arbell killed him, but I believe that she had a secret meeting in the little temple with a lover, a man who did kill Tib. Why he should do so drastic a thing, I cannot think. . ?'

Her voice still thick with unshed tears, Bess stopped.

Drew stared at her, his brain whirling. Finally he said, his voice nearly as unrecognisable as his wife's, 'Did you say nothing because you thought that Tib's murderer might have been me? That the word betrayal, coupled with Arbell, might have meant that? And then kept quiet to protect me? Or did you not believe that I was Arbell's secret companion, but that others would?'

'Oh, Drew, heart of my heart, I knew not what I thought when Tib died in my arms. Forgive me for that. Later, knowing you, I could not believe that you would kill Tib, nor could I think why Arbell's secret lover should wish to do so, either.'

Drew took her by the shoulders, ungently for him, and looked deep into her eyes. 'I shall not try to defend myself. You said that you believed that I was not responsible for Tib's death, and I can understand why, for a moment, you thought that I might have been. No forgiveness is needed. You were right to say nothing of his last words, and you must continue to be silent. Now I must question you. Was that all he said? Think carefully before you answer.'

'He said nothing more, alas! He tried to speak when he first saw me, but could not, and I fear that when he did, the effort killed him.' She gave a little sob.

Drew pressed her hand again and said, 'Bear with me whilst I ask you one more thing. How near was Tib to the temple when you first saw him?'

Bess thought for a moment before answering. 'Quite near. This morning, on pretence of going for a walk, I followed the track he had made and it led to the undergrowth not far from the temple where the fence meets the wilderness beyond—and that is all I know, Drew, and God help me, I wish I did not!'

Drew loosened his hands from her shoulders and kissed her in mercy and pity, not in passion. 'And, knowing this, you have said nothing, but carried this burden on your own.'

It was almost a question, and Bess answered it as such. 'I have spoken to no one, not even to Philip who was with me, and whom I trust. A secret is not a secret if one talks of it—but I owed it to you to tell you the truth.'

'For which I honour you, wife. Now, lie down beside me, not to make love but to be comforted. I thought that you were brave, but you are braver than I knew.'

Bess turned into his arms. A great weight had rolled from her shoulders. It had not gone completely, but the knowledge that her burden was shared had lightened it.

Presently she said, 'Drew? Who could it be? I have thought and thought, but I can come to no conclusion. I cannot believe that it was anyone we know, but consider, would the Lady Arbell be trysting with someone we do not know?'

'I wish,' began Drew, stroking and petting her as he spoke, 'but that is foolish of me—to wish that this had never happened. I fear that Tib's murderer is among us, smiling as he speaks, and it behoves us all, especially yourself, to be careful. In future you must never be alone. I know that you often prefer your own company, but you must forfeit that for your own safety. Consider that the man who killed Tib did not intend him to crawl away and speak to anyone.

'Now let us sleep, for tomorrow is another day.'

After a little space, Bess, emotionally drained, fell asleep in his arms, but Drew could not find oblivion for, on hearing of Tib's last words, he was sure that the Lady Arbell's lover must be the spy whom he and Captain Goreham were seeking—and he still had no notion of who he might be.

'So, your brave lady heard what her servant said as he died, and told no one but yourself of it. Forgive my frankness, but she is a shrewd piece, and no mistake. Most women would have run about Buxton blabbing of what they had been told to all and sundry.'

Drew was secretly pleased by this flattery. 'Yes, I am a lucky man, Captain. She has had a hard life, and that perforce makes her wary, you understand. She has never been pampered.'

'Exactly so, and this puts a new complexion on things. We now know one conspirator, the Lady Arbell—but not the important one—the one who takes the letters from the satchel and hands them to Nau.'

He thought a moment. 'You still have no notion

of who that might be—and whether he is the Lady Arbell's lover?'

'None, and you are not to ask me to use Bess to find out. I will not have her put in danger.'

'Oh, agreed as to that. But we are in the dark, and have no means yet of finding light.'

'Except that I shall try to intercept the courier carrying the satchel when he returns so that I may examine it before anyone else does. With luck it may contain a letter.'

Goreham nodded. 'Good, very good—we shall make an intelligencer of you yet.'

'God forbid,' riposted Drew fervently. 'I have had a deal of trouble in thinking of an excuse for me to intercept the courier myself—pray God it works. The sooner this wretched affair is over, the villains are found, and my name is cleared, the better.'

'Oh, my master will want this plot to continue for a little while longer in order to net as many traitors as possible.'

This news singularly failed to cheer Drew. Rightly or wrongly, he believed that there might be more to this affair than the Captain thought. It seemed to him that he had become a target for the plotters and for the life of him he could not think why. They could have no way of knowing of his involvement with Walsingham, for according to the Captain only he, Walsingham and Drew himself knew of that.

'Plays his cards very close to his chest, does Sir Francis,' had been the Captain's comment when telling Drew this. 'No one is allowed to know of anyone else's complicity and God help the poor devil who talks out of turn. He might soon lack a tongue.'

Another cheerful thought. But that aside, all that

remained for him was to try to reach the courier before anyone else did. Which might be difficult, since no one would expect m'lord Exford to hang about the stables waiting for one of his servants to arrive from London. One of his many underlings would be expected to do that for him.

No one watching Bess and Drew could have guessed from their behaviour that between them they harboured a number of secrets which might have been expected to leave a shadow on all their doings. Drew never ceased to marvel at the resilience and common sense of his wife. She said nothing further to him on the subject of Tib. For some days she wore a black dress in his memory and attended his funeral at the little church in a nearby village.

Aunt Hamilton remonstrated with her over her brief mourning. 'Whatever will people think, my dear? After all, he was only an underservant. The Lady Arbell. . .'

'Do not tell me what the Lady Arbell is saying,' Bess retorted. 'I have no wish to hear it. And you, of all people, know that Tib has been my friend since childhood, and was more of a true gentleman than half the men boasting that title in Buxton. My husband approves of my behaviour and that is enough for me.'

Aunt Hamilton said no more. Bess wondered wryly what aunt Hamilton's reaction would be if she knew the true story of Tib's death—which she was determined to avenge. But for all of her and Drew's care in listening to what was said—and half-said—they were no nearer to solving the mystery.

No matter. Patience was all, and to soothe her troubled spirit she decided that when she next met Philip she would ask him to read some of his latest poetry to her.

Yet the mystery might be nearer to being solved than she thought.

Later that afternoon, alone in his room—for Bess had finally snared Philip and was seated in the open at the back of the Hall, gilded by the sun and listening to his latest poem—Drew stared at the courier's satchel which he hoped would give up his secrets to him.

By pure chance—that chance of which Machiavelli had often written, and which the gods were said to favour mere mortals with—he had been in the stableyard when the courier had arrived from London.

It had been the easiest thing in the world to take the heavy satchel from him and declared that he would deliver it to Charles, whilst the courier refreshed himself in the kitchen after his long ride north. But Charles, out somewhere in the grounds, would have to wait until his master had inspected the satchel himself.

Drew began to loosen the buckles of the bag. It was full of letters and papers which he carefully removed before inspecting an inner pocket which was sewn into one of the bag's sides.

It was fastened by a button which Drew undid before putting his hand inside to find—nothing.

Nothing, it seemed, was straightforward in this Machiavellian game in which Sir Francis Walsingham had ensnared him. Of course, an almost open pocket which the courier—or anyone else—could easily inspect, would not carry a secret letter. It must be elsewhere—but where?

At the bottom of the pocket was a piece of fine linen, a lace-edged kerchief. Drew pulled it out and felt it carefully. Nothing.

Disappointment rode on his shoulders. He put his hand

deep into the pocket and felt around it carefully before examining the outside of the satchel again. To notice something odd about it. The external stitching of the pocket continued to the bottom of the satchel, but the pocket he had been examining stopped halfway down it.

There must be a pocket beneath the obvious one—but how would one open it? Drew ran his fingers carefully along the pocket's bottom. Its seams were thick. Inspiration struck. He pulled one of the seams back a little and found three tiny buttons set between the seam and the bag's side. He undid them carefully to reveal a long thin opening, inside which a sheet of paper lay.

It was the secret letter contained in a version of what was commonly called a poacher's pouch.

He had started well, but his task was only half done. The letter must be copied, and carefully replaced before he passed the bag on to Charles with some witless joke to the effect that he was becoming one of his own servants these days, but the poor devil of a courier had looked quite done up, so he had saved him the stairs.

Again he considered telling Charles of what was passing, but he remembered what Captain Goreham had said to him of the wisdom of Sir Francis Walsingham in playing his cards close to his chest by telling as few as possible of his suspicions—or his knowledge—and desisted.

I am become a true intelligencer, Drew thought wryly when, later, after copying the letter and replacing it, he joined Philip and Bess beneath the trees and laughed and talked with them and promised to take Bess to see Wilton, Philip's beautiful home, before the summer was over if their circumstances allowed.

But he did not fool Bess. As he had walked towards them she had, for a brief moment, espied a hagged look on his face, but at the sight of her it had vanished as though it had never been.

Whether Philip had seen it or no, he ceased to read the poem he had embarked on, and welcomed Drew as he sat down on a grassy bank facing them.

Drew waved an idle hand. 'Continue, Philip. I would hear your latest tropes.'

Philip obeyed. His beautiful voice soothed both Bess and Drew as he spoke of requited and unrequited love. So absorbed were they both that the arrival of Sir Henry and the Lady Arbell went unnoticed. They sat by Drew until, on Philip pausing for breath, Arbell interrupted him to exclaim, 'Oh, fine, oh, passing fine, Master Sidney.'

'Even finer, madam,' remarked Bess coldly, unable to stomach the sight of the woman who must have stood by and allowed Tib to be murdered—and then said nothing, 'if you had waited until Master Sidney had finished his poem!'

'Oh, had you not done so? Pray accept my apologies, sir, and continue.' This was said with a gracious simper as though she was conferring on the poet a favour of the greatest magnitude.

Still seething, Bess welcomed the sight of Charles arriving. He, at least, sat down quietly beside the Lady Arbell, and allowed Philip to finish before joining in the general applause when he did so.

'Bravo, Master Sidney,' was Sir Henry's contribution, echoed by the rest of the party, including Charles who asked for another verse to be read, if the poet had another with him, that was.

Arbell's simper became a pout. Listening to poetry was not her notion of a pleasant way of passing an afternoon. She placed a light, proprietory hand on Charles's knee. 'Come, Master Breton, your admiration of the

Muse does you credit, but I have had sufficient of sitting about. Perhaps you would do me the honour of taking a turn about the garden with me.'

Something about Arbell's familiar manner to Charles, and his easy acceptance of it, grated on Bess. Which was perhaps, she thought wryly, not surprising since nearly everything the lady did grated on her.

Charles, apparently her admirer, like all the other men in Buxton, sprang to his feet and obeyed her command with 'You will allow?' to Sir Henry, who waved a complaisant hand at him, apparently pleased that every man below the age of sixty admired his wife.

Which made it all the more difficult to decide precisely which one had been with her in the temple!

Their going broke up the party. Drew, his copy of the letter burning a hole in his pocket, excused himself from escorting Bess back to the house, leaving Philip to do so. He strode off in urgent search of Captain Goreham with whom he said that he had business, watched by a puzzled Bess.

Yes, there was something afoot, no doubt about it, something which had Drew making an unlikely confidant of the Captain. But Drew was not telling her what it was. She was so intrigued by this new mystery that she scarcely heard a word Philip spoke to her. When she reached her room she bade him farewell most absently in a manner not at all like her usual effervescent self, so that Philip began to wonder what was wrong with *her*!

Still musing, Bess walked over to the window which overlooked the grounds, to see Drew talking intimately to Captain Goreham. Stranger and stranger, particularly when he took the Captain by the arm in a familiar way and walked him away from the house, out of sight of its windows. Towards the butts, she supposed. But he had not taken his bow with him, nor any attendants, so he could scarcely be about to challenge the Captain to yet another match.

Almost before they had disappeared into the trees Charles now came into view, escorting Arbell, and talking animatedly to her—yet another poor fish whom she had hooked and was drawing in, no doubt.

The oddness about them which had troubled Bess earlier, troubled her again. They were plainly about to part when Arbell said something at which Charles laughed, bowed his head and took her hand—to kiss it most reverently. Before he could lift his head again, Arbell leaned forward and carelessly ruffled his hair. He caught the caressing hand and kissed it again, passionately not reverently, his eyes hard on the face of the woman before him.

The hairs on the back of Bess's head stood on end. There was something so revealing in the little scene before her that it was apparent that this was not the first occasion on which they had exchanged similar intimacies. It was as though a flash of lightning, arcing in the dark, had displayed before her, not the landscape which she had always known, but one so different that all her understanding of the world about her was completely altered.

Not Charles! No, it could not have been Charles who had killed poor Tib! But, yes, there was little doubt that Charles was Arbell's lover. A thousand small things, half-seen, half-heard and half-understood, told Bess that she was not wrong in that assumption. She had believed from the moment that she had heard Tib's last words that Arbell's secret lover had killed Tib, but did that mean that, if Charles was Arbell's lover, *he* had necessarily done so? She could well have more than one.

Which was unlikely. Given the open circumstances of their life at Buxton, to run one secret lover demanded the powers of a Machiavelli—to run several would be impossible.

Her next problem was a grave one. How to tell Drew? She had no real evidence of Charles's guilt, and Charles was the cousin with whom he had been brought up, and who was his closest, nearest friend.

Yet the more Bess thought it over, the more convinced she became that Charles *was* Arbell's secret lover and therefore, inevitably, Tib's murderer. He had not gone on the deer hunt, but had asked to stay behind—to tryst with Arbell in the temple, no doubt. But why had it been necessary to kill Tib? Surely no one would be very surprised or shocked to learn that Arbell had a lover— even Sir Henry didn't seem to care greatly whether his wife was faithful to him or not.

Whilst she was worrying over these new and painful thoughts, Charles and Arbell had walked out of her line of sight. She was left to wait for Drew's return when she must decide whether she ought to tell him of her suspicions.

Drew was wrestling with his own suspicions. Once they were out of the sight of the house, he had handed to Captain Goreham the copy of the letter from the satchel. The Captain had grunted after giving it a quick cursory glance.

'I need more time to examine it,' he had said, 'although it's written in a simple code. But from what I can see it tells us nothing that we do not already know. Only that the conspirators are urged to continue, and that, at the appropriate moment, the French will provide them with aid. There's mention of a possible attack on Queen Elizabeth—but no names, and no dates. We shall have to keep this correspondence going in order to learn who is involved—and we must continue to keep careful watch on the Lady Arbell.'

So, if Drew had hoped that the letter might reveal his innocence and bring the whole affair to a conclusion he had been mistaken! They were no further on.

'And you still have not yet discovered the name of the Lady Arbell's lover?'

Drew had shaken his head. 'As I gather you have not?'

It was the Captain's turn to shake *his* head, saying, 'I think that you are in a better position to discover that than I am.'

Which was a damned ambiguous statement, and left it open that the Captain might still consider Drew to be the guilty party!

Altogether he was not in the best of tempers when he joined Bess again, and the sight of her worried face served to depress him even further. 'What is it, wife?' he asked. 'What new horrors have you for me?'

'Do you read me so easily?' Bess shook her head. 'Nay, Drew, that is not important. I hardly know how to tell you what is important.'

She sat down, her face away from him. Improbably, there had been tears in her voice. She could feel them and Drew could hear them.

He sat down beside her on the settle. 'Nay, sweeting, do not cry. I know that Tib's death has overset you, but it is not like my brave girl to go on grieving for what may not be mended.'

Bess pulled her handkerchief from the purse at her girdle and wiped her eyes with it. 'No, Drew, it's not that. I hardly know how to tell you of my suspicions because I have no real evidence to offer for them. But tell you I must. It has been borne in upon me by their behaviour that Arbell's lover is none other than your cousin Charles!'

Drew sprang to his feet. 'No, never. I would as lief suspect myself!'

Bess could not help it. She, who never cried, now began to cry in earnest. 'There,' she said through her sobs, 'I knew that I should have kept quiet. But, oh, husband, the feeling is so strong and grows stronger. So strong that I had to tell you of it. If you think me wrong, or mistaken, you must forget what I have said.'

Drew stared down at her. Not long since he had been admiring her courage, her resilience and—face it, Drew—her cleverness. Why had he denied what she had told him with such speed? Why had he answered in a manner which precluded further discussion? Was it because, if one looked at it coolly and logically, the person most likely to be the one who placed the letter going to London in the satchel, and took out the one coming from London, must be no other than his cousin Charles?

Was that the explanation for his own recent ill humour with the world? He had been enraged that the Captain could consider him a traitor. Was he so enraged with himself for thinking that Charles might be the traitor that he refused to contemplate the evidence which showed that he must be? And was that why he was so angry with Bess? Because she had said the unsayable?

He sat down beside her again, put his arm around her shoulders, and kissed all that he could see of her cheek.

'Forgive me, wife, for being overhasty in my answer to you. What is it which makes you think Charles might be Arbell's lover?'

He did not add, And the traitor who is plotting against the Crown, for if Charles was guilty it explained why it had been necessary for him to murder Tib. It also explained why Tib's last words had been of betrayal.

Bess turned her tear-drenched face towards him. 'Everything and nothing,' she said, before telling him what she had seen that afternoon, and had half-sensed on previous occasions.

'You see,' she explained, 'Charles excused himself from going on the hunt—which gave him and Arbell a good opportunity to be together. You, and the rest of the hunt, had scarce time after you had returned to meet her in the temple, pursue an amour with her, and then murder Tib. So, it seemed to me, as doubtless it did to you, that it must have been one of the men who stayed behind who was with her. I cannot believe that it was someone unknown from outside who killed him.'

'Nor I,' said Drew sadly, for the more he thought about it, and the more Bess had told him of her vague inklings which had brought her worries about Arbell and Charles to a head when she had seen them alone together, the more he considered that the most unlikely suspect of all was the most likely.

After all, Charles had every opportunity both to play the traitor and to run the secret correspondence between Nau and the London Embassy. And how many others were involved? Both in his household and outside it?

Drew's face was so grim that Bess put a tentative hand on the arm which had fallen away from her shoulders. 'Drew? What are you thinking? Have I been a complete fool?'

'Alas, I fear not. But you must understand that we have no evidence, no evidence at all, that Arbell and Charles are either guilty lovers, or that Charles killed Tib. We should be laughed at for accusing them on such flimsy evidence. And supposing that we were proved to

be wrong? Charles was my childhood's friend and playmate as Tib was yours. Am I to kill a long-standing love
between us by accusing him of murdering Tib—and then
discover that he was not the murderer at all?'

Oh, dear God, how hard this was. He could not tell
Bess why his suspicions had begun to match hers. He
had kept from her the knowledge of the plot against
Queen Elizabeth and the knowledge that, if Charles was
the traitor, he was not only Arbell's lover, but also her
fellow conspirator, and that by some mischance Tib,
overhearing them talking had had to be killed to
silence him.

Worse than that, if Tib's words about Arbell and
betrayal were true, then it was Charles who was arranging
matters so that he, Drew, appeared to be guilty.

He could understand Bess's tears only too well. He
wanted to scream at the sun and the moon, at the Christian
God and all the gods in the Pantheon, his rage and terror
on learning that the man who was trying to consign him
and Bess to the block on Tower Hill was none other than
his old friend and playmate.

Every camp has its traitor, Walsingham had said,
doubtless believing that he, Drew, was the traitor. Or
did he? Did the wily devil who masterminded Queen
Elizabeth's security know more than he was telling Goreham and himself? Had he, perhaps, chosen Drew to
unmask Charles because it would have been almost
impossible for anyone else to do so?

He tightened his arm about Bess, who had ceased
crying and had turned her head into his chest for comfort.

'What are we to do, then?' she asked him.

'Nothing. Lacking evidence, we can do nothing.'

Which was not quite true, because now he and
Goreham must find evidence by trapping Charles, not

only to prove that Drew was not the traitor, but also because he must avenge Tib's cruel death.

This led him to draw another unhappy conclusion from these latest revelations. Was it possible that Charles had been the man who had shot at him and killed Cicero? But why should he do that? If he wished Drew to be suspected as the traitor, then why kill him? Or was the shot to warn him? But of what?

Mystery upon mystery, and all of them defying logic. There was only one sane thing left in this mad world and that was the woman who lay so confidingly in his arms. The woman whom he had once rejected and who was now the centre of his being.

Chapter Fourteen

What gave him, and his knowledge of the plot against him, away to Charles, Drew never knew. Later he was to ask himself whether it was something he—or perhaps Bess—had said or done. Or was it Captain Goreham, who had known it was Charles all the time, and who had hinted of it to him, in order to force an ending to the matter? Drew thought not, for Goreham's instructions were to the contrary. Sir Francis wished to keep the plot in motion.

On the surface, indeed, everything went on as before. The three of them, Drew, Bess and Charles, Philip sometimes with them, patronised the Baths, drank water from the Holy Well and practised at the butts. Bess even brought herself to speak civilly to Arbell, to play at *Troule in Madame* with her as though Tib had not died and her and Charles's treachery was unknown.

Philip Sidney, indeed, was the only person to note that something ailed Drew and he bearded him about it. To be told shortly that he 'was over-exercising his poetic imagination' annoyed him more than a little, for Philip was emerging from his prolonged state of calm melancholy into that of fervid excitement in which he found difficulty controlling the hot temper which went with it. He had been subject to these mood swings from childhood.

It was Charles who was agitated. He had need to be, for although Drew had replaced the letter most carefully in the satchel's hidden pocket, on fetching it out, once he was alone, Charles had had the strangest sensation that someone had been there before him.

The Bible says that the wicked flee when no man pursueth. Charles was being pursued, but did not know it, and wished to flee all the same. Ever since he had killed Tib, his guilt had begun to haunt him. On the spur of the moment fear of what Tib might have overheard had driven him to commit murder, but he had regretted his hasty action ever since, for as a result he lived in the shadow of an even greater fear.

The fear of being revealed not only as a murderer but as a traitor. Every word spoken to him seemed to carry a hidden, hideous, meaning. Every joke, every sidelong glance, seemed to say to him, Thou art the man. He knew how Cain felt after he had killed Abel, and his self-love had turned to self-loathing.

Down in the stables, after his fit of unreasoning fear over the letter, he met the courier who was helping Walter with the horses. Fear had him saying abruptly, 'Come here, man. I know that you were attacked on the way to London, and lucky you were to survive it, but was there aught amiss on your return journey? Did anyone try to stop you? Did anyone but yourself handle the satchel you carried?'

A little bewildered, the man stared at him. 'No, sir. Nothing untoward at all. No man but myself touched the satchel until I reached Buxton when m'lord himself took it from me. Most particular he was that I should give it to him for safekeeping so that he might hand it directly to you.'

So, Drew had been 'most particular,' had he? And why was that? It was not in Drew's habit to act as a messenger boy. The black imp which had sat on Charles's right shoulder since that dreadful afternoon when he had murdered Tib, whispered in his ear, 'And why should Drew be "most particular"? Is it possible that he suspects something?

But if so, why and how? Had any other of Drew's habits changed recently? The imp whispered, What of his friendship with Captain Goreham? Well, what of it? Simply that, first of all, he had plainly detested the man, but, quite suddenly, his manner to him had changed, and he had become friendly—if not intimate—with him. But why not? After all, the Captain had helped him home again after the abortive attempt on his life.

And only Charles knew that it had not been an attempt on Drew's life at all. Instead, in a fit of anger that fate had given everything to Drew, and nothing to him, he had on an impulse shot to kill Cicero. At worst, he was destroying something which Drew loved, at best Drew might have broken his neck when the horse, in falling, brought him down, too.

The imp grumbled at him all the way back to his room. It muttered, You are forgetting something important. Drew must have done something which might throw light on why he should suspect you.

Oh, be damned! He was no Walsingham, to be seeing plots everywhere.

Walsingham! That was it. Drew had visited Walsingham before he had decided to go north to see his wife. He had even told him that his real reason for going north at all was to visit Buxton, which he had often longed to see.

And be damned to that, too! Drew, he uncharitably thought, was hardly the kind of world-weary grandee who needed to refresh his ageing mind and body by drinking stinking water in a damned dreary village! Never mind that it had suited him to have Drew there. He had even remonstrated with him a little, saying that the place would bore him, which statement, to Charles's great relief, Drew had dismissed with a laugh.

And it was Walsingham who had invited Drew to supper, not the other way round. And Walsingham was the Queen's spymaster.

Nothing for it now but to test Drew. To listen most carefully to him, and alas, to his wife—whom Drew did not deserve. And also to voice his suspicions to Arbell.

Neither Bess nor Drew was sleeping well. Soon after she had told him of her suspicions, Bess had awoken shortly after midnight one morning to find herself alone in bed. She sat up and looked about her.

Drew was standing in the window, with his back to her. He had parted the heavy curtains so that the moonlight shone on him, gilding his hair. He was motionless, one hand holding the curtain. His whole stiff posture told of his distress

Bess slipped silently from the bed and walked to his side to take the lax hand which was not holding the curtain. 'What is it, Drew? Are you finding sleep difficult, too?'

As though her words had broken some spell which was holding him in thrall, he turned to take her in his arms, burying his head in her soft bosom after a fashion which was almost childlike. It was, Bess knew without being told, the posture of every babe seeking comfort from its mother.

'Oh, Bess,' he said, his voice muffled, 'simply to touch you gives me ease, and that is why I have been standing here, debating with myself. For there is something which I know that you do not, and which I have now persuaded myself that you should. I have been trying to shield you from the evil deeds of the wicked world, but I know that I have married a strong woman, and so I will share my burden with you. You may even be safer if I do.'

What in the world was he about to say? Bess stroked his head gently. 'Do not tell me if it distresses you. I have every faith in your judgment.'

Drew looked up at her, his eyes tender. 'And I in yours.' He took a deep breath, and without further ado told her of Charles and his treachery, and his involvement with Walsingham and Captain Goreham.

He ended by saying to her with the most passionate conviction, 'From now on you must be even more careful than you have been. To share such knowledge with me is to share the danger which I am in.'

Bess was silent when he had finished. 'Alas, that explains what Tib was trying to tell me. I am glad that you have confided in me. You should not have to bear this burden alone—whatever danger it puts me in.'

In one passionate movement Drew stood up and lifted her into his arms. 'You are my treasure,' he told her hoarsely, 'and had not Walsingham asked me to go to Buxton I should never have met you, never have known you. Oh, Bess, you are my heart's darling, the other half of myself whom I never hoped to meet. You are the only good thing to have come out of this tangled mess.'

Kissing and petting her, he carried her to the bed. This was neither the time nor the place to discuss the meat of what he had told her. Rather, Bess thought, before thought ceased altogether in the throes of their mutual passion, it was the time to give him surcease from the pain which Charles's treachery was causing him.

But he, and his treachery, had to be faced, and at the same time life had to go on. Drew had made it plain to Bess that her life, as well as his, lay in the balance if he could not unmask Charles and present Captain Goreham with enough proof to convince him of their innocence. He had urged Bess to caution, bidden her to take no risks, but he had privately conceded that, strong-willed as she was, she might dare to do and say more than he thought wise.

He was right. The very next morning Bess confronted the Captain. 'You are a bigger fool than I took you for,' she said bluntly, 'if you think that my husband could ever be a traitor.'

Captain Goreham could not have been more surprised if a pet rabbit had bitten him. He gave a short laugh. 'Oh, I honour a woman who supports her husband, dear Lady Exford, but do admit it, it takes more than a wife's word to convince a court of his innocence.'

'Nothing to that,' retorted Bess spiritedly, 'for you know that my husband could not have killed Tib and that Charles Breton most certainly did.'

'There is that,' the Captain agreed, 'and perhaps you could now tell *me* exactly what the poor young man said to you when you and Master Sidney found him.'

'Assuredly,' and presently they were engaged in as eager a tête-à-tête as he and Drew had shared. The Captain tactfully complimented Bess on her memory and on her *savoir-faire* when she had found her playmate dying.

'Well, I shouldn't have been much use to him if I had engaged in a fit of the vapours or fainted, or done something equally stupid.'

'Exactly so, m'lady. I see that your husband is coming in search of you. Need I tell you that whatever is said between the three of us over this sad matter must remain a secret?'

'I am not a fool, sir. And I must tell you that my eye will now be secretly upon the Lady Arbell and all her doings. One false step and I shall loose you at her throat!'

A spirited lady, indeed, was Drew's seemingly demure young wife. The Captain briefly envied him his bedmate. In his experience, high spirits in one area of life were like to be found in another!

'So, wife, I looked for you in our room to be told that you were gone, and behold, I find you dallying with the Captain. Go to, you should be dallying with me!'

M'lord Exford's voice was jovial, but the look he gave the Captain was a hard one, and probing. The Captain knew why the look was there.

'No dallying. M'lady and I were speaking of matters of state. Was not that so, madam?'

Before Bess could answer him, Drew was speaking again. 'I thought, wife, that I had advised you to speak of matters of state to no one but myself.'

This time it was the Captain's answer which was forestalled. 'Why, husband,' Bess said, her face aglow, 'I thought that for me to listen to the opinions of a fresh mind on the subject would be most useful.'

'And useful to me also,' added the Captain. 'For it was most enlightening to hear from m'lady's own lips the last words of her unfortunate servant.'

'I can think of two other people who might be unfortunate if I had my way,' growled Drew, 'and neither of them is above ten paces from me.'

The Captain took him by the sleeve in the most familiar manner. 'Come, m'lord, seeing that m'lady has been involved in this wretched business by accident and by her ability to read the minds and acts of others correctly, there is no way in which she can be returned to her previous situation of fortunate ignorance. That being so, it would be stupid for us not to take advantage of her abilities. By doing so, she will be in no more, and no less, danger.'

'So you say.' Bess was fascinated to note that Drew was still growling. 'But seeing that we are about to be discovered, I will say nothing further to either of you. At present, that is. Later, why, later, will be quite another matter.'

They were being approached by the Lady Arbell, who was escorted by the two squires, Masters Blagg and Bown. Sir Henry was in the rear, attended by Claude Nau and Charles. Charles, on seeing Drew, exclaimed cheerully, 'Oh, there you are, cousin. I have received two letters this morning, both by special messenger and both of which need your urgent attention.'

'Not so urgent that they cannot wait upon my pleasure.' Drew's annoyance with Bess for involving herself with Goreham still held him in thrall and was making him short with everyone.

She had no business putting herself at risk, none at all, and that coarse schemer, Goreham, had no business to be taking advantage of her ignorance of the danger in which she might be.

'Come, wife,' he said, seizing her by the hand and half-dragging her away, 'I have a mind to refresh myself in the Baths. I will do the honours with you all later. Until then, adieu.'

Exeunt left, m'lord and m'lady Exford, he thought grimly, remembering the plays and masques he had seen when he had been at Oxford University with Philip Sidney, as he walked Bess rapidly away.

'Now what bee has lodged itself in his bonnet?' queried Arbell, her brows raised as she watched the pair of them disappear rapidly from sight. Two people were not surprised. They were an amused Captain Goreham and an alarmed Charles Breton.

So, thought the Captain, m'lord Exford's Achilles' heel is his clever young wife: that is a thing to remember, whilst Charles concluded bitterly that Drew's odd conduct was one more piece of evidence to lead him to conclude that Drew was suspicious of him and that it was affecting his behaviour.

As Bess, tactlessly, was busy warning Drew once they were safely out of sight of the others. 'What ails you, husband, to be so short with everyone? You are in danger of starting your fox by warning him that the hounds are after him.'

Without letting go of her hand, Drew stopped short suddenly, so suddenly that Bess almost fell over.

'I will tell you what is wrong, madam wife. It is wrong that you should run to the Captain at the first opportunity and begin to meddle in this matter, something I most expressly told you that you were not to do! *That* is what is wrong.'

Bess gave him her most wounded stare. 'You forget, husband, that it was I who alerted you to the possibility of Charles's treachery and that, being your wife, I am thus in as much danger of ending up on the block on Tower Hill as you are. Since I assume that the Captain had feared that you might be the traitor, I assured him most solemnly that you were not.'

'A most valuable ploy, wife, seeing that a wife's word about her husband has no force in law.'

'But Captain Goreham is not the law. . .'

Her face was so rosy and indignant, so alight with a combination of love and determination, that Drew was quite overset. He gave a little cry of thwarted indignation mixed with lust, and pushing her into the shade of a small dell, sheltered from observation, he bore her to the ground.

'Is this the only way in which I can silence you, madam?' he groaned at her, stopping her mouth with a kiss.

Bess struggled her mouth free, 'I will not be silenced. . .' she began, then, as Drew began to pull her skirts up, 'No, no, we shall be seen. Drew, think where we are, what you are doing.'

'I *am* thinking of what I am doing. I am pleasuring a naughty wife and silencing her—if only for the time that I am doing so! And if you keep quiet whilst I am about this happy business, no one will know that we are here because no one will be able to see or hear us.'

It was impossible to try to prevent him. He had but to touch her and she was on fire. And, despite what she had said, he had been right when he had said that they were not likely to be seen. But to keep quiet when all her senses were alive and thrilling was almost impossible. And when she reached climax and opened her mouth to shout her joy, his hand was over it, silencing her—so she bit him. Not hard, but enough to break the skin slightly.

Drew reared up, and hissed at her after he had inspected his damaged thumb. 'Vixen! I shall punish you for that this night when we are quite alone.' But he was laughing quietly after he spoke, all his recent ill humour gone, whilst Bess, happy that he was not irredeemably angry with her, began to laugh too, her head in his chest to muffle the noise she was making.

Sitting up, they clung to one another as they heard the party which they had left behind them walk past their hiding place. Arbell was trilling, the Captain was booming, and Charles's light baritone was acting as counterpoint to him.

'And now to the Baths, else I am foresworn,' laughed Drew, watching Bess set herself to rights again. 'But confess, wife, love in the open is a fine thing.'

'Not so very open,' retorted Bess saucily. 'Another day we must go alone to the hills and play at nymphs and shepherds there—when all is safe again, that is.'

'Aye, if that happy day ever arrives.'

Which was a sombre note on which to end, but as Bess said to him when they walked sedately along to the Baths, 'We are not really nymphs and shepherds but, like the lovers in Philip's poems, we may pretend to be—if only for a short time.'

Charles, despite his outward calm, was in ferment. He was sure that Drew knew of his treachery, and sure also that Captain Goreham had a hand in the game. There was something present in Drew's eye when he spoke to him, as well as something lacking in his voice. The quiet confidence which had always lain between them had been shattered.

The only question was, How soon would Drew move against him? That question haunted him. If Drew had discovered the secret compartment and the strange letter in it, one way of allaying his suspicions might be to ensure that when the satchel went south again in a few days time, the compartment was empty. But Arbell had already told him that Nau would have another letter ready before it left.

That letter must be stopped, and the only way to ensure that it was, must be to tell her that for their own safety's sake it would be necessary for it to be held back for the time being. So sure was he that he—and possibly Arbell as well—was being watched that, meeting her by chance in the Baths on the day before the courier was due to leave, he asked that they might meet privily for he had something urgent to tell her.

'Privily, sir? Why privily? Ah, I see you mean in the little temple.'

Charles shuddered. 'God forbid.' The place was anathema to him—how could she make such an insensitive suggestion? Had she no remorse? No feeling for the poor dead boy? And what a hypocrite he was to mourn over having killed Tib when he was so busy trying to consign his cousin to a brutal death!

But all he said was, 'No, not there. I have reason to believe that we are being watched. This afternoon, let us ride separately and secretly to the hills above Buxton, for I have somewhat to tell you that might alter all our plans.'

The Lady's beautiful eyebrows arched in surprise. 'How so? Our enterprise has gone well so far—save for the unfortunate episode of which you know. But if it will make you happy, then I will give way. Although I shall find it difficult to ride out without an escort.'

'This afternoon, then, at two of the clock, at the Holm oak beyond the brow of the hill where the footpath forks. We shall not be seen from the village.'

She was late, of course. She would be, would she not? The festering anger with which Charles was beginning to view life was ready to transfer itself to Arbell. Particularly when she rode into his view and he saw that she was accompanied by that complaisant and cuckolded clown, her husband.

Charles tethered his horse to a tree and walked towards her, his face thunderous. It was not until he was near to her that that he saw that she looked rather less than her usual haughty and impudent self. She also read his angry face correctly, and began with an uncharacteristically nervous rush of words. 'My husband, I must now confess, is party to our enterprise and has insisted that he accompany me.'

This put a totally different complexion on things. When Arbell had recruited him earlier in the year, having become aware of his dissatisfaction with his life with Drew, and also that he had secret hankerings after the restoration of the Catholic faith, she had said nothing of her husband's involvement and much of her recluse brother's.

Did she ever speak the truth? Sir Henry, who had also dismounted, waved a hand to silence her for she would have continued. He stared Charles coldly down.

'You have matters of urgency to tell me relating to our noble enterprise, Master Breton. Pray speak on, my time is valuable.'

He was quite unlike the amiable fool and nonentity whom the world thought it knew. Charles began slowly, 'The Lady Arbell. . .'

Sir Henry waved a contemptuous hand. 'Oh, we have no time for that—or her. Arbell, my dear, pray ride a little way into the nearest copse and admire the scenery from there. I would talk privately with Master Breton.'

He smiled at Charles. 'She has been a useful—and pleasant—go-between, you will allow.'

Oh, he had been roundly tricked into this murky

business, had he not? It was becoming plain to Charles that he had been bought with Arbell's body. But there was no time to think of that. He had to consider instead his own safety, and theirs.

'He suspects,' Charles said slowly. 'My cousin Drew suspects that I am involved in the plot on behalf of the Queen of Scots and may even know that I killed his wretched servant.'

Sir Henry said dispassionately, 'And a careless fool you were to put yourself in the way of being vulnerable to such an underling. For once I have not chosen my tool well. What, may I ask, makes you believe that you are blown?'

'I have no direct evidence, but I am sure of it. I have come to ask that the letter from Nau to our allies in London shall not go south in the Exford courier's satchel. If it does I believe that my cousin will intercept it, read it, and send it on, thus enabling Walsingham to monitor our doings and prove that he is innocent of wrongdoing when one of our aims was to implicate him if the correspondence was discovered.'

'*Our* aims, Master Breton? *Our* aims? You are mistaken. That was *your* aim, and yours alone. *I* am not interested in Exford's fate or future.'

Charles's face was ghastly. 'You have tricked me. . .'

Sir Henry smiled sweetly at him. 'No, no, sir, you tricked yourself. And the letter will go south to London. I order it so done.'

'Then I shall not obey you.'

'How fortunate that I discover your cowardly folly thus early on in this great enterprise,' said Sir Henry, still sweet, 'for I can dispose of you as neatly as you killed that poor fool of Exford's—and with less chance of discovery.'

He had moved closer and closer to Charles, until, on his last words, he drove the dagger he had taken from his belt into Charles after the same fashion as Charles had despatched Tib.

Without a sound Charles fell forward. Sir Henry stared down at him. 'A pity,' he said to himself, 'that that had to be done, but necessary. Now to dispose of the evidence.

Arbell had not dismounted. She had found a small plateau from which there was a view away from Buxton and she rode round and about it until Sir Henry, leading Charles's horse and riding his own, came into view again.

'Where is Charles?' she asked, her face fearful.

'Now that, my dear, you do not need to know. Suffice it that he will not be returning to Buxton and that we shall need to use another messenger. He had grown fearful and tiresome, and therefore dangerous.'

He paused. 'You are sure that no one knew that you were meeting him here?'

'Quite sure—but his disappearance will be most remarked on. He is, after all, not a nobody of a groom, but a Breton and an Earl's cousin.'

'Oh, my dear, think nothing of that. Remember, Exford has been shot at, the groom was killed, and all, you must understand, by the disaffected who roam these parts, who frequent the hills and the woods looking for victims to kill and rob. They have grown bolder of late, one must admit. Now we will loose his horse—to gallop home riderless, and puzzle everyone.'

'But the letter? With Charles gone, how shall that be sent south?'

'No matter. I have another who will do the business as well as yon poor fool. In these enterprises one must always be ready to change one's plans.'

Arbell stared at the husband whom everyone believed
to be her dupe, when the matter was quite otherwise. Oh,
he thought of everything, did he not? And disposed of
everyone who stood in his way. Now and in the past. It
did not do to ask how two of his older brothers had died
in accidents before him and he had inherited all. His
pretence of being a kindly, bumbling cuckold had been
the ploy of a cunning man who had allowed his wife to
betray him only with those he wanted to use. It also
allowed those whom he wished to betray to underesti-
mate—nay—to pity him.

For the first time Arbell, who was not quite so stupid
as she seemed, asked herself a question. How safe am I
if he comes to think that I stand in his way? Thinking
this, she sniffled miserably all the way back to Buxton.
But it was for herself that she grieved, not Charles.

Halfway down the cliff from which Sir Henry had thrown
him, caught on bushes before he had reached the ground,
still alive and still hoping to be saved, Charles prayed
for deliverance from the nightmare which his life had
become, but not a deliverance which would end in
his death.

He could hear woodsmen far below him, felling trees,
and began to shout feebly in the hope that he might yet
be saved. . .

Chapter Fifteen

'**D**rew?'

'My love?'

Bess decided that she would be daring. After all, she had nothing to lose. 'When this is over, may we go back to Atherington? We could enjoy ourselves there, nearly as well as we have done this afternoon.'

Drew looked over to where she sat, looking out of the latticed bedroom window towards the hills.

'No baths?' he suggested naughtily.

'What? Oh, you mean that we have no baths at Atherington. But there is a lake but half a mile from the house. We could take our pleasure there.'

'So we could. And if you look at me like that, wife, I shall take my pleasure now—and yours, I hope. But I dare not since I have been expecting Charles's arrival this last hour.' He frowned. 'It is not like him to be behind time. I trust. . .' He fell silent.

'Yes?'

'I trust that he has not discovered that we suspect him. His manner to me has been most constrained these last few days.'

'The bell will chime for supper shortly,' Bess said

somewhat slyly. 'He will be sure to be there for that, and you may speak to him then.'

But he wasn't. And it was as they were leaving after one of Lord Shrewbury's less interesting meals that Walter, the Great Hall's chief groom, came up to them, his face grave.

'I would, if you please, have a word with you alone, m'lord.'

Drew was about to reply that anything which Walter had to tell him could be said before his wife, when something in Walter's steady look stopped him.

'Forgive me, wife, if I ask you to go to your room. I will join you there later.'

Walter waited to speak until Bess was out of earshot. 'It's Master Breton, m'lord. I fear that some accident may have befallen him. He took his horse out when the tower clock chimed two, and rode off towards the hills without a groom and never returned. But—and this is the troublesome part, m'lord—at the hour of five by that same clock, his riderless horse returned, all of a lather.'

'And no sign of Master Breton?' Which was a stupid question, Drew owned, but was forced from him by the serious nature of Walter's story.

'None, m'lord. But, knowing that an unknown marksman had made you a target, I took the liberty of sending two of the grooms into the hills to look where I knew he might have ridden by the direction he took. They are not back yet, but I must humbly urge you to send another party out in the opposite direction as soon as maybe.'

'Do that, Walter. I will come to the yard myself. Was there anyone with you when Master Breton set out?'

'Only one of the lads, Jem by name.'

Drew thought a moment. Charles, the potential traitor and the possible murderer of young Tib, was now missing himself. Which could mean that he, Bess and the Captain were mistaken as to his treachery. . .but he thought not.

He followed Walter to the yard where the boy Jem was caring for Charles's spent horse. 'Tell me, lad,' he ordered, still abrupt—Walter thought that he had never seen m'lord so disturbed—'did anyone join Master Breton when he rode out.'

'Nay, m'lord. I watched him ride off towards the hills. He was quite alone.'

'Nor did anyone follow him?'

'Not in my sight, m'lord, no.'

Drew looked around at the grooms and servitors of Lord Shrewsbury's other guests. Philip had just ridden in, late for supper, and on seeing Drew, he dismounted and walked over to him.

'What's amiss?' he asked. 'You look troubled.'

Drew told him. 'And it seems that he was alone. Jem here says he rode towards the hills.'

Philip frowned and said idly, 'He was not the only one. What time did he leave?'

Walter told him. 'Hmm.' Philip thought for a moment. 'It must have been some short time later that I saw Sir Henry and his wife set off in that direction. Best ask if they caught a glimpse of him.'

'Arbell? The Lady Arbell set off in that direction?' Drew was so eager that Philip stared at him.

'Aye, with her husband,' he repeated.

'I shall question them forthwith. And you, Walter, send out another party and let me know immediately if there is any news.'

He swung round. 'Forgive me, Philip, if I leave you on the instant but I must away. Some accident has befallen him, and the sooner we order things so that he might be recovered, the better.'

He found Sir Henry and his wife in the Great Parlour next to the dining hall, Bess was with them. It seemed that they had stopped her on the way to her room and asked her to join them in a jug of mulled wine. Arbell was, for once, being civil to Bess. Drew was not civil to any of them.

He interrupted Arbell's long-winded welcoming of him by waving a hand at her. 'No time for that. My cousin Charles went riding early this afternoon into the hills. He has not returned but his horse has—riderless. Some accident must have befallen him. Philip Sidney believes that you might have seen in which direction he went since you set out shortly after him. . .'

He got no further. The Lady Arbell gave a strangled cry and covered her face with a fine lace-bordered handkerchief, emerging from it long enough to say, 'Oh, no, not another terrible mishap after your's and that poor boy's—I forget his name.'

'Tib,' Bess reminded her sharply. 'His name was Tib.' She was not in the least deceived by Arbell's meretricious goings-on. She would have been equally overset if she had spilt wine down her elaborate gown. 'And did Charles take no groom with him after all he said to you about the folly of riding out alone?' she asked Drew.

Bess could plainly see that this aspect of the matter had not struck him before.

'I had not thought of that,' he replied. And, indeed, it suggested to him immediately that Charles might have set off on an errand to meet someone in secret. Someone whom he did not wish his groom to know of.

Bess meantime watched Sir Henry clumsily comforting his wife in his usual kind manner. 'There, there, my dear, we must hope that his horse threw him, and that he will be found safe and sound.'

To no avail. Arbell continued to sob bitterly, shedding the mock tears for Charles which she had not offered Tib, being Bess's cynical thought. Yet when her husband neglected her for a moment to ask Drew grave questions about search parties, and she dropped her handkerchief again, Bess was surprised to see that she had been weeping real tears, not the pretend ones which she usually went in for.

Another unwelcome thought struck her. If she and Drew were right, Arbell knew of Tib's murder even if she had not actually watched the deed being done, and now here she was, placed not far from Charles before he disappeared. This was either an unfortunate coincidence, or something worse. But surely Arbell couldn't have killed Charles, or engineered his death, could she? No, it was her tongue that was long and strong, not her body.

Further thought was stopped by Arbell suddenly descending, or ascending, Bess was not sure which, into real hysterics. Aunt Hamilton, who had been hovering whilst all this was going on, looked reproachfully at the men for talking so frankly of death or injury before the women. She put an arm around Arbell and said comfortingly, 'Let me help you to your room, my dear. We are not needed here.'

She seemed to be asking for Bess to help her with the stricken Arbell, but Bess shook her head. She felt that she needed to speak to Drew at once, if not sooner.

'Oh, you do not need me, Aunt. See, here is Arbell's woman. Drew may need comforting, too. After all, Charles is his cousin.'

Sir Henry, beneath his outward appearance of loving care, was beginning to be annoyed with Arbell, fearing that she might yet say or do something incriminating, and was only too happy to have her led away to collapse

in private. It was as though what might have happened
to her late lover had only become real to her when Drew
had spoken of his riderless horse.

Once she had been removed, the men, for Philip had
joined them, began to plan how they might yet recover
Charles, either dead or alive, injured or non-injured.
Drew finally took Bess by the arm to lead her to their
room so that he could change into clothes and boots
suitable for riding out himself.

He also knew Bess well enough to be aware that she
was big with something which she wished to tell him in
private!

'Drew,' she said breathlessly the moment that they
were alone. 'Arbell was crying real tears over Charles,
I know she was. She must know that something serious
has happened to him, and that is why she was crying.'

Drew stopped in the middle of pulling on his boots.
'That's a big jump to make, wife, although I give you
that she seemed genuinely distressed.'

'So?' Bess challenged him.

'So, I believe that one of two things occurred. Either
Charles had a genuine accident, nothing to do with any
plot, or else he met someone who is also in the plot
and something went wrong, resulting in Charles disappearing.'

'Well, we do know that Arbell was in the plot, so
perhaps she was meeting Charles.'

Drew stood up. 'But, Bess, can you see Arbell killing
Charles and disposing of his body?'

'No. But think, she was riding out with Sir Henry.
Suppose he was in the plot all the time and it was he
who . . .disposed, as you say, of his body. And that is why
Arbell is so upset. She knows the truth about Charles's
disappearance.'

Drew sat down heavily on the bed. 'You are sure that she was crying real tears?'

'Quite sure.'

'She could have been pretending—and still crying real tears.'

'She has never cried real tears before. I know that because I have been watching her like a hawk ever since I first met her. In the beginning because I thought that either you were already lovers, or that she was determined to seduce you, and later when we suspected that she was with Charles when Tib was murdered.'

What a woman! She was as shrewd as the Queen was said to have been when she was Bess's age. A true Bess, indeed!

'Yes,' he said slowly, 'it make more sense to believe that Sir Henry is running the plot, using Arbell to tempt Charles into helping them, and keeping secretly in touch with Nau and enlisting the other conspirators who are here. They would scarcely follow a woman. We have been thinking of Charles as the leading conspirator. Suppose that he was Sir Henry and Arbell's dupe?'

'And,' said practical Bess, who was not remembering with sorrow, as Drew was, the days when he and Charles had been happy boys together, 'suppose their bait was that they would pretend you were the organiser so that if Sir Francis discovered the plot he would go after you, not them? Charles must have thought that either way he gained. If the plot succeeded, he would be rewarded with your lands and title; if it failed and you were arrested and convicted, he is your nearest relative, even if on your mother's side, and he might gain what was left over after your attainder—since you would leave no heir.'

'True. And if we are right, then whilst Philip and I are searching for Charles, you must go to Captain

Goreham and tell him of our suspicions. And, Bess, remember that they are suspicions only. We have not the slightest scrap of hard evidence which would convince Sir Francis or a High Court of their guilt.'

And so Captain Goreham also told her when she found him. 'No, m'lady, I believe that we may have reached the truth of the matter, but nothing can be done until we have some hard proof, which at the moment is missing. Do you go back to the house and watch the Lady Arbell lest she and her husband commit some action or some folly which might enable me to act. Until then we must bide our time.'

Which was roughly what Drew had said to her. He said it again when he returned from searching for Charles. 'We have not found him,' he told her sadly, for he still had a faint hope that his cousin might not be the traitor he thought him. 'But we have found this,' and he handed to Bess the small gold medallion showing St George killing the dragon which Charles had worn on a chain around his neck.

Bess took it, her own face as distressed as Drew's. 'Where was it?' she asked.

'Caught on a bush, on the edge of the cliff which faces away from Buxton. The odd thing about it was that there was no sign of hoofprints there. Just the faint impression of a pair of boots belonging to a larger and heavier man than Charles.'

He decided to tell her the worst of it. 'There was also the tracks made by a man being dragged along the ground, a man who must have been Charles. We rode to the bottom of the cliff, but there was no sign of him there. Which, all things considered, is passing strange, for he could not have survived the fall. After that we searched around, but could see no other sign of him.

There were some evidence that woodcutters had passed that way, but we could not discover where they had encamped. By then it was growing so dark and the terrain so treacherous, that we decided to return and try again tomorrow.'

He fell silent before bursting out with, 'Oh, Bess, I do not know whether I wish to find him. To do so would help to clear us, but if he were alive, what is his end likely to be—given all that he may have done?'

Bess put her arms around him. 'Oh, Drew, you are magnanimity itself, seeing that he has tried to kill you— and you must remember that he did kill Tib. To that extent he deserves what is coming to him.'

'He was my childhood friend.' Drew's voice was muffled.

'True. And there is the other thing. We now know that it must have been Sir Henry, not Arbell, who dragged him to the cliff and threw him over. She could not possibly have done that. Have you told the other searchers of our suspicions?'

'No, for I remembered Captain Goreham's dictum, "The less said the better."'

He looked so tired that Bess said gently, 'Let's to bed, my love, to sleep. Remember that tomorrow is another day.'

'You are my comforter and my strength,' he muttered into her ear as they lay quietly down, 'and come what may, together we shall face down the world—and bring down Sir Henry and Arbell into the bargain, praise God.'

It was true that the less said the better, but there were those who were shrewd enough to read a puzzle and Philip Sidney was one of them.

Eating his poached eggs at breakfast, the eggs which

the good physician Jones had recommended to those who took the waters, but over which both Philip and Drew had pulled wry faces, Philip remarked, apparently casually, 'Would it be wrong of me to assume that there is rather more to the recent odd events than meets the eye? After all, it is not every day, nor even every month or year, that one hears of an attempt to kill a man—yourself— an actual murder—that of your page—and the disappearance of a man of substance—like your cousin Charles. London itself would be proud of such record of crime over such a short space of time!'

'True,' Drew replied, as, to his profound disgust, egg yolk dribbled down his chin. 'But these things happen.'

'Aye, mayhap. But when they happen in the vicinity of a lady around whom countless plots have been hatched, a man of sense might find himself asking question.'

'True again, but that does not mean that another man of sense might be able or willing to answer them.'

'Oh, that is an answer in itself, is it not?' Philip smiled. 'For were nothing untoward happening you would be willing to speak the truth to me, but seeing that you are not, then I must believe that there is more to all this than mere coincidence, sent by the gods. Take my kerchief, Drew, and use it before the egg yolk leaves your chin and stains your ruff. It is a most devilish stain, very difficult to remove—or so my valet tells me.'

Drew wiped his chin clean, and grumbled, 'You are a damnably persistent fellow, but I am an obstinate one— and that is all that you learn from me.'

'Not even if I tell you that I have reason to know that Sir Henry is a secret Catholic sympathiser and that is why Arbell's relatives allowed him to marry her?'

Bess, sitting on Philip's left, said brightly, 'Goodness, we are serious today, Philip. Must we discuss religion at breakfast? I had much rather not.'

As a ploy to silence Philip this was singularly unsuccessful.

He waved a long-fingered hand at her. 'You are, m'lady, as devious as your husband. Else you would not have watched the Lady Arbell this last week as keenly as a dog watches a rabbit hole, waiting for his prey to appear.'

'Dear me,' said Bess, a trifle mortified, 'was I as obvious as that?'

'No, I doubt whether any others saw. But Drew will tell you that I have more senses than five.'

'Amen to that,' and Drew clapped Philip on the back. 'And will pay for that one day, no doubt. Forgive me, old friend, if I say no more.'

'Indeed—If you will bet with me over whether Master Charles Breton is alive or dead, and that the question of religion, with deference to you, m'lady, is germane to the matter.'

'No, not even with you will I bet on my cousin's life.' Drew threw down Philip's stained kerchief. 'And now I must go to the stables to begin the search for him again. Will you accompany us?'

'And will you ask Sir Henry. . .?' Philip paused significantly.

'Ask him what?'

'Why, whether or no he wishes to join us, what else?'

Philip's smile was so oversweet, Drew thought, that it bordered on the rancid. *He suspects a plot. Why else would he tell me of Sir Henry's secret Catholic leanings? And how many others are beginning to guess the truth? Say what you will, murder and treason smell to high heaven and will not be suppressed.*

He kissed Bess openly, so that all the world might see

that he loved his wife. She was looking pale this morning. The strain of her secret knowledge was beginning to tell, even on her brave spirit.

Bess watched them go. Moved by some urge that she did not understand, she decided to follow them, even though it was plain that Drew wished her to remain behind. To watch Arbell, no doubt.

Instead, despite wearing thin slippers, she walked to the stable yard. The day was a dull one, and a light drizzle was falling. Their golden summer had turned as dark as the day's news. In the bustle of the yard Drew and his fellow did not see her as horses were brought out, grooms shouted and the business of the day began. Others were also riding out, although not to look for Charles. Sir Henry and Arbell were not among them, for even as Bess had left the dining-room they had passed her on the way into it.

Drew's party were all mounted and ready to start. A great train of grooms was going with them so that they might search more places than one at the same time. But, at the very last moment, Walter, at the head of them all, shouted 'Hola, someone comes. Stop a moment, m'lord.'

Through the arched opening to the yard walked a small party of artisans and peasants. Most of them were shouldering axes, some carried large wicker baskets. One of their number was leading a donkey on which a man was slumped. The man was only just identifiable as Charles Breton, so torn and stained was his clothing. The worst stains of all were of blood. His head and chest had been bandaged with dirty cloths, and he had been roped to the donkey to keep him on it. Even so, every now and then one of the peasants steadied him so that he might not fall off.

The leading man said, speaking with an accent that

was barely understandable, 'Be my lord of Exford here?'

Drew dismounted and walked towards him.

'I am Lord Exford. What would you have with me?'

The man waved a hand at Charles. 'We found this fellow halfway down the cliff late yesterday after we had finished our work. We brought him down and tended him overnight. He seems like to die. He can speak, but would not give us his name. All he would say was that we were to bring him to Lord Exford at the big house in Buxton. Here he is, and if he dies of his journey we are not to blame.'

'Indeed not.' Bess watched Drew walk over to where Charles sagged in the arms of the man sustaining him. He said in a low voice that none but Charles could hear, 'Is this truly what you want, Charles?'

'Truly, yes, truly,' Charles mumbled. 'Sanctuary.' He fell silent.

This last word came out so loudly that all present heard it. Captain Goreham had joined Drew, and spoke to him briefly ending with, 'Agree to his wishes, m'lord.'

Drew waved a peremptory hand at Walter, who had also dismounted and had come over to him. 'See that he is carried to his room, and a physician sent for.'

Charles must have heard him, for he gave a moaning sigh and fell into Walter's arms, unconscious.

Bess had slowly advanced until she was in Drew's line of sight.

'You should not be here,' he told her, but he did not sound angry.

'He is not dead, then?' Bess asked; which was a stupid thing to say, to be sure, but Drew did not seem to think so.

'Almost, by the look of him,' he replied. 'He is not conscious, nor, I think will he recover himself soon. It is useful that you are here, for you may go and tell Sir

Henry and his wife that Charles has been brought back alive, but is unable to speak. That should give them food for thought. They may try to leave, but they will be stopped.

'I shall give orders that no one is to leave until my cousin recovers sufficiently to tell his story. Captain Goreham tells me that he has already sent word to the High Sheriff of the county, asking either that he comes to Buxton himself or that he sends his senior officers and tipstaffs here as soon as possible. He has given no reason beyond the simple one of the recent criminal acts which have taken place and which need investigating.'

Bess needed no second bidding. She ran back into the Hall to find that Sir Henry and the Lady Arbell were already leaving the dining-room.

Arbell caught her by the sleeve, her voice high and stammered out, 'Is is true? Is it true that Charles Breton is alive and has been brought back to the Hall?'

'Quite true,' said Bess, and then, naughtily, but in order to see how Arbell responded. 'With him being such a friend of yours, you will doubtless be greatly relieved and will wish to see him as soon as possible. But, alas, he is gravely injured and is at this moment unconscious.'

The conflicting expressions of apprehension mixed with relief on Arbell's face when she heard this last piece of news told Bess everything.

'Oh, no,' she said swiftly. 'Now that we know that he is safe and sound we may leave at once. Sir Henry has had urgent news from home which requires his presence there immediately. You may give Master Breton our best wishes for his speedy recovery, of course.'

Bess was about to inform them that their leave-taking would not be possible, for no one would be allowed to leave until the High Sheriff or his officers arrived, and then only with their permission, when Drew came in and saved her the trouble.

'This is preposterous,' Sir Henry exclaimed, speaking at last. 'What possible reason could you have for detaining me and my wife?'

'What, indeed?' said Drew smoothly. 'But take heart. You are not alone in this. All now present in the hall must remain, including those who were about to set out this morning and must now delay their journey.

'The claims of justice are strong—as are those of your safety—who knows what murdering outlaws may be hiding in the hills?' he ended as Sir Henry opened his mouth to challenge him again.

Arbell's face was ghastly. She appealed to Bess. 'Can you not persuade your husband to change his mind, m'lady? It is imperative that we leave immediately.'

Indeed it was! For was not the game now up? Bess was not averse to playing cat and mouse with the woman who had stood by when one man was murdered and another was sent to his probable death.

'If you have aught to argue, madam, that would enable m'lord Exford and the High Sheriff to look kindly on you, then say it now.'

This was a direct invitation to her to confess and, by her expression, Arbell took it as such. But before she could answer Bess, Sir Henry seized her wrist in a grip of iron.

'I will not have my wife beg on my behalf,' he said, still playing the mild and amiable buffoon. 'I can speak for myself, and she can surely have nothing to say that I cannot say for her.'

'Truly spoken,' answered Drew, who was also beginning to enjoy playing the cat and watching the mice wriggle. 'For the meantime I have ordered the stables closed until the High Sheriff and his officers arrive and have sent word to Lord Shrewsbury at Chatsworth as to what has passed here. I am determined to smoke out those who have treated my cousin so cruelly.'

No word had been spoken of plots or treason, but like Philip Sidney, who had arrived to stand at Drew's elbow, lending him the weight of his powerful family name, Sir Henry knew full well why Drew was behaving as he did. As did Arbell, whose face was ghastlier than ever, and who was now caressing the wrist which Sir Henry had twisted when it was behind her back but had now freed.

Bess's hawk eye could see bruises on it, and she wondered what Sir Henry would say to his wife when they were alone.

The unofficial meeting was over. Sir Henry, muttering, 'I know not who gave you authority to be in charge at Buxton, Exford, but of course, I will do my duty and remain here,' walked away, his dignity still intact. He was grasping Arbell firmly by her other wrist and her face was set in a rictus of pain which passed as pity for Charles among those who were watching and were not in the know.

'Well done, wife,' said Drew quietly. 'You almost frightened Arbell into giving herself away. Philip,' he added, 'I should like to speak to you privily.'

Captain Goreham had agreed with him that, under the new circumstances of Charles's return, it would not hurt for another person to be aware that there was a conspiracy brewing. Besides that, Philip would be available to keep another watchful eye on Sir Henry and his wife, lest they try to escape.

'All will be over for them,' he said to Drew, 'if your cousin recovers sufficiently to be able to tell us who attacked him. His room must be guarded so that none might enter secretly and dispose of him and his evidence.'

'I have already arranged for that to be done.'

'Good, good.' The Captain nodded approvingly at Drew. 'And guard yourself and your good lady, too, for there are others here besides our chief suspects who may be in the plot, and might wish to take any action designed to save their necks from the block or the hangman's noose.'

Bess shivered at his words. Both then and later, when she sat at an early afternoon repast, she looked at those around her with new eyes.

Drew was telling Philip and Captain Goreham that he had spoken with the wood cutters and although they had told him in detail where they had found Charles, halfway down the cliff with a great wound in his chest, they had no notion of how he came to be there.

'So that is a dead end, my masters. I have seen the physician caring for Charles, and he is hopeful that he may live and speak to us, but for the moment he is out of his wits.'

Philip lifted his goblet. 'I'll drink to that. For the rest, Nau has had the impudence to commiserate with me on the assault on a friend, and bade me pass that message on to you, Drew, which I now do. He also said that his mistress, the Queen of Scots, was shocked to hear of such barbarism being practised in this fair country. She also asks you to attend her so that she may offer you her sympathy in person.'

'Does she so?' Drew's voice was savage. 'The same sympathy, I suppose, which she offered her own murdered husband, Henry Darnley!'

'Come, come, Drew. That remark goes under the heading of those which are thought but never said. The lady was a Queen—you must swallow your just indignation and go through the forms of ceremony which imprison us all.'

Bess put a quiet hand on Drew's arm to quieten him. They were no longer beleaguered, no longer suspected of monstrous treachery, so there was no need for him to lose his temper.

Drew shook his head as though to clear it. 'You are right, Philip, and I am wrong to rail at you. I must do my duty and visit her, but I shall not ask Bess to join me. You, wife, will need to be ready to go to Charles's room should he regain consciousness during my absence, and wish to speak. Since we are telling no one of the conspiracy, it would not do for us to behave as though Charles were a prisoner.'

So it was agreed, and Drew, changed into his most magnificent attire, repaired to the Queen of Scots's quarters to receive her lengthy commiseration with a straight face. Bess, an anxious aunt Hamilton by her side, remained in her room. Her aunt had just returned from caring for Lady Arbell who, she informed her niece, was most distressed.

'You were somewhat unkind to her, my dear,' she reproached Bess. 'It was not like you at all.'

Bess could make no reply that would satisfy her aunt, so, surprisingly for her, she kept silent, stitching away at her canvaswork, her head bent, listening for the messenger who might come to tell her that Charles had regained consciousness.

She shook her head at Drew when he returned and looked questioningly at her.

'Philip came, not ten minutes ago, to tell us that Charles was still unconscious, but that he showed signs of returning to life.'

'Good,' said Drew, but his approval was not, as aunt

Hamilton thought, for Charles's showing signs of improvement, but rather for the hope that he might soon be able to tell them who had tried to kill him and why.

The bell rang for the midday meal, but Bess had ordered food from the Talbot Arms to be served in their room. Before they could begin to eat, Charles's page ran in, shouting breathlessly, 'The physician has sent me to tell you that my master has regained consciousness and has asked to speak to you. He is very weak, and the physician told me to warn you that he might swoon again before you reach him.'

Drew was out of the door like a scalded cat, all his ceremonial lordship forgotten in his urgency, was Bess's irreverent thought.

He found Charles propped up against pillows, his face ghastly, his breathing shallow. The physician stood by him, looking anxious.

'He wishes to speak to you, m'lord, but I have warned him that overmuch exertion might prove fatal.'

'Be damned to that,' whispered Charles. 'If it is the last thing I do I must speak to you at once, cousin, privately.'

Weak though he was, he stressed the words cousin and privately.

The physician immediately began to warn him against doing any such thing. 'I need to be with you,' he said.

Drew shook his head at him. 'You heard my cousin,' he said. 'If he wishes to be alone with me, then Amen to that.'

'I must warn you—' the physician began.

'You have already done so.' Drew's voice was stern. 'For once, let the patient decide. If you continue to defy us, I shall have my footmen remove you.'

Grumbling, the physician left at last. Charles gave a

weak smile. 'It would not do for him to hear what I have to tell you.'

'Nothing to that, cousin. Speak.'

Charles's smile was now deathly weary. 'I never thought that you would call me cousin again after what I have tried to do to you.'

'Nothing alters our relationship, even treachery.' Drew was as cool as he could be.

'True.' He sighed. 'Now let me tell you all of my wicked folly—even unto this last.'

Haltingly, stopping occasionally to allow Drew to hold a goblet of water to his cracked lips, Charles told his whole sad tale. Drew, Bess and Captain Goreham had already guessed the gist of it. He named the names of those whom he had contacted both in London and in Buxton. Drew was a little relieved to hear that young Master Blagg was not one of them—he had taken a liking to him and his wife. Master Bown, however, was involved and several others with whom neither Drew nor Bess were intimate.

'I thought that I was the prime player in the game, using Arbell, not being used by her. And all the time that apparent dotard and cuckold, Sir Henry, was pulling the strings. He used Arbell as bait, no doubt of that. . .I thought that she loved me. We were to marry when the plot succeeded after her marriage to him was annulled. It was forced on her, she said.'

This last confession set off a fit of coughing so strong that Drew, out of pity, was constrained to hold him up, finally lying him back on the pillows.

'But why, Charles, why? I know your family were devout Catholics so I can understand your wishing to restore the faith, but why did you try to betray *me* so cruelly? We were close friends from boyhood on.

I thought that you loved me, as I loved you.'

Charles lay silent and spent, moving his head restlessly on the pillows. Drew rose from the seat he had taken by the bed. 'No, do not answer me if it pains you. I have no right to—'

Charles reared up and caught him by the wrist. 'No, stay, and I will try to explain. Was I not merely the poor relation of the wrong religion, lucky to have you as a patron? You always had so much and I so little. You were Earl and I was nothing. Everything which you touched turned to gold. Every woman I ever wanted fell into your arms, not mine. Every game I played, you could beat me at. Even at University you outshone me.

'And your wife, she whom you had named monkey and vilely deserted for ten long years, proved to have turned into a beauty. Worse than that, she took one look at you when you arrived to claim her and became yet another worshipper of the god named Andrew Exford. She never looked at me, although when I looked at her I would have worshipped *her*, not required her to worship *me*. Even if I had not already begun to betray you, I would have done so after we came to Atherington. . .'

He stopped to cough, to turn his head away before beginning to speak again. 'Oh, God, how I grew to hate you. I would have done anything to bring you low, anything. But I could not even do that properly, but fell victim to another who used me only to throw me away. And then, today, knowing what you do, you speak to me kindly, call me cousin. You will, I'm sure, even offer me forgiveness—as much as you can with that man of Walsingham's after me, that is. And what does your kindness make me but an even worse cur and traitor than I already am?'

What could Drew say? Nothing. He had his duty to

do, and that entailed handing over to Walsingham and the State not only Sir Henry, Arbell and the others, but also Charles, who, now that he had confessed all, might earn a little, a very little, in the way of mercy.

The urgent knocking on the door which had begun whilst Charles was speaking, and which Drew had scarcely noticed, became even more urgent, and only stopped when Captain Goreham entered the room.

The Captain took one look at Drew, saw him nod, heard him say that Charles had confessed all, and now must give all the details to the Captain as Walsingham's representative.

'Not now,' he said. 'There's no time for that now. Sir Henry, aware that his game is up, has made a run for it. He has bribed one of the grooms to get him a horse and you and I must be after him.'

'And Arbell?'

'Not to be found. She was not with him. The thing is, he must be captured secretly, for this whole business must be kept undercover until we are ready to tell all— if we ever do have to tell all. Do you post guards on this room and come with me. I have told Master Sidney to begin a search for the Lady. She cannot have gone far. He will also speak privily with the High Sheriff's officers if they arrive in our absence.'

Drew took one last agonised look at Charles, who was now lying back with his eyes closed, called for his page who had been lurking anxiously in the corridor, and then set off for the stables—this time still in tne court finery he had worn to visit the Queen of Scots.

Bess, although anxious to know what was passing in Charles's room, stitched steadily on. Aunt Hamilton excused herself after a short time. Bess was, for once, pleased by her absence, mostly because she could not speak the truth to her aunt, and she was growing tired of dissembling.

I would not make a conspirator, she decided, it's too much like hard work! What I want to do is to go home to Atherington with Drew, and then, later on, perhaps, visit Wilton, which Philip has persuaded me is as near to Arcadia as any place on earth.

To think of Philip was to bring him into the room, enquiring hastily, without a by-your-leave or any of his usual courtier-like gravity, 'Have you seen the Lady Arbell lately?' and immediately that she said him nay, he was gone again, and she could hear him running down the corridor.

Straightway after that, which was odd enough, aunt Hamilton almost fell into the room. She had a great bruise on her face and her farthingale's hoop had been knocked awry. She was breathing so shortly that when Bess ran at her, asking 'What's amiss, Aunt?' it took her several minutes to regain the power of speech.

'Oh, Bess,' she said at last, 'you were right about Arbell all the time. I have just met her in the lower corridor outside the Great Parlour and stopped to pass the time of day with her and tell her the good news, that dear Charles had recovered his senses again and that Drew was with him. You may imagine my surprise when she immediately shouted, "Out of my way, you silly old woman. I've no time to lose", and struck at me so hard that I fell to the ground, before she ran off with her skirts held high like any rustic milkmaid!'

Poor aunt Hamilton's senses were even more confounded when her niece, throwing down her canvaswork, shot past her through the door, hurling at her as she went,

'Forgive me, but if that is so, I have no time to lose, either.'

The poor lady collapsed into a chair, exclaiming, 'What, has all the world suddenly run mad?' before shouting in her turn, this time for her woman to come bathe her face.

So that was what Philip had been about, thought Bess, running down the corridor, looking for Arbell. And her silly aunt had had nothing better to do than tell her that Charles was likely confessing everything to Drew.

Where could she have gone? Escaped with Sir Henry, perhaps. That notion was knocked on the head when she met Philip in the Entrance Hall.

'Have you seen Arbell?' they both asked together.

Bess shook her head, 'I only know that she is not to be found. Perhaps she and her husband are trying to escape.'

'No, he has escaped on his own, on horseback. Captain Goreham and Drew are after him.'

So he had deserted Arbell; left her to her fate. Which was all of a piece, coming as it did from a man who had callously used his wife as bait to catch careless and greedy fish like Charles.

'Useless to stand here talking,' said Philip. 'She cannot have gone far. I will go to the stables; she might be trying to bribe a groom. You had best return to your lodgings, my dear, and wait for Drew. This is no work for you.'

Was it not? Bess did not argue with him. She tried to think what she would do in Arbell's shoes. The trouble was that she was so unlike Arbell she had difficulty in doing any such thing.

Suppose Arbell thought that now Sir Henry had deserted her, one way of escaping from imprisonment and death was to go into Buxton itself and try to hire a horse, or a carriage at the inn. She could then make for the home of a Catholic family in the area who might be ready to hide her. She would probably think the gamble worth the taking.

Moreover, Bess was sure that the villagers did not know of the secret goings-on in Lord Shrewsbury's Great Hall and therefore they would not try to stop her from leaving. Both Captain Goreham and Drew wanted to keep the conspiracy from public knowledge as long as possible.

What to do? There was no time for her to find grooms or pages in order to send them into the village, for if she took too long Arbell might yet escape. There was only one thing for it. She must go after Arbell!

No sooner thought than done. If she did not exactly raise her skirts like a milkmaid, Bess half-ran, half-trotted into the village street and made for the Talbot Inn. . .

Chapter Sixteen

Meantime Drew and Captain Goreham were on Sir Henry's trail. He was not so far ahead of them that they might not catch him up. He would, the Captain guessed, make for the byway which led to the road to Derby, not only because it ran south to safety, but because he would need fresh horses which could only be found on a road with post houses on it.

Reaching the byway, which wound uphill out of Buxton, they could see Sir Henry ahead of them, riding hard. For a time they could only match his speed, but gradually they began to gain on him, until he could hear them close behind him. He turned once to look at them when they were almost on him, and seeing who it was following him, he realised immediately that he was like to be the victim of a relentless Nemesis.

He reined his horse in, leaped from it and ran off the road and into the scrub and forest which bordered it, in the hope that he could somehow elude them in it.

Drew and Captain Goreham followed suit, only staying tether their horses to a nearby tree. Both of them had armed themselves before leaving the stables, and found, as they ran through the undergrowth and between the trees, that their swords were a drawback in such conditions. They had little difficulty in tracking Sir Henry, although they were unable to see him, since it was impossible to run quietly through such rough terrain.

Slowly the forest began to thin out until, finally, Sir Henry found himself on a large plateau, covered in scrub and heath, with the forest continuing again some half a mile away. Wishing to regain its shelter, he ran swiftly towards it, following a track which ran parallel with the edge of the cliff which had created the break in the forest. Far below him he could see the road to Derby winding into the blue distance.

Drew, with Captain Goreham, a much heavier man, labouring in his rear, was almost upon him, his youth and strength giving him an advantage over both the older men. He caught up with Sir Henry at the point where the scrub met the forest.

'Hold,' he cried, drawing his rapier. 'I bid you stop and surrender yourself in the name of the Queen.'

Realising that he was cornered, Sir Henry turned and drew his own sword, 'No. For you hold no office which gives you the right to arrest me.'

'I have the right of a trueborn Englishman to arrest anyone he suspects of treason and murder and you have committed both. Be sensible and surrender so that you may throw yourself upon the Queen's mercy.'

'Oh, I know right well what *her* mercy might be,' retorted Sir Henry, advancing on him, rapier at the ready. 'I see that your ally has fled the field. If you wish to take me you must kill me first,' and drawing his dagger, he thrust at Drew without delay.

Drew only had time to draw his own dagger before Sir Henry was upon him. He had no doubt at all that Sir Henry meant it to end in the death of one or other of them, and he defended himself vigorously against a man who had been a master swordsman in his youth. He could only hope that his own youth, and his skill, would sustain him.

And what had he meant by saying that the Captain had fled the field? It was true that he had not appeared to help him in his fight with Sir Henry. Where could he have gone?

He was soon to find out.

In the to and fro of the duel he was turned until he was facing the direction by which he and the Captain had come and, true enough, there was no sign of him. Drew could not believe that he had been left to deal with Sir Henry alone, but he had no choice but to act as though that he had.

Youth and strength at last began to prevail. Sir Henry, almost overcome by the ferocity of Drew's attack, was compelled to retreat backwards towards the forest. Twice Drew caught him, first with his sword and then with his dagger, drawing blood, but he could not quite follow up his advantage. So engrossed were both men in their struggle for mastery that neither of them realised that the path of the duel had brought them dangerously near to the cliff edge.

And then Drew saw Captain Goreham. He was down on his hands and knees in the scrub, advancing slowly towards the pair of them. Drew, by measured feints, kept Sir Henry in front of the approaching Captain so that he should not espy him until, seeing his enemy beginning to falter, he prepared to deliver the *coup de grâce* which would kill him.

But he was never to do so. Captain Goreham, having crawled and slithered to a point immediately behind Sir Henry, suddenly rose and gripped him round the waist.

Surprised at this attack from such an unexpected quarter, Sir Henry cried out and dropped his sword, preparatory to tackling this new threat.

The Captain, his face savage, gave him no chance to launch a counter-attack. He whirled his prey round and, with one mighty heave, flung him over the cliff's edge.

Drew, dropping his sword, joined the Captain where he stood, looking at Sir Henry who lay still, some hundred feet below them, his neck broken. He had suffered the face which he had destined for Charles.

He took the Captain by the arm and said half-angrily, 'Why did you do that? I was about to finish him off.'

The Captain answered him softly, 'Do but think, m'lord. This matter must not become public—which it would have done if you had killed him in a duel. Now there are no marks of a sword or dagger on him, only those of his fall. An accident, was it not? You are safe and innocent of causing another's death, and so am I, for you'll not talk, I'll be bound. My master Walsingham would not approve of that. No, no, this was the better way. We are not even here. We rode out by quite another route. Others shall find him for us.'

'But Charles and Arbell—what of them and the other conspirators?'

'Why, m'lord, we shall speak of that later. Now we must return to Buxton and pretend to have enjoyed our ride.'

Drew sheathed his sword. He would have liked to have had his revenge for Tib and the duping of Charles, but life was not necessarily arranged for the benefit of those who lived it. He listened to the Captain as he outlined their next steps.

* * *

Philip Sidney's errand to the stables in order to find whether there was any news of Arbell turned out to be fruitless. It occurred to him that she might not have have tried to escape at all, and that it would be as well to go to Bess's lodgings to discover whether she might have seen her.

He bounded up the stairs like a very greyhound to visit her. Alas, when he shot into the Exfords' room, he found no Bess, but only a dishevelled aunt Hamilton, who was being tended by one of her ladies who was holding a wet cloth to her bruised cheek.

'Tell me, madam,' he asked, breathless, without any of his usual elaborate courtesy. 'Is Lady Exford here— and have you seen the Lady Arbell?'

'Questions, questions,' returned aunt Hamilton crossly. 'The world is full of them today. The Lady Arbell I do not wish to speak of, and as for Bess, when I told her that Arbell had run off after attacking me, why, what must Bess do but run after *her*, incontinent.'

'But where, madam, did they go?'

Aunt Hamilton murmured, 'I have no idea, none in the world,' before she lay back and closed her eyes, seeking some relief from a day gone mad. But she was not destined to find it. The door opened again. This time to let in one of the pages. 'Oh, Master Sidney, the grooms told me that you would be here. They said you were looking for the Lady Arbell. Not ten minutes ago I saw her run out of the gates and down the road to the village. I thought that was strange, indeed, but stranger still, not long after that, I saw m'Lady Exford running in that direction. . .'

He was not allowed to finish. Philip pushed past him without a word and ran down the stairs even faster than he had come up them, shouting for his horse and grooms as he approached the stable.

Aunt Hamilton opened her eyes and said faintly to her lady, 'Child, fetch me a tisane. I must try to sleep at once and try to recover from the insults of a world turned upside down. I thought that Master Sidney was the most courteous of men, but he is no better than the rest, alas.'

Watched by curious eyes, Bess ran down the village street towards the inn. And there, just as she had supposed, was Arbell, arguing with the landlord and a groom who was holding a flighty horse. It seemed that her ladyship having no money or servants with her they were loath to let her leave on a valuable horse

In the middle of their noisy bickering Arbell turned and saw Bess running towards her, calling her name.

'No!' she cried, before pulling up her skirts. To the astonishment of the landlord, who was still refusing to let her mount his horse, she turned and ran, away from Bess, away from discovery and ruin, down the village street towards the road out of Buxton and the river which ran beside it. Where she thought that she was going, the good God alone knew. Panic had Arbell in its grip and flight was her instinctive response.

Panting with effort, Bess ran after her. Her heavy clothing hampered her, and, oh, how she wished she was in the boy's clothes which she had always worn when she rode out with Tib.

Tib! The very thought of him was a spur to her tired legs. She reminded herself that Arbell was similarly hampered, took no exercise and was doubtless finding flight even more difficult than Bess was finding pursuit.

She was slowing down and Bess was visibly gaining on her. They were soon out of the village and on the road, or rather the track, which ran by the river. Sobbing, tears of fear and rage streaming down her face, Arbell turned to face her pursuer. She could run no more.

'What do you want of me? In the name of heaven, let me go.' Her voice was a croak; her whole appearance was of such utter despair as to invite pity.

Bess felt no pity for her. She thought of Tib and, yes, of Charles, traitor and dupe though he was, and her heart hardened against the woman before her.

'No,' she said sternly. 'Come back with me and face your fate.'

'Never,' shrieked Arbell, and turned to run again, but she only managed a few yards before Bess was upon her. She caught Arbell round the shoulders to stop her, but Arbell, desperate, twisting, tore herself loose and tried to run away again. Bess, fired by rage and revenge, caught her again, this time around the waist. They struggled together for a few moments before Arbell lost her footing and fell to the ground, dragging Bess with her.

Side by side, entwined, they rolled down the bank towards the river—and into it, Arbell giving one last agonised shriek as she entered the icy water, Bess, silent, still grimly holding on to her prey. She had swum in cold water before and was by no means as shocked as Arbell was by its cruel clutches.

'Dear God, save me, I cannot swim. Oh, help me, help me.' Arbell's cries were for anyone, even Bess.

The summer had been a dry one, and the river was low, but their heavy skirts encumbered both women. Bess, realising that their summary ducking had ended Arbell's resistance, made for the river bank, dripping water, leaving Arbell behind her.

Why should she not leave Arbell to her fate? Just think, she told herself, of all the trouble that would save

Drew, and the state. But she could not. To do any such thing would make her as bad as Arbell, whom she so despised. Wearily, Bess returned to help her out, a task rendered difficult by Arbell's refusal to help herself in any way.

Somehow Bess dragged and hoisted her out of the water, and laid her on the grass, gasping and panting, all her resistance gone, destroyed by her involuntary ducking.

Bess, trying to wring the water out of her skirts, said, her voice as severe as she could make it, 'If you try to get up and run, Arbell, I shall either sit on you, or push you back into the river, so you had better behave yourself.'

Even as she spoke she could hear hoofbeats and voices shouting her name. Help was at hand. Help in the shape of Philip Sidney and a couple of grooms.

Bess thought that the long day would never end. Philip had escorted her and Arbell back to the Great Hall, each of them riding pillion and dripping wetly over an unlucky groom. Arbell had been handed over to her ladies, and Philip had bid a pair of grooms guard her door so that she might not escape again.

Bess's ladies had stripped her of her wet clothing, and then bathed and dressed her in all her best finery. All the time poor aunt Hamilton had moaned and clucked over her as though she were twelve again.

The tisane her waiting woman had brought her had barely had time to take effect before Bess's arrival in such disarray set the seal of unlikeliness on her already unlikely day.

'I cannot imagine what you think you have been doing,' she wailed as though Bess were a child again.

'Saving Arbell from the river,' returned Bess briskly, but somewhat unhelpfully. She didn't think that it would be wise to inform her aunt how Arbell had come to fall in.

She was still being chided and wailed over when Drew came in from his ride.

'Such a pother as we have been engaged in today, you would never believe. You were well out of it,' aunt Hamilton told him. 'You have missed all the excitement,' and she gave him her version of Bess's heavily laundered tale about following Arbell and rescuing her from the River Wye.

She ended by complaining of Master Sidney's sudden loss of courtesy, and by demanding that Drew reprimand his wife for being such a hoyden.

'Seeing that she is in your care now, not mine! Oh, what a day it has been! I am like to die of excitement and shall need a holiday to recover from this one.'

'Yes, indeed, I have certainly missed all the excitement,' Drew told her gravely and untruthfully. 'And you would scarcely have me reproach my wife for carrying out such a noble deed. She almost certainly saved Arbell's life.'

Something in his voice alerted Bess. She said to her aunt, 'My dear, I think that it is you who ought to take a rest, not me, and recover from the exertions of your day.'

Still grumbling, her aunt left them. As the door shut behind her, Bess took Drew by the hand,

'And now, husband, is it not time that we told the truth to one another?'

'No hope of deceiving you, my dear, I see,' and he launched into the tale of Sir Henry's attempt to escape and his subsequent death, before listening to Bess's story. Philip had already told him the gist of it.

He took her into his arms as she finished. 'Dear heart,

you are never to do such a thing again. You should not have followed Arbell at all, let alone ended up in the water with her, but, all things considered, it was for the best,' was all that he had to say.

Bess, who had been waiting for him, a little fearful that he might disapprove of her headstrong goings-on, was mightily relieved. Drew laughed a little as her face brightened visibly.

'But you are never to do such a thing again,' he repeated, kissing her. 'You were lucky that neither of you drowned.'

'Little likelihood that I should, seeing that I am able to swim!' Bess was dismissive. 'Arbell, now, was quite another matter for she could not. Have you had time to see Charles again? The physician says that he is fast recovering.'

Drew shook his head, 'No, alas, and this afternoon must be given over to help the Captain concoct some sort of explanation for the wild happenings of the last few days. We may have to call on Philip's lively imagination.'

'But even he could scarce have foreseen Sir Henry and his plotting.'

'No, indeed. And a search party will have to be sent to find him since he has not returned from his ride. And, of course, Captain Goreham and I have said nothing of what actually happened to Sir Henry on the hill beyond Buxton. Needless to say he had not informed his servants or grooms that he had no intention of returning at all!'

Bess shivered, her face solemn again. 'He might have killed you, Drew. Now *you* must promise me that *you* will never do such rash thing again.'

'My answer will be the same as yours—which was no answer at all!'

'And in the end he found the death he would have

given Charles. There's a kind of divine justice about that. Arbell does not know, of course?'

'Nor anyone else.'

'But when the High Sheriff's men arrive, everything will come out, will it not?'

Drew began to laugh. 'Which was my thought, too. But, no, the Captain says that they will be given an explanation which will have nothing to do with any conspiracies against the Queen's Majesty. He has, he said, already prepared the ground for that. Do not ask me how—he is to tell me later.'

'I would not like him for an enemy.'

'Nor I.'

'And Charles and Arbell—if all is to be kept quiet, what will happen to them?'

'I don't yet know. Now that I have found you dry, rosy, and as impertinent as ever, with no need of succour from me, I am to meet the Captain and Philip for a final council of war. He will advise us on how best to explain the odd happenings of the last few days in such a fashion that no one will ask any further questions.'

'Although they might think a lot,' Bess added, 'and, Drew, when we are finally alone together tonight, there is something I must tell you.'

'Now, lady wife, you have whetted my appetite, I shall hurry back as soon as possible.'

But as soon as possible for Drew was a long time coming. First of all there was the council of war to attend, and when that was over, the search party arrived back with Sir Henry's body, which caused more than a little to-do. Not long after that the High Sheriff's men arrived and joined in yet another council at which the Captain produced witnesses who gave evidence that there was a party of bandits, landless men of straw, roving this part of the Peak District and who were preying upon those who were foolish enough to ride out alone.

As for preventing any of the guests from leaving until the High Sheriff's men arrived, the Captain explained that as a precaution against further attacks until action was taken against them. It was agreed that a party of armed men would be assembled as soon as possible to scour the district and rid them of this plague.

'And, of course,' the Captain had said privately to Drew and Philip, 'they are bound to find some sturdy beggars playing at Robin Hood, and will hang them out of hand, even though they will deny all knowledge of the deaths of your page and Sir Henry and the attack on Master Breton. So everyone will be happy.'

Drew told all this to Bess when he finally arrived back in their rooms at midnight, having had an audience with the Queen of Scots and her secretary Claude Nau in order to tell them the unlikely story which the Captain had concocted.

'Whether the Queen knew aught of what passed is a moot point, but her secretary undoubtedly did. Nevertheless he smiled and congratulated us, even though he must have known that we were lying in our teeth. Dear God, Bess, I shall be glad to see the back of this vile business. This is the last enterprise I shall undertake for Sir Francis.'

'And Arbell and Charles, what will happen to them—seeing that they cannot be accused of treason?'

'Arbell will be confined, as the Queen of Scots is, in the care of a distant relative who is a loyal servant of the Crown. It will be given out that her health has failed. She will not argue against her confinement—she knows that she is lucky not to be sent to the scaffold on Tower Hill.'

'And Charles, will he go to the scaffold? After all, he did murder Tib most cruelly.'

Drew shook his head in sorrow, thinking of his boyhood friend who had been willing to use disaffected Catholics in order to injure him. He also thought of the many loyal English Catholics who quietly practised their faith in secret, who did not deserve to be persecuted for the actions of the few.

'Not so,' he said, 'since all is to be kept secret. No, if he recovers from his wound, he will be taken to the Tower of London as soon as he is fit to travel. Once there he will be offered a choice between a secret death in its dungeons or working as a double agent for Walsingham.

'I think myself I would prefer the first choice—but that is up to Charles. He and Arbell are both fortunate that the Captain's orders were to keep this plot, and the identities of the plotters, secret, if he could, for there have been too many plots lately. Since this one was so feeble in execution, and involved so few persons of any consequence—apart from Sir Henry, who is conveniently dead—the Captain is able to carry out Walsingham's decision. He will keep an eye on the minor members like Master Bown, you may be sure.'

'So, it is over, Drew?'

Drew, who was lying in a great armchair, exhausted, nodded his head in agreement. Bess was already in the Great Bed, and had been there for some hours, waiting for him.

'Yes, dear wife. It is over. Thanks be to to God.'

'And we may go home—soon?'

Drew came over to sit beside her. He clasped her face

in his two hands and asked her gravely, 'Home, wife? And where is that?'

'Why, husband,' she told him, looking deep into his eyes, 'it is where *you* are. But I like to think that you could call Atherington home.'

He relinquished her face and lay down beside her, clothed though he was.

'Dear wife, until I came to Atherington I never had anywhere which I could call a true home. My father's house in the country which I inherited is half a ruin, left over from the Wars of the Roses. The other half is new built, but bleak and bare. My mother died early and no woman ever made it comfortable. I have a small house in London and some rooms at court—when I attended there.

'The only home I have ever known is Atherington. For that I would bid God's blessing on Walsingham for sending me north on this mission, and for suggesting that if I visited Buxton with you no one would think that I had an ulterior motive. Without that we might never have met again The few days I spent at Atherington with my new wife were the happiest I have ever known—once you and I came to terms.'

Bess's face was rueful. 'Came to terms, Drew? Is that all that we have done?'

He pulled her down beside him. 'No, indeed, my darling hussy. Let me say the words to describe that which I once thought existed only in the imagination of poets like Philip. I love you, Lady Exford, more than I ever thought to love any woman, and I wish to live with you, where you will, whether it is at Atherington, or Exford House when we visit it. I am tired of Queens and courts, of intrigue and jockeying for position. Something which Charles said to me, when he explained why he became a traitor, made me ask myself whether, in the pride of my rank, I rode roughshod over the wishes and desires of others, as though only I existed in the world. My one wish now is to raise a family and safeguard the interests of the people who serve Exford and Atherington.'

He fell silent. Bess kissed him on the cheek. A friendly kiss, not a passionate one. She had just gained her heart's desire—the knowledge that he loved her as she loved him. It was true that he had only come to claim her because of the suspected plot, but that meant nothing in the light of what had passed between them since. She gave a quiet little laugh.

'Why, husband, it is my turn to say that I love you, and happy I am that your monkey wife turned out to be the one woman in the world with whom you wish to live. And as for raising a family, then I have to tell you that you may be nearer to achieving that wish than you might think. I have reason to believe, my Lord of Exford, that I am already increasing, and that, boy or girl, your first child is on the way.'

Drew sat up and clasped her in his arms again. 'Oh, my darling, what a clever wife you are! And what a naughty one, to follow Arbell into the river knowing that.'

'And no harm done, husband. I have observed that the wives of my humble people at Atherington who continue to work have easier births than the fine ladies who live about me and do nothing for nine months. So do not expect me to sit at home with my feet up.'

'No, indeed, I would never expect that of you! But neither must you be rash. And we shall certainly return to Atherington now, for it has all the comforts for a breeding wife that Exford lacks.'

Bess lay back on her pillows as Drew began to pull

off his clothing preparatory to coming to bed—to celebrate her news, no doubt.

'I promise to behave myself on one condition,' she said, as he jumped in beside her.

'Anything, I will grant my dear wife and the future mother of my child, anything.'

'That next year we visit our good friend, Master Sidney, at Wilton.'

'Oh, is that all! I had expected you to demand the equivalent of the Crown jewels at least.'

Which had Bess laughing as they prepared to enjoy the first of many happy nights together, now knowing that each truly loved the other, and that their love was strong enough to sustain them through good times and bad.

The deserted bride was deserted no longer.

Historical Romance™

Coming next month

MISS HARCOURT'S DILEMMA
by Anne Ashley

A Regency delight!

Verity's life was not simple. Somehow she'd
become involved in unmasking a spy and
fallen in love with two men—Brinley Carter
and the mysterious Coachman. How would she
ever choose?

TRUE COLOURS
by Nicola Cornick

A Regency delight!

James wanted to know why Alicia had ended
their engagement and why she'd rather risk
another infamous scandal than marry him,
especially when he was *sure* she still loved him.

MILLS & BOON®

Makes any time special™

On sale from 4th May 1998

Available from WH Smith, John Menzies and Volume One

INTERNATIONAL BESTSELLING AUTHOR

Karen Young

Good Girls

When they were good...

Jack Sullivan is an ambitious and painful presence in
the lives of three prominent Mississippi women.
He made Suzanne a prisoner of violent memories,
used Taylor as a lonely trophy wife and drove
Annie's mother to suicide. When Jack is murdered,
each wonders who finally pulled the trigger...

"Karen Young is a spellbinding storyteller."
—Romantic Times

MIRA®

1-55166-306-6
AVAILABLE FROM MAY 1998

SUSAN WIGGS

The Lightkeeper

Lighthouse keeper Jesse Morgan's reclusive life is
changed forever when he finds Mary Dare washed up on
the shore one morning—unconscious and pregnant.
She's keeping a secret—one that puts them both in
terrible danger.

*"A classic beauty and the beast love story...
A poignant, beautiful romance."*
—bestselling author Kristin Hannah

1-55166-301-5
AVAILABLE FROM MAY 1998

MIRA®

DANCE FEVER

How would you like to win a year's supply of Mills & Boon® books? Well you can and they're FREE! Simply complete the competition below and send it to us by 31st October 1998. The first five correct entries picked after the closing date will each win a year's subscription to the Mills & Boon series of their choice. What could be easier?

OBLARMOL
AMBUR
RTOXTFO
RASQUE
GANCO

KOPLA
OOOOMTLCIN
MALOENCF
SITWT
LASSA

EVJI
TAZLW
ACHACH
SCDIO
MAABS

G	R	I	H	C	H	A	R	J	T	O	N
O	P	A	R	L	H	U	B	P	I	B	W
M	O	O	R	L	L	A	B	M	C	V	H
B	L	D	I	O	O	K	C	L	U	P	E
R	K	U	B	N	C	R	Q	H	V	R	Z
S	A	N	I	O	O	N	G	W	A	S	V
T	S	I	N	R	M	G	E	U	B	G	H
W	L	G	H	S	O	R	Q	M	M	B	L
I	A	P	N	O	T	S	L	R	A	H	C
S	S	L	U	K	I	A	S	F	S	L	S
T	O	R	T	X	O	F	O	X	T	R	F
G	U	I	P	Z	N	D	I	S	C	O	Q

D8C

Please turn over for details of how to enter ⇨

HOW TO ENTER

There is a list of fifteen mixed up words overleaf, all of which when unscrambled spell popular dances. When you have unscrambled each word, you will find them hidden in the grid. They may appear forwards, backwards or diagonally. As you find each one, draw a line through it. Find all fifteen and fill in the coupon below then pop this page into an envelope and post it today. Don't forget you could win a year's supply of Mills & Boon® books—you don't even need to pay for a stamp!

Mills & Boon Dance Fever Competition
FREEPOST CN81, Croydon, Surrey, CR9 3WZ
EIRE readers send competition to PO Box 4546, Dublin 24.

Please tick the series you would like to receive if you are one of the lucky winners

Presents™ ❑ Enchanted™ ❑ Medical Romance™ ❑
Historical Romance™ ❑ Temptation® ❑

Are you a Reader Service™ subscriber?   Yes ❑   No ❑

Ms/Mrs/Miss/Mr ....Intials ...(BLOCK CAPITALS PLEASE)

Surname...

Address ....

....

....Postcode.........................

(I am over 18 years of age)   **D8C**

Closing date for entries is 31st October 1998.
One application per household. Competition open to residents of the UK and Ireland only. You may be mailed with offers from other reputable companies as a result of this application. If you would prefer not to receive such offers, please tick this box. ❑

Mills & Boon is a registered trademark of Harlequin Mills & Boon Ltd.